READATHON 1998
TAKE A
READING **SAFARI**

Neary Students
EARNED THIS BOOK
FOR THE NEARY SCHOOL LIBRARY
BY
READING

Here's what kids have to say to
Mary Pope Osborne, author of
the Magic Tree House series:

When I read those books, I feel like I'm in a different world where I could be what I want to be and do what I want to do and go where I want to go.—Ross E.

Out of the 3,000 books I've read, your books are the best.—Lauren S.

I love your books so much that I could read them with my eyes closed.—Gabriel R.

I normally like to watch TV, so my mom likes it when she sees me reading your books. Please write some more.—Brian B.

I love your books. I feel like I am Jack and Annie. I like reading like Jack. I like pretending like Annie.—Robin P.

Your books are so educational.—Allan D.

I don't like reading. But your stories are so interesting that I love reading them.—Katy P.

I wish I could spend my life reading the Magic Tree House series.—Juliette S.

Parents and teachers love
Magic Tree House books, too!

[After reading Pirates Past Noon*], I
realized we were "in the middle" of the
series, so I ordered all the other books...
I wish you could have seen my children's
reactions to seeing the other books. It does a
teacher's heart good to see children "fighting
over books"!*—D. Bowers

*I thank you for your wonderful contribution
to children's literature—and to my classroom
as well.*—E. Mellinger

*Your series is named correctly, having the
word* magic *in the title. They truly are
magical books.*—J. Royer

I use the Magic Tree House books as enrichment in my curriculum. When I assign the children to read from one of your stories, it's one of the quietest times of the day!—J. Korn

Please continue to write more stories! You're doing a great job helping children to learn to love reading.—J. Arcadipane

Having children beg to read "just one more chapter" is a reading specialist's dream, and with your books, my dream is coming true.—K. Letsky

Dear Readers,

 I have long wanted to send Jack and Annie to China, but I couldn't figure out what period of history they should visit. Then one day, when I was reading in my local library, I stumbled across some amazing information. In the 1970s, archaeologists began excavating a great wonder in China: an ancient burial tomb with over 7,000 statues of soldiers and horses. The tomb was more than 2,000 years old and had been built for the first Chinese emperor.

 After I learned this, I found other library books about that period of Chinese history, and I spent days reading and taking notes. From these notes, I fashioned <u>Day of the Dragon King.</u>

 Have I told you before that libraries are very important to me? They are <u>my</u> magic places...where I dream and wonder...and spin my stories.

 Visit <u>your</u> library and I bet you'll find the same magic!

 All my best,

 Mary Pope Osborne

Day of the Dragon King

by Mary Pope Osborne

illustrated by Sal Murdocca

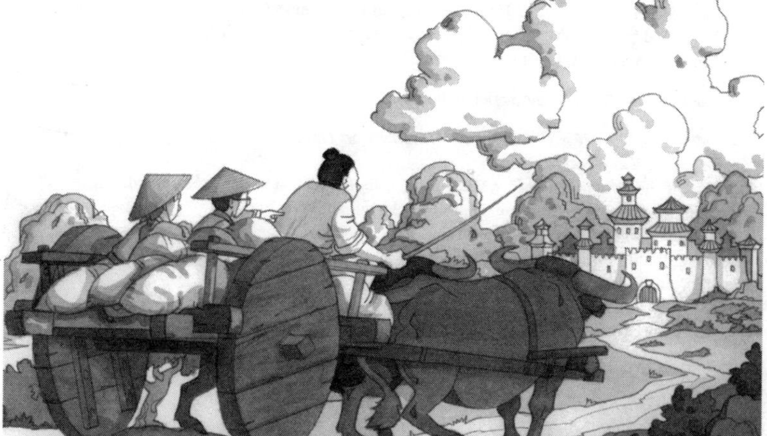

A STEPPING STONE BOOK™

Random House 🏠 New York

For Peter and Andrew Boyce

Text copyright © 1998 by Mary Pope Osborne
Illustrations copyright © 1998 by Sal Murdocca
All rights reserved under International and Pan-American Copyright Conventions.
Published in the United States by Random House, Inc., New York, and
simultaneously in Canada by Random House of Canada Limited, Toronto.

www.randomhouse.com/magictreehouse/

Library of Congress Cataloging-in-Publication Data
Osborne, Mary Pope.
Day of the Dragon King / by Mary Pope Osborne ; illustrated by Sal Murdocca.
    p.   cm. — (Magic tree house ; #14)   "Stepping Stone book."
Summary: The magic treehouse takes Jack and Annie back two thousand years to
ancient China where they must find the original copy of an old legend before the
Imperial Library is burned down by the evil Dragon King.
ISBN 0-679-89051-3 (pbk.) — ISBN 0-679-99051-8 (lib. bdg.)
[1. Time travel—Fiction. 2. China—History—Han dynasty, 202 B.C.–220 A.D.—
Fiction. 3. Magic—Fiction. 4. Tree houses—Fiction.] I. Murdocca, Sal, ill. II.
Title. III. Series: Osborne, Mary Pope. Magic tree house series ; #14.
PZ7.081167Day   1998   [Fic]—dc21   97-49199

Printed in the United States of America 10 9 8 7 6 5 4 3 2 1

Random House, Inc. New York, Toronto, London, Sydney, Auckland
A STEPPING STONE BOOK is a trademark of Random House, Inc.

Contents

Prologue

One summer day in Frog Creek, Pennsylvania, a mysterious tree house appeared in the woods.

Eight-year-old Jack and his seven-year-old sister, Annie, climbed into the tree house. They found that it was filled with books.

Jack and Annie soon discovered that the tree house was magic. It could take them to the places in the books. All they had to do was point to a picture and wish to go there.

Along the way, they discovered that the

tree house belongs to Morgan le Fay. Morgan is a magical librarian from the time of King Arthur. She travels through time and space, gathering books.

In Magic Tree House #12, *Polar Bears Past Bedtime*, Jack and Annie solved the last of four ancient riddles and became Master Librarians. To help them in their future tasks, Morgan gave Jack and Annie secret library cards with the letters <u>M L</u> on them.

Jack and Annie's first four missions as Master Librarians are to save stories from ancient libraries. When their first adventure ended (Magic Tree House #13, *Vacation Under the Volcano*), Morgan asked them to return to the tree house in two weeks to go to China and save another story.

Now the two weeks are over…

Day of the
Dragon King

1

The Bamboo Book

Annie peeked into Jack's room.

"Ready to go to China?" she asked.

Jack took a deep breath.

"Sure," he answered.

"Bring your secret library card," Annie said. "I have mine in my pocket."

"Yep," said Jack.

He opened his top dresser drawer and took out a thin wooden card. The letters <u>M L</u> on it shimmered in the light. Jack dropped the card into his backpack. Then he threw in his notebook and a pencil.

"Let's go," said Annie.

Jack pulled on his pack and followed her.

What are we in for today? he wondered.

"Bye, Mom!" said Annie as they passed their mom in the kitchen.

"Where are you going?" she asked.

"China!" said Annie.

"Great," said their mom. She winked at them. "Have fun."

Fun? thought Jack. He was afraid that *fun* wasn't quite the right word.

"Just wish us luck," he said as he and Annie headed out the front door.

"Good luck!" their mother called.

"If only she knew we aren't pretending," Jack whispered to Annie.

"Yeah," said Annie, grinning.

Outside, the sun shone brightly. Birds sang. Crickets chirped. Jack and Annie walked up their street toward the Frog Creek woods.

"I wonder if the weather will be this nice in China," Annie said.

"I don't know. Remember, Morgan said this would be a very scary adventure," said Jack.

"They're always scary," said Annie. "But we always meet animals who help us, or people."

"True," said Jack.

"I bet we meet someone *great* today," said Annie.

Jack smiled. He was starting to feel excited now instead of scared.

"Let's hurry!" he said.

They ran into the Frog Creek woods. They slipped between the tall trees until they came to a huge oak.

"Hello!" came a soft voice they knew well.

They looked up. Morgan was peering down from the magic tree house.

"Ready for your next mission as Master Librarians?" she asked.

"Yes!" said Jack and Annie.

They grabbed the rope ladder and started up.

"Are we still going to China?" asked Annie when they had climbed into the tree house.

"Indeed," said Morgan. "You're going to *ancient* China. Here is the title of the story you must find."

She held up a long, thin strip of wood. It

4

looked like a ruler, except it had strange writing on it instead of numbers.

"Long ago, the Chinese discovered how to make paper. It was one of the world's most important discoveries," said Morgan. "But you are going to a time earlier than that, to a time when books were written on bamboo strips like this one."

"Wow," said Annie, pointing at the figures on the bamboo. "So *this* is Chinese writing?"

"Yes," said Morgan. "Just as we have letters, Chinese writing is made up of many characters. Each one stands for a different thing or idea. These characters are the title of an ancient Chinese legend. You must find the first writing of the legend before the Imperial Library is destroyed."

"Hurry, let's go," said Annie.

"Wait, we need our research book," said Jack.

"Yes, you do," said Morgan.

From the folds of her robe, she pulled out a book. On the cover was the title: *The Time of the First Emperor.*

Morgan handed the book to Jack.

"This research book will *guide* you," she said. "But remember, in your darkest hour, only the old legend can *save* you."

6

"But we have to find it first," said Annie.

"Exactly," said Morgan.

She handed Jack the bamboo strip, and he slipped it into his pack.

Jack pushed his glasses into place, then pointed at the cover of their research book.

"I wish we could go there!" he said.

The wind started to blow.

The tree house started to spin. It spun faster and faster.

Then everything was still.

Absolutely still.

2

The Cowherd

"Oh, wow," Annie said. "These clothes feel so soft. And look, I have a pocket for my secret library card."

Jack opened his eyes. Their clothes had magically changed.

They no longer wore jeans, T-shirts, and sneakers. Instead, they had on baggy pants, loose shirts, straw shoes, and round hats. Annie's shirt had a pocket in it.

Jack saw that his backpack had become a

rough cloth sack. Inside were his research book, his notebook, his library card, and the bamboo strip.

"Cows," said Annie, looking out the window.

Jack looked out, too. The tree house had landed in a lone tree in a sunny field. Cows grazed, and a young man stood watching over them. At the edge of the field was a farmhouse. Beyond the house was a walled city.

"It looks so peaceful," said Annie.

"You can never be sure," said Jack. "Remember, Pompeii looked peaceful before the volcano went off."

"Oh, yeah," said Annie.

"Let's see what the book says," said Jack.

He reached in the sack and pulled out the China book. He opened it and read aloud:

9

Over 2,000 years ago, China was ruled by its first emperor. Because he chose the dragon to be his symbol, he was called the "Dragon King." In China, dragons are seen as brave and powerful creatures.

"Dragon King? That sounds a little scary," said Jack.

"I like his outfit," said Annie.

Next to the writing was a picture. It showed a man wearing a rich, flowing robe with wide sleeves. He also wore a tall hat with beads hanging from it.

Jack pulled out his notebook and wrote:

first emperor called Dragon King

"The book we need must be in the Dragon King's library," said Annie. "I bet his palace is in that city."

Jack looked up.

"Right," he said. "And that's how to get there." He pointed across the field to a dirt road that led to the walled city.

"Good plan," said Annie.

She climbed out of the tree house and started down the rope ladder.

Jack threw the China book and his notebook into his sack. He slung the sack over his shoulder and followed Annie.

When they reached the ground, they started through the field.

"Look, that guy's waving at us," said Annie.

The man tending the cows was shouting and waving. He started running toward them.

"Uh-oh, what's he want?" said Jack.

A moment later, the man stood in their path. He was young and handsome with a kind face.

"Can you do me a great favor?" he asked. "I would be most grateful."

"Of course," said Annie.

"Give a message to the silk weaver. You will see her at the farmhouse," said the young man. "Tell her to meet me here at twilight."

"Sure, no problem," said Annie.

The young man smiled.

"Thank you," he said. Then he started to leave.

"Wait, excuse me—" said Jack. "Do you know where we can find the Imperial Library?"

A look of horror crossed the man's kind face.

"Why?" he whispered.

"Oh, I—I just wondered," said Jack.

The young man shook his head.

"Beware of the Dragon King," he said. "Whatever you do, *beware*."

Then he turned and ran back to his cows.

"Oh, man," whispered Jack. "Now we know one thing for sure."

"What?" asked Annie.

"This place is *not* as peaceful as it seems," Jack said.

3

The Silk Weaver

Jack and Annie kept walking across the pasture toward the road. Annie stopped when they neared the farmhouse.

"We have to find the silk weaver and give her the message," she said.

"Let's do that on our way back," said Jack. "I'm worried about finding the Imperial Library."

"What if we don't have time?" said Annie. "We promised. And he was so nice."

Jack sighed.

"Okay," he said. "But let's find her fast. And remember to keep your head down so no one will notice us."

Jack and Annie bowed their heads as they headed toward the house.

As they got closer, Jack peeked out from under his hat. An ox pulled a cart filled with hay. Men hoed the ground. Women pushed wheelbarrows piled high with grain.

"There!" said Annie. She pointed to an open porch where a young woman was weaving cloth on a loom. "That must be her!"

Annie ran to the silk weaver. Jack looked around to see if anyone was watching. Luckily, all the farmworkers seemed too busy to notice anything. Still looking around carefully, Jack walked toward the porch.

Annie was already talking to the silk weaver.

"What did he say?" the young woman asked. Her voice was soft but strong. Her dark eyes glowed with happiness.

"He said you should meet him in the field at twilight," said Annie. "He's so handsome!"

"Yes, he is." The silk weaver gave Annie a shy smile. Then she reached down to a basket near her loom and picked up a ball of yellow thread.

"It was very brave of you to bring the message," she said. "Please accept this silk thread as my thank-you."

She handed Annie the ball of silk.

"It's beautiful," said Annie. "Feel."

She handed it to Jack. The thread was smooth and soft.

"How do you make silk?" said Jack.

"It is made from the cocoons of silk-worms," said the weaver.

"Really? Worms? That's neat," said Jack. "Let me write that down."

He reached into his sack.

"Please don't!" said the silk weaver. "The making of silk is China's most valuable secret. Anyone who steals the secret will be arrested. The Dragon King will have him put to death."

"Oops," said Jack.

He dropped the ball of silk into his sack.

"I think you must leave quickly," whispered the silk weaver. "You have been seen."

Jack looked over his shoulder. A man was pointing at them.

"Let's go," he said.

"Bye!" said Annie. "Good luck on your date!"

"Thank you," the silk weaver said.

"Come on," said Jack.

They hurried away from the silk weaver.

"Stop!" someone shouted.

"Run!" said Annie.

4

The Great Wall

Jack and Annie ran around the farmhouse. At the back was an oxcart filled with bags of grain. There was no one in sight.

The shouting behind them got louder.

Jack and Annie looked at each other, then dived into the back of the wooden cart. They buried themselves in the middle of the bags of grain.

Jack's heart pounded as the shouts came closer. He held his breath and waited for the people to leave.

Suddenly the cart lurched forward. Someone was driving them away!

Jack and Annie peeked over the bags.
Jack saw the back of the driver. He was calm-
ly steering the oxcart over the dirt road.
They were on their way to the walled city!

Jack and Annie ducked down again.

"This is great!" whispered Annie. "All we
have to do is jump out when we get into
the city."

"Yep," Jack said softly. "Then we'll find the Imperial Library, find the book, and get back to the magic tree house."

"No problem," whispered Annie.

"Whoa!" The cart slowly came to a halt.

Jack held his breath. He heard voices and the heavy tramping of feet—lots of feet. He and Annie peeked out.

"Oh, man," he whispered.

A long line of men was crossing the road in front of the cart. They carried axes, shovels, and hoes. Guards marched alongside them.

"Let's find out what's happening," said Jack.

He reached into his sack and pulled out the China book. Pushing his glasses into place, he found a picture of the workers. He read:

**The Dragon King forced many of his
subjects to start building a wall to
protect China from invaders. Later
emperors made the wall even longer.
Finally, it stretched 3,700 miles along
China's border. The Great Wall of China
is the longest structure ever built.**

"Wow, the Great Wall of China," said Jack.

"I've heard of that," said Annie.

"Who hasn't?" said Jack. "Those guys are going to work on it right now."

Just then, someone grabbed Jack and Annie. They looked up. It was the driver of the cart.

"Who are you?" he asked angrily.

"We—uh—" Jack didn't know what to say.

The man's gaze fell on the open book in Jack's hands. His mouth dropped open. He let go of Jack and Annie. Slowly he reached out and touched the book. He looked back at Jack and Annie with wide eyes.

"What is *this?*" he said.

5

The Scholar

"It's a book from our country," said Jack. "Your books are made of bamboo, but ours are made of paper. Actually, *your* country invented paper. But later, in the future."

The man looked confused.

"Never mind," said Annie. "It's for reading. It's for learning about faraway places."

The man stared at them. Tears filled his eyes.

"What's wrong?" Annie asked softly.

"I *love* reading and learning," he said.

"So do I," said Jack.

The man smiled. "You don't understand! I am dressed as a farmer," he said. "But in truth, I am a scholar!"

"What's a *scholar?*" said Annie.

"We are great readers, learners, and writers," he said. "We have long been the most honored citizens in China."

The scholar's smile faded.

"But now scholars are in danger," he said. "And many of us have gone into hiding."

"Why?" said Jack.

"The Dragon King is afraid of the power of our books and learning," said the scholar. "He wants people to think only what he wants them to think. Any day he may order *the burning of the books!*"

Annie gasped.

"Does that mean what I think it means?" said Jack.

The scholar nodded.

"All the books in the Imperial Library will be burned," he said.

"That's rotten!" said Annie.

"Indeed it is!" the scholar said quietly.

"Listen, we have a mission to get a book from that library," said Jack.

"Who are you?" asked the scholar.

"Show him," said Annie.

She reached into her shirt pocket as Jack reached into his sack. They brought out the secret library cards. The letters shimmered in the sunlight.

The scholar's mouth dropped open again.

"You are Master Librarians," he said. "I

have never met ones so honored who were so young."

He bowed to show his respect.

"Thank you," said Jack and Annie.

They bowed back to him.

"How can I help you?" asked the scholar.

"We need to go to the Imperial Library and find this book," said Jack.

He held out Morgan's bamboo strip to the scholar.

"We will go to the Imperial Library," said the scholar. "As for the story, I know it well. It is a true one, written not long ago. But I warn you. We will be in great danger."

"We know!" said Annie.

The scholar smiled.

"I am happy to be doing something I believe in again," said the scholar. "Let us go!"

They all climbed into the front of the cart. The long line of wall builders was marching in the distance. As the oxen started forward, the scholar turned to Jack and Annie.

"Where are you from?" he asked.

"Frog Creek, Pennsylvania," said Annie.

"I have never heard of it," said the scholar. "Do they have a library there?"

"Oh, sure, there's a library in every town," said Jack. "In fact, there are probably thousands of libraries in our country."

"And millions of books," said Annie. "And no one burns them."

"Right," said Jack. "Everyone gets to go to school to learn to read them."

The scholar stared at him and shook his head.

"It sounds like paradise," he said.

6

The Dragon King

The oxcart bumped across the wooden bridge that crossed over a moat. Then it passed guards standing by giant wooden gates.

"Are the gates ever closed?" Jack asked.

"Oh, yes, every day at sunset," said the scholar. "When the gong sounds, the gates close. The bridge comes up. And the city is sealed shut for the night."

"I guess visitors have to leave before that happens," Annie said. "Or they'll be stuck here for the whole night. Right?"

"Yes," said the scholar.

The cart bumped between the city gates.

Rows of small houses were bunched together on either side of the street. They were made of mud with straw roofs. People cooked over outdoor fires. They washed their clothes in wooden tubs.

As the oxcart bumped along, the houses got larger. These were made of painted wood and pottery tiles. They all had curved roofs.

"Why are those roofs like that?" asked Jack.

"To keep away the bad spirits," said the scholar.

"How do they do that?" said Annie.

"The spirits can only travel in straight lines," said the scholar.

"Wow," whispered Annie.

The cart went by some open tea shops. Then it passed a large market square filled with stalls and shoppers. People were buying and selling fish, chickens, firewood, wagon wheels, silk cloth, furs, and jade jewelry.

Some people were lined up at a stall filled with tiny cages.

"What's for sale there?" said Annie.

"Crickets," the scholar said. "They make good pets. You can feed them tea leaves and enjoy their delicate song."

The cart moved on toward the Dragon King's walled palace. They stopped in front of the palace gates.

"Grain delivery!" the scholar shouted up to the guard at the tower.

The guard waved them through. Inside were beautiful gardens and huge mounds of earth surrounded by a low brick wall.

"That is the Imperial Burial Grounds," said the scholar, pointing at the mounds.

"Who is buried there?" asked Jack.

"The ancestors of the Dragon King," said the scholar.

"What are *ancestors?*" Annie asked.

"They are the people in your family who lived before you," said the scholar. "Someday the Dragon King himself will be buried there. Three hundred thousand workers have been building his burial tomb."

"Oh, man," said Jack.

He looked over his shoulder at the burial grounds. He wondered why it took so many workers to build a tomb.

"*No!*" said the scholar.

Jack whirled around.

"What's wrong?" he asked.

The scholar pointed at the palace court-yard. A dark cloud of smoke was rising into the sky.

"*Fire!*" said the scholar.

"*The books!*" said Jack.

"*Hurry!*" said Annie.

37

The scholar snapped the reins. The oxen trotted up the stone path. When the cart rolled into the courtyard, soldiers were everywhere.

Some threw wood on a huge bonfire. Others were carrying bamboo strips down the steep stairs that led from the palace.

"Are those books?" asked Jack.

"Yes. The strips are tied together into different bundles," moaned the scholar. "Each bundle is a book."

"Look!" said Annie, pointing to the palace entrance.

Stepping outside was a man in a rich, flowing robe and a tall hat. Jack knew him at once—*the Dragon King!*

7

The Burning of the Books

The Dragon King watched the bonfire as it blazed up toward the sky. Around the fire the air was thick and wavy. Bamboo books were stacked beside the fire, waiting to be burned.

"Hurry!" said the scholar.

They jumped down from the cart and joined the crowd by the bonfire.

The Dragon King shouted to the soldiers. They began throwing the books into the fire. The bamboo crackled as it burned.

"Stop!" cried Annie.

Jack grabbed her.

"Quiet!" he said.

Annie pulled away.

"Stop!" she shouted again. But her voice was lost in the noise of the roaring fire.

"*There's* your story!" said the scholar.

He pointed to a bamboo book that had fallen off a waiting stack.

"I'll get it!" said Annie.

She dashed over to the book.

"Annie!" cried Jack.

But she had already snatched up the bundle of bamboo strips and was charging back to them.

"Got it! Quick, put it in your sack!" she said.

Jack put the bundle of bamboo strips in his

sack. Then he looked around fearfully. He gasped.

The Dragon King was glaring at them! Then he headed their way.

"Seize them!" the Dragon King shouted.

"Run through the burial grounds!" the scholar said to Jack and Annie. "The soldiers will be afraid to follow. They fear the spirits of the ancestors!"

"Thanks!" said Jack. "Thanks for everything!"

"Good luck!" cried Annie.

Then she and Jack took off. Soldiers shouted after them. An arrow whizzed by.

But Jack and Annie kept running. They ran down the path to the burial grounds. They jumped over the low brick wall and ran between the huge mounds of earth.

Suddenly arrows filled the air around them. The archers were shooting from the tower!

"Look!" cried Jack.

There was a doorway in one of the mounds. Jack and Annie ducked inside.

They were in a long hall lit with oil lamps.

"It's so quiet," said Annie. She walked down the passageway. "Hey, there are some steps here."

"Don't go any farther!" said Jack.

"Why not?" said Annie.

"We don't know what's down there," said Jack. "This is a burial tomb, remember? It's creepy."

"Let's just take a quick look," said Annie. "Maybe it's the way out of here."

Jack took a deep breath.

"You might be right," he said. "Okay, but go slow." He didn't want to stumble upon a dead body.

Annie started down the steep steps. Jack followed. The lamps lit their way as they kept going down and down. Finally, they reached the bottom.

Jack blinked. Even though oil lamps glowed everywhere, it was hard to see at first.

When Jack's eyes got used to the strange light, his heart nearly stopped.

"Oh, man," he breathed.

They were in a room *filled* with soldiers— thousands of them.

8

The Tomb

Jack and Annie stood frozen.

The silent soldiers did, too.

Finally, Annie spoke.

"They're fake," she said.

"Fake?" whispered Jack.

"They're not real," she said.

"They *look* real," said Jack.

Annie walked straight toward the front row of soldiers.

Jack held his breath.

Annie pulled the soldier's nose.

"Fake!" she said.

"Oh, brother," said Jack. He walked over to the soldier and touched his painted face. It was as hard as stone.

"It's amazing," Jack said.

Annie nodded. "It's like a museum."

She walked down a row between two lines of soldiers.

"Wait. This is spooky," said Jack. "What *is* this place?"

He put down his sack and pulled out the China book. He found a picture of the frozen army and read aloud:

> The Dragon King had 7,000 life-size clay figures made for his burial tomb. The clay was baked and painted.

The Dragon King hoped that the clay army would protect him after he died.

"It's like the pyramid in ancient Egypt," said Jack. "Remember? The queen was buried with a boat and lots of things to take to the afterlife." He looked around. "Annie?"

"I'm here," she called. She was far down another row.

"Come back here," yelled Jack.

"No, *you* come here," said Annie. "It's so cool. All their faces are different."

Jack threw the book into his sack. Then he hurried down the row to Annie.

"Look," she said. "Just look."

In the flickering lamplight, they wandered down the rows of soldiers. No two soldiers had the same nose, the same eyes, or the same mouth.

"Oh, man. No wonder so many people had to work on this tomb," said Jack.

"They really did a good job," said Annie.

"Yeah," said Jack.

There were kneeling archers and foot soldiers dressed in red and black armor.

There were real bronze swords, daggers, axes, spears, bows, and arrows.

There were even life-size wooden chariots with horses. The horses looked completely real. They were different colors with white teeth and red tongues.

"I have to take some notes about all this," said Jack.

He pulled out his notebook and pencil. Then, kneeling on the brick floor, he wrote:

*no two faces the same
not even the horses*

"Ja-ack," said Annie. "You know what?"

"What?"

"I think we're lost," she said.

"Lost?" Jack stood up. "We're not lost."

"Yeah? Then which way is out?" said Annie.

Jack looked around. All he could see were rows of soldiers. In front of them, to the right, to the left, behind them—nothing but clay soldiers.

"Which way did we come?" said Annie.

"I don't know," said Jack.

All the rows looked the same. They stretched out endlessly.

Jack tried not to panic.

"I'd better look this up," he said.

"Forget it," said Annie. "Morgan said the research book would *guide* us. But in our darkest hour, only the ancient legend would *save* us."

"Is this our darkest hour?" asked Jack.

Annie nodded. "Yeah, it's pretty dark."

It does seem to be getting darker in here, thought Jack. The air was getting thicker, too. It seemed harder to breathe.

"Let's ask for help," said Jack.

He reached into the sack and pulled out the bamboo book. He held it up and said,

"Save us!"

As Jack waited, the tomb seemed unbearably quiet.

Jack held the book up again. "Please help us find our way out," he said.

He and Annie kept waiting. But nothing happened.

The air was growing even thicker. The light was getting dimmer. The countless rows of soldiers seemed creepier.

Help did not come.

Jack felt faint. "I—I guess we'll just have—have to—"

"Look!" Annie said.

"What?"

"The ball of thread! It rolled out of your sack!" she said.

"So what?" said Jack.

He looked at his cloth sack lying on the floor. The ball of yellow silk thread *had* rolled out. And it was *still* rolling, leaving a trail of yellow thread!

9
The Silk Path

"What's going on?" said Jack.

"I don't know," said Annie. "But we'd better follow it."

She hurried after the ball of silk thread.

Jack put the bamboo book into his sack and took off after her.

They followed the trail of thread down the row, where it turned down *another* row.

"Hey, that's impossible!" said Jack. "That's scientifically impossible!"

"I told you, it's magic!" cried Annie.

Jack couldn't believe it. But he kept following the thread.

Suddenly the trail of thread was gone. The ball had completely unrolled.

Jack and Annie stood still for a moment and caught their breath.

"What—what now?" said Jack.

"I guess we go up those stairs," Annie said.

"What stairs?" said Jack.

"There."

Jack looked through the dim light and saw the entrance to a stairway only a few feet away.

"Let's get out of here!" he said.

They ran up the stairs. At the top, they saw that they were in the hall that led to the entrance of the mound.

They walked and walked and walked down the lamp-lit passage. Finally, Jack stopped.

"I don't remember this hall being so long," he said.

"Me neither," said Annie. "I guess those weren't the same stairs that we went down."

"What should we do now?" said Jack.

"We'd better keep going," said Annie.

"Yeah, we don't have much choice," said Jack.

They started walking again. They rounded a corner and came to a door.

"Oh, great!" said Annie.

"Wait. We don't know what's on the other side," said Jack. "Go slow. Be careful."

"Okay," said Annie.

Slowly and carefully, she opened the door. Then she peeked out.

"Yippee," she said softly.

Annie stepped into the fading daylight. Jack stepped out after her.

The sun had gone down.

They were standing *outside* the gate of the Dragon King's palace. They could see the market not far away. The stalls were closing for the day.

"We're safe!" said Annie.

Jack breathed a huge sigh of relief.

Just then, a gong sounded. It was coming

from the tower of the city walls!

"Oh, man! They're going to close the gates!" said Jack.

He clutched his sack as they took off. They charged up the street. They ran past the market. They ran past the rich houses...past the poor houses.

Their straw shoes fell off. But Jack and Annie kept running barefoot.

Just as the giant wooden gates started to close, they tore through them.

They charged across the bridge and kept running up the dirt road, past the farmhouse, and through the field.

By the time they reached their tree, Jack's lungs ached. His heart pounded. His feet burned.

He followed Annie up the rope ladder. When they got inside the tree house, Jack collapsed.

"Let's—go—home," he said, out of breath.

He reached for the Pennsylvania book.

"Wait," said Annie, looking out the window. "They found each other."

"Who—found—who?" said Jack, panting.

He dragged himself to the window and looked out.

Two figures embraced at the edge of the field.

"The silk weaver and the man who takes care of the cows!" said Annie.

"Oh, yeah," said Jack.

"Bye!" Annie called to them.

The couple waved back.

Annie sighed happily.

"We can leave now," she said.

Jack opened the Pennsylvania book and pointed at the picture of the Frog Creek woods.

"I wish we could go there," he said.

The wind started to blow.

Jack looked out one last time at the Chinese couple. They seemed to be glowing like stars.

The tree house started to spin.

It spun faster and faster.

Then everything was still.

Absolutely still.

10

The Ancient Legend

Jack opened his eyes. He was wearing his own clothes and his sneakers. The cloth sack had turned back into his backpack.

"Welcome home, Master Librarians," said Morgan.

She stood in the tree house, smiling at them.

"Hi!" said Annie.

"We brought you the ancient legend," said Jack.

"Wonderful!" said Morgan.

Jack reached into his pack. He took out the China book. Then he pulled out the bamboo book. He handed them to Morgan.

"What's the legend about?" said Annie.

"It's called *The Silk Weaver and the Cowherd*," said Morgan. "It's a very famous Chinese tale."

"Guess what, Morgan?" said Annie. "We actually *met* them! We helped them get together!"

"Oh, did you?" said Morgan.

"Yes!" said Jack. "The silk weaver's ball of silk saved us!"

"What does the legend say about them?" asked Annie.

"It says that long ago they were heavenly beings who lived in the sky," said Morgan.

"When they came to earth, they fell in love."

"That's when we met them!" said Annie.

"Yes, I imagine so," said Morgan. "The book you brought back tells about their happiness on earth. But I'm afraid a later legend tells us that when they returned to the sky, the king and queen of the skies separated them by a heavenly river called the Milky Way."

"Oh, no," said Annie.

"They get back together once a year," said Morgan. "On that night, birds make a bridge in the sky over the Milky Way."

Jack and Annie gazed up at the bright summer sky.

"Go home now," said Morgan. "Come back two weeks from today. Next you're going to find a book in the country of Ireland, over a thousand years ago."

"That sounds like fun," said Annie.

Morgan frowned.

"I'm afraid it was a very dangerous time," she said. "For Viking raiders often attacked the seacoasts."

"Vikings?" said Jack. He'd had enough danger to last a long time.

"Don't worry about it now," said Morgan. "Just go home and rest."

Jack nodded.

"I'll try," he said, pulling on his backpack.

"Bye," said Annie. "See you in two weeks."

"Thank you for your help," said Morgan.

"Anytime," said Annie.

They headed down the rope ladder.

From the ground, they waved to Morgan. Then they started for home.

As they got to the edge of the woods, Annie stopped.

"Listen to the crickets," she said.

Jack listened. The cricket chirps sounded louder than usual.

"Their ancestors lived in the time of the Dragon King," said Annie.

"Oh, brother," said Jack.

"Right now the grownups are telling the little crickets a legend," said Annie.

"Yeah, sure," said Jack.

"A legend passed down from their ancestors," said Annie.

Jack smiled. He didn't want to admit it, but the cricket noise *did* sound like storytelling. He could almost hear them saying, *Dragon King, Dragon King, Dragon King.*

"Jack! Annie!" came a voice.

It was their mother calling them.

The spell was broken. The cricket stories were just plain old cricket sounds again.

"Coming!" Jack shouted.

Jack and Annie ran down their street and across their yard.

"Did you have a good time in China?" their mom asked.

"It was pretty scary," said Annie.

"We got lost in a tomb," said Jack. "But we were saved by an ancient book."

Their mom smiled and shook her head. "My, books are wonderful, aren't they?" she said.

"Yep!" said Jack and Annie.

And they followed her inside.

Don't miss the next Magic Tree House book,
when Jack and Annie are whisked back to
ancient Ireland to find another book in

MAGIC TREE HOUSE #15

VIKING SHIPS
AT SUNRISE

(August 1998)

The Mystery of the Ancient Riddles
(Books #9–12)

☐ **Magic Tree House #9, DOLPHINS AT DAYBREAK,** in which Jack and Annie arrive on a coral reef, where they find a mini-submarine that takes them underwater into the home of sharks and dolphins.

☐ **Magic Tree House #10, GHOST TOWN AT SUNDOWN,** in which Jack and Annie travel to the Wild West, where they battle horse thieves, meet a kindly cowboy, and get some help from a mysterious ghost.

☐ **Magic Tree House #11, LIONS AT LUNCHTIME,** in which Jack and Annie go to the plains of Africa, where they help wild animals cross a rushing river and have a picnic with a Masai warrior.

☐ **Magic Tree House #12, POLAR BEARS PAST BEDTIME,** in which Jack and Annie go to the Arctic, where they get help from a seal hunter, play with polar bear cubs, and get trapped on thin ice.

The Mystery of the Lost Libraries
(Books #13–16)

❑ **Magic Tree House #13, Vacation Under the Volcano,** in which Jack and Annie land in Pompeii during Roman times, on the very day that Mount Vesuvius erupts.

Read all the Magic Tree House books!

Available wherever books are sold...OR
You can send in this coupon (with check or money order)
and have the books mailed directly to you!

❏ Magic Tree House #1, DINOSAURS BEFORE DARK
(0-679-82411-1) $3.99

❏ Magic Tree House #2, THE KNIGHT AT DAWN
(0-679-82412-X) $3.99

❏ Magic Tree House #3, MUMMIES IN THE MORNING
(0-679-82424-3) $3.99

❏ Magic Tree House #4, PIRATES PAST NOON
(0-679-82425-1) $3.99

❏ Magic Tree House #5, NIGHT OF THE NINJAS
(0-679-86371-0) $3.99

❏ Magic Tree House #6, AFTERNOON ON THE AMAZON
(0-679-86372-9) $3.99

❏ Magic Tree House #7, SUNSET OF THE SABERTOOTH
(0-679-86373-7) $3.99

❏ Magic Tree House #8, MIDNIGHT ON THE MOON
(0-679-86374-5) $3.99

❏ Magic Tree House #9, DOLPHINS AT DAYBREAK
(0-679-88338-X) $3.99

❏ Magic Tree House #10, GHOST TOWN AT SUNDOWN
(0-679-88339-8) $3.99

❏ Magic Tree House #11, LIONS AT LUNCHTIME
(0-679-88340-1) $3.99

❏ Magic Tree House #12, POLAR BEARS PAST BEDTIME
(0-679-88341-X) $3.99

❏ Magic Tree House #13, VACATION UNDER THE VOLCANO
(0-679-89050-5) $3.99

Subtotal ....$ _____
Shipping and handling..............................$ __3.00__
Sales tax (where applicable)............... _____
Total amount enclosed............................$ _____

Name _____

Address _____

City_____ State _____ Zip _____

Prices and numbers subject to change without notice. Valid in U.S. only.
All orders subject to availability. Please allow 4 to 6 weeks for delivery.

Make your check or money order (no cash or C.O.D.s)
payable to Random House, Inc., and mail to:
Magic Tree House Mail Sales, 400 Hahn Road, Westminster, MD 21157.

Need your books even faster? Call toll-free 1-800-793-2665
to order by phone and use your major credit card.
Please mention interest code 049-20 to expedite your order.

Do you love the Magic Tree House books?

**Do you want sneak previews
of the next book in the series?**

Climb the ladder into
The Magic Tree House Club!

You'll get:
- three newsletters filled with fun facts,
  games, puzzles, and a note from author
  Mary Pope Osborne
- a super Magic Tree House surprise
- plus chances to win free books and prizes

SIGN ME UP! I want to be a member of
The Magic Tree House Club.

MY NAME: _____

MY ADDRESS: _____

_____

Have an adult write a $1.50 check or money order
payable to Random House, Inc., for shipping and
handling. Send this coupon and your check or money
order to:

The Magic Tree House Club
Random House, Inc.
201 East 50th Street
Mail Drop 30-2
New York, NY 10022

Visit the

MAGIC TREE HOUSE

website

at

www.randomhouse.com/magictreehouse/

MORE FACTS FOR YOU AND JACK

1. Chinese writing has over 50,000 characters. According to legend, the first characters were devised from the tracks of birds and animals.

2. In 221 B.C., China was divided into many kingdoms. Under the leadership of the first emperor, Shi Huangdi (who called himself the Dragon King), China became a united country. Afraid that Chinese scholars were a threat to his power, he ordered all their books burned.

3. Silk thread comes from the cocoon of the silkworm, which feeds on mulberry leaves. The art of making silk was kept a secret because the Chinese once depended on silk for foreign trade.

4. The first emperor built the Great Wall to protect his empire from northern invaders. According to Chinese legend, the wall is a dragon that has turned to stone.

5. Since the 1970s, archaeologists have been investigating the Dragon King's tomb and have unearthed over 50,000 artifacts.

6. The Chinese legend of the silk weaver and the cowherd is connected with the stars Vega and Altair. The two were married on earth. But when they returned to heaven, they were so happy that they refused to work. The king and queen of Heaven grew angry and separated them by the Milky Way. But once a year, they are together. On the seventh day of the seventh moon, magpies make a bridge between them.

DATE DUE			
FE 19 02	15		
FE 5 03			
FE 26 '03			
MR 27 03			
5			
25			
13			
24 2000			
DEC 9 2003			

DEMCO 128-5046

The Last Yankees

Gathering hay by hand. USDA Farm Security Administration; photo by Jack Delano, 1941.

The Last Yankees

*Folkways in Eastern Vermont
and the Border Country*

Scott E. Hastings, Jr.

University Press of New England   Hanover and London

#20391959

UNIVERSITY PRESS OF NEW ENGLAND
Brandeis University
Brown University
Clark University
University of Connecticut
Dartmouth College
University of New Hampshire
University of Rhode Island
Tufts University
University of Vermont
Wesleyan University

© 1990 by Scott E. Hastings, Jr.

Designed and produced by Christopher Harris/Summer Hill Books
Perkinsville, Vermont
Printed in the United States of America
∞

Library of Congress Cataloging-in-Publication Data

Hastings, Jr. Scott E.
    The last Yankees: folkways in eastern Vermont and the border
country / Scott E. Hastings, Jr.
        p.   cm.
    ISBN 0–87451–510–6. — ISBN 0–87451–511–4 (pbk.)
    1. Vermont—Social life and customs.   2. New Hampshire—Social
life and customs.   3. Material culture—Vermont.   4. Material
culture—New Hampshire.   5. Vermont—Industries.   6. New Hampshire—
Industries.   I. Title.
    F55.H37   1990
    974.3—dc20   89–24785
                                                            CIP

This publication has been supported by the National Endowment
for the Humanities, a federal agency which supports the study of
such fields as history, philosophy, literature, and languages.

5 4 3 2 1

To Elsie Elizabeth Hastings for all the sunshine and flowers,

and to
Josephine and Scott Hastings,
Maurice Page, Edward Clay,
and
Mary and Laurance Rockefeller

I have suggested that the old rural society was society's unconscious, possessing two more-or-less distinct levels like the unconscious of the individual: the preconscious into which sink outdated customs, half-forgotten science, outmoded fashions, and words and phrases once the coin of polite conversation but gradually demoted into the rural dialect; and beneath this at a level more rarely exposed the true phylogenetic unconscious where the most archaic beliefs and modes of thinking have lasted until recent years. This level is a rich repository of much of the rural history of these islands.

George Ewart Evans, *The Pattern Under the Plough,* London, 1966

Contents

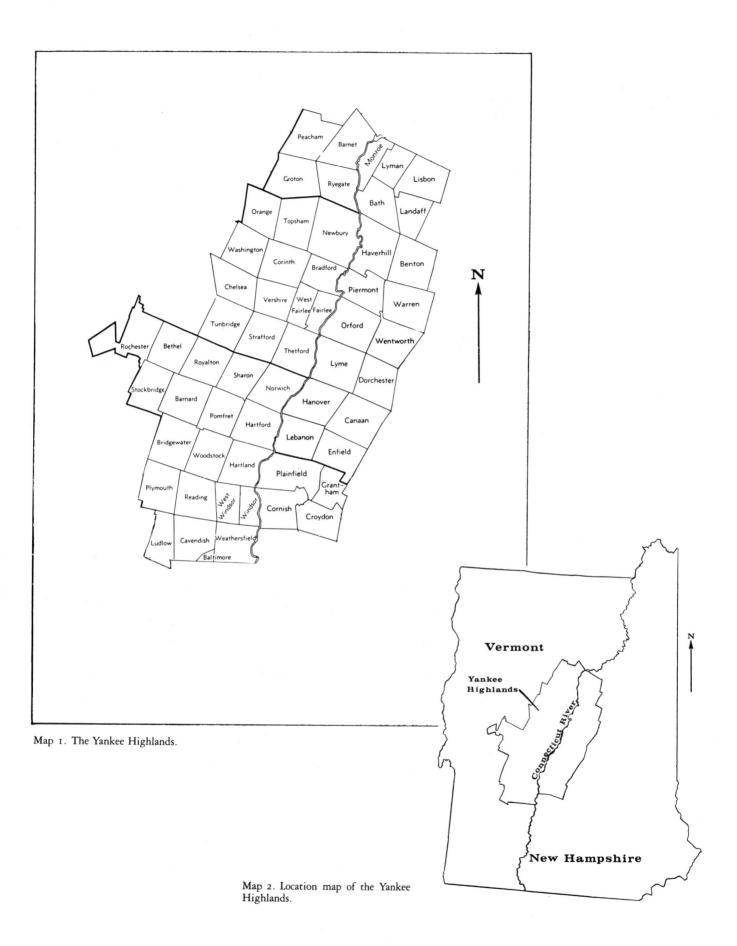

Map 1. The Yankee Highlands.

Map 2. Location map of the Yankee Highlands.

Preface

What is folklife? As a discipline, it embraces the spectrum of life for pre- or partially industrialized groups living submerged on the fringes of the industrial revolution and in isolated corners of the planet. Its interests lie equally in how things are made and used and the end results of that use—be they built objects such as a basket or a woods sled; less tangible phenomena like the telling and playing of tales and tunes; or something in between, say the planting, harvesting, and processing of crops. We are also interested in the traditional lore and folk wisdom governing all of this.

By comparison with European nations, the United States is so vast and diverse that relatively little has been done with folklife studies. The country is full of unexamined, regional folk worlds: unknown, mysterious, and therefore full of fascination.

Since the 1950s, firsthand, practical knowledge of folk trades and small local industry has diminished sharply. This decline in knowledge has been directly proportional to the death rate of the men who followed this way of life. Their tools and jigs and patterns, except for the comparative few saved by collectors, have vanished by the hundreds of thousands. It is the same for the shops, mill buildings, farms, and roadsides where they worked. The machinery and plenishings have long ago been broken up and scattered—the structures demolished or left to rot down.

This book deals with men who spent their lives working at archaic folk trades and small industry in a hilly patch of northern New England, which I call the Yankee Highlands. Their skills and wisdom, and those of the women who shared in this life, reflect the life of the farms, forests, and tiny mills that once defined the place. These livelihoods were passed down over many generations. Some date to before the Civil War—a few to early settlement times. Because of people like these, as well as effects of cultural factors and isolation, these trades and industries survived until recently. In each instance, they continued in practice substantially unaltered, save for the occasional, inevitable incorporation of technological change along the way.

A word concerning the background of this book might be of interest. By the end of the 1950s, a very old way of life was teetering on the edge of extinction in much of east central and northern Vermont and the New Hampshire border country. In the late 1960s, I began to record as much of it as I was able, given the demands of full-time work in another field. I took photographs (which, together with my maps and drawings, illustrate the book except where other sources are indicated in the captions), found good informants, and collected a great deal of now irreplaceable material. Nevertheless, I could see that much was steadily slipping away.

In 1970, I hit upon the idea of contacting Laurance S. Rockefeller, who owned an old vacant mill site in Woodstock, Vermont. It seemed to me an ideal location for a museum of Vermont's regional folklife. I wrote to him outlining the possibilities for such a museum, but there was no interest in the project at that time. Mrs. Rockefeller's family, however, still owned the farm and estate of her grandfather, Frederick S. Billings, which is located at the edge of the village. By 1972 she and Mr. Rockefeller had decided to purchase all the family shares in the farm and were thinking about how best to secure its future. At this point, they recalled my letter and offered to hire me for a year while I proved that enough artifacts and knowledge yet remained in the countryside to make establishment of a folklife museum at the farm a practical undertaking.

At the end of that year, the Rockefellers commissioned the Vermont Folklife Research Project, which I directed for ten years. During this time, I located and purchased more than twelve thousand museum-quality, folk artifacts of farm, forest, and mill, ranging in size from a sewing thimble to a functioning, water-powered mill. I also implemented a cataloging system and organized a fully equipped workshop to order and preserve the items, and I put together a far-ranging library of folklife and agricultural history. I hired and trained a small staff and helped form a master plan for the museum.

The initial years of the project were devoted to garnering as much as possible of the seamless and intricate web of folk knowledge still lodged under the white thatch of old heads. These people were the ones who owned, or discovered for me, the archaic objects and implements they alone remembered how to use. My days (and long days they were, too) were filled with establishing contacts and trust. Then came months of recording sessions, while I gathered information over a cup of tea in a farm kitchen or on the floor of an old mill filled with the muted thunder of water falling over a wooden dam.

Before my work could begin, however, it was necessary to establish geographical boundaries for the region I intended to study. The Yankee Highlands will not be found on any map but the one in this book. The territory is some thirty or forty miles wide by sixty miles long, the western border lying along the crest of the Green Mountains in Vermont. Eastward, the land descends in a confusion of rough, broken hills and mountains. These promontories are intersected and pushed back by a labyrinthine maze of deep, narrow valleys, through which rush swift streams and rivers—the watershed of the Connecticut. With this river, the concept of a culturally cohesive region spills over into the valley towns of New Hampshire. Close ties have always existed between Vermont and New Hampshire river towns.

The population of the Yankee Highlands is concentrated in the towns and large farms along the river. In the hills rising steeply from the river intervales, farms and villages are smaller. A few farms are sited on the hilltops, the valley slopes being given over to rough pasture and woodlots. This backcountry exists on a scale nicely fitted to humans, a fact often commented on by the observant outsider. The hills confine the sky so that it is small. Fields are small, too, and often stony and sharply tilted. Fields encompass every bit of arable land. For that reason they fit no standard field pattern but are irregularly shaped. Along the valley bottoms it is the same—here the fields assume their shapes from being crowded against the wooded ridges. It is no uncommon thing to find that a hill has pinched off a field, pushing the narrow dirt road beside it onto a slim overhang above the stream below.

Prolonged isolation on remote mountain farms and villages helped pre-serve the patterns of life originally brought from the British Isles, then sub-jected to one hundred and fifty years of adaptation to conditions of life in the Atlantic littoral. Vermont, with parts of New Hampshire and Maine, was the first American frontier after the initial settlement of the colonies. It is this fact, together with a harsh climate and a loose settlement pattern of scattered farms and villages (quite unlike the tight, English-style farm/village clusters of south-ern New England), that has been responsible for the persistence of an indepen-dent frontier cast of mind lasting well into the twentieth century. Even now, among the older generation, this mindset has not entirely disappeared.

As with Vermont's Northeast Kingdom, the Yankee Highlands is both a real place and a working concept. While its interior glows with a fine clear color, its joinings with neighboring realms are not the reassuring, precisely inked black lines of a map, instead they fade and blur in hazy meldings. Nonetheless, overall similarities in climate, geographic features, and cultural traits (speech patterns, household practices, woods craft, work opportunities, farming prac-tice, and world view are examples) make this a definable place. It is real—for all that its borders occasionally fall off the map.

This place held a culture marked by tenacity, independence, ingenuity, and individualism. The first three traits gave rise to the myth of the archetypal north country Yankee. The latter two ensured that, in reality, no two were ever alike.

Acknowledgments

I would like to offer my sincere thanks to the following persons and organizations for the use of materials, which add so much to this book (listing is alphabetical):

The Billings Farm & 1890 Museum for the use of photographs taken by the author during fieldwork, 1973–1983.

William Gove, Randolph, Vermont, for several photographs of bateaux on the Connecticut River log drives.

The Historic American Engineering Record and the Library of Congress for the architectural drawings of Ben Thresher's Mill, West Barnet, Vermont.

Mary Anne O'Hara, when she was a fieldworker for the Vermont Folklife Research Project in the mid-1970s, conducted several excellent interviews with elderly farm women. I am grateful to be able to include her insightful interview with Nettie Adams in chapter 13, under the title, "Recollections of a Farm Woman."

Maurice Page, East Corinth, Vermont, for the photograph of three generations of Pages who operated Page's Box Shop.

William S. Richards, Fairfax, Virginia, for his patient searching of the archives of the Farm Security Administration in the Library of Congress and for sending me samples from which to choose a selection of photographs for this book.

John St. Croix, Hartford, Vermont, for photographs of log drive bateaux near White River Junction, Vermont, c. 1912.

With sincere thanks to my editors, Jeff Grathwohl and Mary Crittendon, who became my friends.

Taftsville, Vermont   S.E.H., Jr.
July 1989

1. Oliver Hastings, a farmer, carpenter,
and mason, McIndoe Falls, Vermont.

Part I

MILLS AND TRADES

2. Page's Box Shop, ca. 1912, showing Maurice Page's father, grandfather, and great grandfather.

1

The Water Tub Maker

Page's Box Shop
East Corinth, Vermont

3. Page's Box Shop, in East Corinth, Vermont.

The Tabor Branch of Waits River rises in a remote area in the northwest corner of Topsham, Vermont. By the time the stream enters East Corinth, a few miles to the south, the Powder Spring, Levi, and Hedgehog streams have added their waters to it and made it a small river.

In 1858, if you were to travel from the southern end of East Corinth and proceed northward along the Tabor Branch, you would find the following small, water-powered rural industries: Page's blacksmith shop, a carding mill, another blacksmith shop, a grist mill, two shoe shops, a blacksmith shop, a carriage shop, a starch "factory," and, finally, a sawmill.

Toward the end of the 1800s, the existing shops were enlarged, or new ones were built, as the older mills disappeared. Among the survivors were the Burgess carriage and buggy shop, Page's Box Shop, the Bowen-Hunter Company cotton bobbin mill, and the Jackman Company woolen bobbin mill.

At the lower end of the village still stands Page's Box Shop, sole survivor of the string of water-powered shops and mills that once lined Tabor Branch. A great wooden pulley, rising vertically through the shop floor, once transferred the water power to a spider web of line shafts and pulleys suspended from the ceiling. Belts drop from the spinning pulleys to turn woodworking machinery a hundred or more years old. Among the machines is one capable of driving several nails at once. A two-bladed circular saw adjusts to cut tub staves and box parts to standard lengths, while a double-spindle shaper is now used mostly as a means of shaping the circumference of water tub bottoms to form a watertight seal with the staved wall of the tub. Thickness planers, a drill press or two, a large bandsaw, and a homemade disk sander complete the machinery roster. In the cellar is a long disused, ancient metal-working lathe, partly built of timber.

Littered work benches line the walls, and hand tools are everywhere. Stacks of cut lumber awaiting assembly vie for space with baskets of shavings and pieces yet to be cut. In winter, heat is furnished by an ancient cast iron box stove in a corner by the stairs. On the second floor are forms for making round and oval

3

cheese boxes. A scrollsaw and a machine for cutting box lock corner joints, both shop built but no longer used, are shoved into a spare corner.

Various shop formulae, stave bevels for different tubs, set dimensions and other data for making boxes, tubs, stanchions, and so on, which have accumulated over the years, have been drawn on boards, written on the walls, and notched or painted on other portions of the building. Parts of the building itself have thus become gauges used when making the shop's products. At its peak, Page's Box Shop employed four men and also sold farm machinery made by Sargent, Osgood and Roundy of Randolph, Vermont, and the Walter A. Wood Company of Hoosick Falls, New York. Today there is only Maurice Page, who has run the place alone since the death of his father, C. M. Page, in 1952. He makes all sorts of boxes and novelty items to order, and he continues to make the traditional tubs that have always been made in the shop. A new use for these tubs has been found in the modern hot tub.

I first met Maurice Page in mid-June of 1973, on the very day I began the fieldwork for Laurance Rockefeller that resulted, ten years later, in the Billings Farm & 1890 Museum. Maurice was the first of my informants. I had passed his place several times while traveling the countryside recording small derelict mills and shops for a course in industrial archaeology at Dartmouth College. Often, as I drove by, I'd catch a glimpse of a tall, spare man dressed in green work clothes with an old feedstore cap perched on his head.

That morning, I rose early, packed my camera, tape recorder, and notebooks in the car and set out for East Corinth. When I got there, Maurice was already hard at work assembling boxes at the old-fashioned nailing machine. The din was deafening. When he saw me standing in the door, he shut it down. Turning, he gave me a long look, trying to place me. When he couldn't, he gave me a small smile and, in one of the most authentic Vermont accents I have ever heard, said,

"And what can I do for you, young feller?"

That day I began a long friendship with Maurice and his wife Ruth. I spent the morning poking around the shop, and he let me eat my lunch there when he went up the hill to his house for dinner—an act of trust, for the place was full of shavings (a fire hazard) and valuable tools. Before I left that afternoon, he agreed to let me record the making of a stock watering tub he planned to begin in a few days.

Shops and mills like these do not make good calendar art. They have no picturesque, overshot mill wheel slowly turning under a sparkling headrace. Instead, their power source, in spite of still being called "the wheel," is the cast iron turbine invented in France in 1827 by Fourneyron. It lays hidden deep in the bowels of the mill—buried in a pit of water in a wooden or concrete enclosure called a press box. By the late 1840s, especially in northern New England with its abundant water power, turbines had made great inroads in the use of the traditional water wheel as a power source. Still in the process of development, the turbines were made throughout the 1890s by "cut and try" methods in a multitude of small foundries and machine shops throughout

4. Typical old-fashioned timber dam, in Bridgewater, Vermont.

Vermont, New Hampshire, and Massachusetts. The extensive use of the turbine during the latter half of the nineteenth century and well into the first half of the present one is a relatively unknown chapter of American industrial history.

Wherever sufficient "drop" was present, a stream or river often carried one mill after another. It was only necessary that the dam of the next mill downstream be located sufficiently distant that the level of its millpond could not choke the tailrace of the mill upstream of it. Dams, especially on small northern streams, were often built of wood (see illus. 4), and such was the dam of choice along Tabor Branch. A great hewn log called the "mudsill" or "tole log," set in a trench dug across the river's width, formed the upstream anchor of wooden dams. To it were fastened heavy, vertical, morticed and tenoned, triangular frames spaced every few feet across the river. The downstream base of these frames rested on ledge or upon a cribwork of logs. To heavy stringers fastened to the upper faces of the frames were nailed the three-inch-thick doubled planking that retained the pond. The upper six feet of the dam was often triple-planked against the ravages of ice "going out" in the spring of the year. The two ends of the dam were tied into thick stone or log abutments built into each bank and projecting well upstream and downstream of the dam. The detail of such dams is clearly shown in the drawings accompanying chapter 4 on Ben Thresher's Mill.

In addition to a Chase turbine built in Orange, Massachusetts, Page's Box Shop possessed a horizontal, double-acting, twenty-five horse power, mill-type steam engine made by the Steam Engine Company of Watertown, New York. It was installed in 1893 when C. M. Page built a milk receiving station in the north end of the box shop. The turbine remained in use until about forty years ago, when the owners of one of the bobbin mills upstream persuaded C. M. Page to switch to electricity because they felt his dam was backing water onto their turbine and lessening its efficiency. The steam engine, originally emplaced to supply power during the annual period of low water in July and August, continued in use through 1943.

The present owner, Maurice B. Page, is the fourth generation of his family to work the mill. He began working with his father in 1924 and is still at it today. During its lifetime, this small enterprise has made countless things of wood. Beehives and cow stanchions were made for use on surrounding farms. Butter boxes of poplar, hand-brushed with wax to prevent the butter from picking up a "woody" flavor, were made by the thousands. Cheese boxes were made of pine. Five-pound butter prints were made of maple or basswood. The market for wooden butter and cheese boxes disappeared about the year 1952, however, because local creameries began shipping their cream and milk to large producers of butter and cheese outside the region.

A great deal of maple sugar was made locally and shipped outside the state. Cast in rectangular blocks using tin molds, the sugar was packed in basswood sugar boxes lined with paper. One year the box shop made more than four thousand such boxes. The great hurricane of 1938 destroyed many sugar bushes, and in ensuing years many farmers stopped sugaring. This, along with the switch to tinned maple syrup, killed the demand for sugar boxes. Very few were made after the death of C. M. Page. During the heyday of hard block sugar, though, the shop made sugar boxes for farmers on Taplin Hill, Corinth Corners, Bradford, Vershire, West Fairlee, East Randolph, Newbury, Goose Green, Wells River, and many other places. The boxes were usually shipped as "shooks," or "knocked down," to save shipping space. Because of their box lock corners, they were easily and quickly assembled by the sugar makers as needed. A printing press on the second floor of the shop printed the sides and ends of the boxes with the name and address of the sugar producer.

In C. M.'s time, the box shop made "steam boxes" for the Maverick Mills of East Boston, Massachusetts. Bobbins of woolen yarn were packed in these boxes and exposed to steam "to take the twist out of the yarn." After his father's death, Maurice made round and oval bentwood boxes for cheese and butter. One-eighth-inch clear basswood was used for the sides, and the bending was done with the aid of hot water. Maurice, himself, made the necessary jigs and fixtures. Shortly after he began making this product, though, the market went to pasteboard, forcing him to cease production of this type of box.

A very old blacksmith shop, attached to the box shop, was the original structure of this Page family manufactory. Inside there was still a standup slant-top desk. I opened it one day and found two old fifes. Maurice told me that his grandfather, Charles Page, and two other Civil War veterans, Captain Stubb and Joe Welch, often played those fifes and a drum in the smithy until after dark. If we could only have recordings of those tunes!

Charles Page carried on the smithy until his death in 1906. Since that time, its only use has been to make hoops for water tubs. Charles Page never shoed horses, but he did repair farm machinery and performed the general blacksmithing work so greatly in demand at the time. He and the men he knew must have chewed a great deal of tobacco, for the smithy wall next to the road was stuck full of hundreds of the brightly colored tin name tags once affixed to cutplug tobacco.

THE GENERATIONS

Reuben Page (1741–1841): Soldier in the Revolutionary War and an early settler of Corinth, Vermont.

William Page (1801–1868): Son of Rueben Page. Built a blacksmith shop on Tabor Branch in East Corinth Village sometime between 1820 and 1830.

Charles Maurice Page (1826–1906): Son of William Page. Enlarged his father's blacksmith shop in 1849 and again in 1874. Did general black-smithing. Sold and repaired farm machinery. Built Page's Box Shop and Cream-ery in 1893.

Charles Maurice Page, Jr. (1871–1952): Son of Charles Maurice Page. Entered the business with his father in 1894. Sold the creamery in 1909. Thereafter he operated the box shop and sold farm machinery.

Maurice Blaisdell Page (1908–   ): Son of Charles Maurice Page, Jr. Entered the business with his father about 1924. Has operated the box shop alone since his father's death. Makes stock watering tubs, wooden boxes and chests, and other wooden items.

MAKING A WATER TUB

To the making of a six- or eight-foot circular watering tub goes a consider-able amount of sound native white pine, three lengths of thick round iron rod and two or three days hard labor, all of it governed by the long years of skill and experience lodged in the maker's brain and fingers. The average tub has well over a hundred running feet of joints, every inch of which must be watertight. Moreover, a glance at the photos shows that the joints in the body of the tub are beveled. This beveling must be done to a nicety, for the slightest deviation from the correct angle results in accumulative error around the tub's entire circum-ference when it is "set up." As if this were not sufficient challenge, consider the fact that each stave must be made a trifle narrower at the bottom so that the tub splays outward at the top.

To my knowledge, there are but two craftsmen left in Vermont who continue to make the now old-fashioned water tub and who have been tradi-tionally trained in the craft. One is Maurice Page, and the other is Benjamin "Ben" Thresher, whose mill in West Barnet is discussed in chapter 4. Though these two men live but thirty-five miles apart as the crow flies and each owns a mill where water tubs have been made well back into the nineteenth century, they use distinctively different methods when putting their tubs together. Neither man was aware of this difference.

The technique Ben Thresher learned seems to have been derived from Yankee ingenuity. He sets the circular bottom of his tub face down on a pair of sawhorses and circles it, tapping the dadoes of the tub's staves onto its rim, one

5. Staves, two of which show the chine or chime.

by one. Afterward, the hoops are put on, tightened, and the completed tub turned upright.

With Maurice Page we find remnants of the traditional cooper's way of assembling a tub. Actually, it is believed that a skilled cooper worked in the shop in the late 1800s, and a very old cooper's long plane, a large set of dividers, and several other dusty cooper's tools are stored in the nooks and crannies of the shop. Maurice Page's tubs are assembled in a manner exactly opposite to Ben Thresher's, although each man ends up with a first-class product.

Maurice proceeds by setting the staves up within the hoops. The last stave must be a very tight fit, so tight that it is necessary to coat its edges with bacon fat to drive it into place, thus wedging the staves in tightly all around the tub. Only then is the bottom made and installed.

As practiced by Maurice Page, the sequence of steps for making a water tub is as follows. The one pictured here is six feet in diameter and two feet in height. It is made of white pine, planed to a thickness of two inches. A few tight sound knots in the pine do not affect the tub's capability to hold water.

1. Once the pine is planed to thickness, the planks are cut to stave width. The stock is then cut into stave lengths. For a tub of this size, each stave is seven inches wide by two feet long.

2. The stave has a groove, called a chine or chime, cut across its lower end to receive the tub's bottom (see illus. 5). This groove is sometimes called the dado because it is sawn using a dado head on an old wood framed machine reserved for this process. The "stops" on the machine are set so that no adjustments need be made during sawing.

3. The bevel is planed on the two long edges of each stave. Planing is done on a machine called a jointer, though originally it was probably done by hand. The correct bevel angles for different stave widths were worked out long ago and drawn on pattern boards, which hang on the shop walls. The angles were determined in this way: The radius of the tub is drawn as a centerline on a wide board. At one end, a line is drawn across the width of the board at right angles to the centerline. Half the width of the stave is then laid off on this short line each side of center. For example, a stave seven inches in width lays three and one-half inches to each side of center. A line drawn from the centerline's other end to either of these two points gives the correct angle for the stave edge. This angle is "picked off" the pattern board using an adjustable square (T-bevel).

4. The fence of a large jointer is then set to this angle, and the bevels are planed on both edges of the staves. A pass or two is sufficient. The dado end of each stave is then turned toward the rear of the jointer, and another cut is taken off the bottom one-third of the stave's length. A second full-length cut, using this initial cut as a guide, establishes the taper of the stave, thus ensuring that after assembly the tub will be slightly smaller at its bottom. If the water in the tub should freeze, then, the ice will push upward and not rupture the tub.

5. After the staves are finished, the hoops are made. In Maurice's grandfather's time, these were made of flat steel, welded together in the smithy. In his father's day, they were riveted. The hoops were painstakingly hammered all

around the top half of the inside edge, giving them a taper to match the taper of the tub. They were driven on from the bottom of the tub and pounded home with a hoop driver until they were very tight, wedging the staves solidly together. About the time of the Second World War, flat steel became hard to get, and hoops bent from round stock were substituted. These hoops are threaded on each end, passed through twin holes in a cast piece, and secured with washers and nuts. The stock for the hoop rods is stored in the narrow stockroom of the blacksmith shop. For a six-foot tub, the rod is cut to a length of slightly more than twenty-one feet. The tub assembly platform, along the front of the shop, has a wooden block nailed to it at one end. This block serves as a stop for the rod, which lies alongside a series of painted figures (with nails for markers) representing the different lengths of rod used. The hoop rods are cut to length using a big set of bolt cutters. In the past, this cutting would have been done using an anvil hardy and a heavy smithy hammer. The rods are carried into the blacksmith shop and fed through the hoop bender (see illus. 6). One pass through this machine results in a perfectly round hoop of the correct diameter.

6. The hoop's ends are fastened, one at a time, in a post vise at the side of the shop and are threaded with a die. Bacon grease is used as the lubricant. When the second end has been threaded, the two ends of the hoop are passed through the holes in the hoop casting, and the washers and nuts are attached. The hoop is now complete and ready for use.

7. Two of the three hoops are brought to the assembly platform and laid down, one atop the other. Three staves, placed equidistant around the inside of the hoops, are fastened with large iron C-clamps to the top hoop. The bottom hoop is then raised two or three inches, and an 8d nail is driven under it into the stave and bent upward to form a crude staple, which holds the hoop in place during assembly. At this point, two hoops are attached to three staves, and the whole affair is rather wobbly. Starting at one of the staves, other staves are set up, side by side, within the hoops (see illus. 7). When another of the staves held by a C-clamp and a bent nail is reached, the clamp is loosened, and that stave is tapped tightly against the others. This process is repeated around the entire tub until the space for the final stave is reached. Ideally, the last stave is a bit too wide for the space available for it, and it must be lubricated with bacon grease and driven downward into place using a four-pound sledge hammer. Wooden wedges, driven down first, spread the opening to aid its progress (see illus. 8). Should the space still prove too small, four staves are taken to the jointer, and a very thin shaving is taken off one side of each stave until the tub fits together.

8. The staves are now driven up or down, as necessary, to bring the ring of dadoes into perfect alignment. The staves are also tapped both inside and outside to align their faces. If alignment is not achieved correctly, the staves will not "close" and the tub will leak.

9. Now the tub is turned bottom side up. The hoop nuts are tightened with a wrench to bring the staves in tight and snug, after which the nails holding the bottom hoop are pulled out. The bottom hoop is tightened the most, since the top of the tub then opens up to ease insertion of the bottom. At each step, the stave ends and sides are being aligned with the hammer. A good

6. Maurice Page and helper bending the tub hoops in smithy attached to box shop.

7. Setting up the water tub.

8. Spreading tub for insertion of the final stave.

9. Figuring radius of tub bottom. Note cooper's dividers behind Mr. Page.

deal of pounding is also done on the hoops, which helps bring the staves into alignment.

10. When the tub is tight and nicely fitted, the radius of the bottom is determined as follows: A large pair of steel dividers (shown in illus. 9) is set by eye, as nearly as possible, to one-sixth the circumference of the dado line of the tub. To do this, a pencil mark is made anywhere on the inner wall of the dado, and from it the distances are stepped off with the dividers. The objective is to set the distance between the divider's points so that the sixth point arrives exactly on the pencil mark, a process that usually takes a few tries. When the points go around the dado ring exactly six times, the radius of the tub's bottom has been established.

11. A two-inch plank, about ten inches wide, is then laid across the upside-down tub and sawn off two or three inches too long. This is repeated with other planks until the opening is covered. A large V is penciled across the entire bottom (which makes it possible, by putting the V back together, to reassemble the pieces exactly as they were laid out), and the edges of the planks are planed straight and square on the jointer.

12. Two boards (anything will do) are laid across the bottom opening of the tub as supports, and the freshly planed planks are reassembled. A pair of trammel points is set to the exact radius of the tub bottom (minus a heavy three-sixteenths of an inch to allow for future tightening of the hoops), and a circle is scribed on the planks (see illus. 10). The ends of each plank are then cut to this line on the bandsaw. This forms the bottom of the tub.

13. The pieces are now carried to a late 1800s double-spindle shaper, and a concave molding is cut on the edge of each end of these bottom planks. This molding makes a wedge-shaped, "pinch" fit between the bottom and the dado, allowing the hoops to be tightened, as necessary, in the future.

14. The tub is turned right side up, and the hoop nuts are eased off. The pieces making up the bottom are laid across two boards over the opening and carefully lined up. A roughly made wooden cross is laid on top, and nails are driven through it into each bottom plank to hold the circle of wood together. The nail heads are left projecting for easy removal later.

15. The tub bottom is now set squarely into the open top of the tub and driven downward into place using the four-pound sledge and a stout wooden block to take the hammer blows. When the bottom has been driven down about five inches, Maurice gets inside the tub and finishes driving it down until it enters the dado (see illus. 11). As the process continues, the hoop nuts are backed off still more. The tub is again turned bottom side up, and the bottom is seated into the dado by tightening the hoop nuts and pounding around the hoops with the sledge. At this time, the upper and lower hoops are persuaded into their final positions, about three inches in from the ends of the staves. The nuts are now turned down very tightly, bringing enormous pressure against all components of the tub. Minor openings in the seams, if indeed there are any, will swell shut when the tub is filled. Illustration 12 shows the tub being turned right side up, after which the middle hoop will be installed.

16. Large tubs, like this one, have a thick piece nailed to the underside of the bottom to keep it from sagging under the weight of water. Tubs should never rest on dirt (although they often did) but should be put on blocking to allow air to circulate freely under and around them. The outside of the tub is painted barn red, but the rim's edge and inside are not painted. Ben Thresher omits the stiffener under the bottom but paints the rim and also the edges of the planks from which the bottom is made. He also joins the bottom planks using hardwood dowels, which he chops out square and then drives through a hole in a steel plate to round them. Maurice Page does not use the dowels.

In the poem with which this chapter begins, the "wife" would feel right at home with these tubs, for, aside from the machine tools used, they were built of easily obtainable local materials and in the same way as the coopered articles she was accustomed to using.

10. Tracing circle of bottom using old set of trammel points.

11. Hammering the bottom down till it pops into the chime of tub.

12. Turning the finished tub right side up for painting. The assembly "cross" will be removed from bottom.

13. Donald Guganig holding an axe with handmade helve.

2

The Ladder Round Maker:
A Primitive Hand Industry

Donald Guganig
Monroe, New Hampshire

Oak of the Clay lived many a day
Or ever Aeneas began.
A Tree Song,
Rudyard Kipling

During the summer of 1984, I chanced to be visiting Ben Thresher at his mill in West Barnet, Vermont. We were sitting, chatting about this and that, on the granite slab that serves as the threshold to the main floor entrance. A car pulled off the main road and drove slowly down the track to stop in front of us. Out stepped a small man dressed in plaid shirt and dungarees. To my considerable surprise, a froe dangled from one hand. For readers who may not recognize the name, a froe is a tool from days long gone. It has a long hand-forged blade, perhaps three inches wide, thin on the bottom and thicker at the top. At one end the iron has been bent back upon itself and forge-welded into an oval loop to hold a short, stout handle of hardwood. At one time, froes were used to split thin pieces, such as roofing shakes, from sections (bolts) of cedar or pine trees.

"'Lo Ben," he ventured, "s'pose you can fix this froe for me? The loop's split."

While Ben carried the tool into the forge and blew up the fire so he could begin work, I asked the man what he was doing that required a froe in good working order.

"Oh," says he, "I make ladder rounds across the river there in Monroe, New Hampshire."

His name was Donald Guganig, and he was retired. He also had cancer and was having more bad days than good ones; nevertheless, he readily agreed to let me visit to watch and photograph him making ladder rounds. He was one of the very last men carrying on the trade, and a year or two later, he died.

"I'll call you a day or so ahead next time I feel up to making some. You can drive up and see how it's done," he said. "I'd like to know it's written down somewhere, and you can take lots of pictures of the whole process."

It wasn't until a Friday night late that fall that the phone rang and Donald said, "If you can get up here early in the morning, we'll shave out some rounds, and if there's time, we'll make a ladder, too. The whole thing—from start to finish." I assured him I'd be there.

Donald's house was just south of the little village of Monroe. I pulled in at eight in the morning and found him in his backyard, the site of his outdoor workshop. Running across the end of the house, under the protection of the eaves, were shelves packed with finished ladder rounds. Tied in bundles of twelve, they had been placed there to dry. Nearby was a stout workbench used for assembling ladders. Just behind that, at the edge of the woods, a tiny shed housed the collection of tools he used in the trade.

Donald had prepared a couple of red oak bolts and was awaiting my arrival. His trade is a very old local hand industry once concentrated in the valley of the Baker River, which rises in the Upper and Lower Baker ponds back of Mount Cube, near Wentworth, New Hampshire. Men in Wentworth, Warren, West Rumney, Rumney, and West Plymouth, using only hand tools and muscle, once made ladder rounds by the hundreds of thousands. The industry was still functioning strongly during the 1920s and 1930s and, probably, had been quite successful during the several decades before that. The men involved were small farmers, loggers, and men working at seasonal trades or mill work, where they might be laid off during part of the year. Youths and old men worked the trade, too. Shaving ladder rounds filled in during slack times and earned badly needed income.

Red oak was the timber of choice, both because it was suitable and plentiful. Hickory is not found north of Bellows Falls, Vermont, and white oak was too scarce to bother with. Most of the completed ladder rounds went to ladder

14. Red oak ladder round bolt, laid out for blanks and partially split.

manufacturers in southern New England. The safety standards in force for firemen's ladders required the use of hand-split rounds. The hand-shaved round is split from the bolt, and its grain runs straight and unbroken from one end of the piece to the other. Sawn rounds, on the other hand, could result in a stock cut across the grain, leaving a dangerously weak spot apt to break under the weight of a man.

The first step in making ladder rounds was getting out the timber. Men accustomed to woods work seemed to acquire an uncanny ability to judge the straightness of grain in a tree. While traversing the woods throughout the year, they took note of suitable trees. In winter, when the ground was covered deep in snow, they entered the woods with twitching horses, two-man crosscut saws, axes, cant dogs, and falling wedges. Once felled, the tree was limbed and bucked into log lengths using the crosscut saw. The logs were then twitched out of the woods and loaded onto drays and sleds for transport to the work area.

The blocks, or bolts, from which the blanks for rounds were split, were measured and cut off the end of a log with the two-man crosscut saw. A man working alone used a one-man crosscut saw. Pains were taken to cut the ends of the bolt as squarely as possible to keep all rounds the same length. Bolts were cut only in quantities that could be worked into rounds while the wood was still green. Since dried oak is extremely hard and difficult to work, the rest of the log was left whole so the wood would remain in its green state longer, and additional bolts were cut only as needed. Some men made ladder rounds in barns and sheds, but many of the work areas were out-of-doors, which left space for the copious litter of red oak shavings generated by the shaving process. Also, the light was better outside, and it allowed for more freedom of movement.

To begin the work, Donald placed an oak bolt upright on a chopping block. The bolt was seventeen inches long, but this dimension can vary with the width and type of ladder. With a sharp steel point and a straight edge, he carefully scribed a center line across the end of the bolt. Using a square, he scribed a second center line at right angles to the first. Placing a wooden pattern 1-1/4 inches wide against the scribed lines, he worked his way out from the center point, laying out a series of parallel lines, to the circumference on each "side" of the bolt. Giving the bolt a quarter turn, he repeated the process from the second center line. When he was done, the top was scribed in 1-1/4-inch squares, each of which would become a ladder round (see illus. 14).

Picking up the froe and hardwood froe club (illus. 15), Donald began splitting off blanks in 1-1/4-inch slabs, starting at the outside lines and working inward. As he worked toward the center of the bolt, its width increased until the slabs became more difficult to split. He then turned it and began to take slabs off one of the narrower edges. This process went on until the bolt had been reduced to slabs, each one the thickness of a round. He then split the slabs, one by one, into single blanks, using a shorter, stouter froe. The result was a pile of 1-1/4-inch square blanks ready for the final shaving.

This particular batch of rounds was to have a center diameter of approximately 1-1/8 inches, thinning to 7/8 inch at the ends. Donald told me that the men who had taught him made their rounds of equal size from one end to the

15. Splitting the blanks using the froe and froe club.

16. The finished ladder showing "swelled" rounds.

17. Seen from the left: a blank, the hand-forged drawknife, three rounds in process, and a jig for sizing the ends of rounds.

18. Shaving horse used by ladder round makers.

other. More time and effort, and a keen eye, are required to put in the center swelling Donald made. He felt the additional strength and ease of standing on a swelled ladder round were worth the extra work. Though he did not mention aesthetics, I am certain he unconsciously factored this into the shaving process: the swelled rounds are far handsomer than those seen on ladders made today (illus. 16).

Rounds were shaved using a specialized local drawknife form shown in illustration 17. These tools were highly valued. They were hand forged and tempered by local blacksmiths out of a worn-out horseshoeing rasp. In the illustration, you can just see where the coarse teeth of the rasp were flattened and forged into the blade's surface by the smith's hammer. The sharpening bevel is its outside surface.

To hold the rough blanks against the pull of the drawknife during shaping, Donald used a special upright shaving horse fastened to the side of his tool house (illus. 18). A narrow steel jaw grips the blank, holding it firmly against the horizontal support board. A foot treadle operates the jaw; the greater the pressure applied, the tighter it holds.

Illustrations 17 and 19 show how the shaping of a round progresses. The rough split blank shown at left in illustration 17 is first shaved so that it has an octagonal cross section, done by removing its corners with the straight portions of the drawknife blade. Using the half circular, center section of the drawknife blade, the blank is then reduced to cylindrical form, and the swell is shaped out and smoothed. Finally, the ends are brought to the finished dimension.

A completed round lies under the handles of the drawknife in illustration 17. The short piece of board with a hole bored through it, nailed to the end of the sawhorse upon which the drawknife and other pieces rest, is a gauge block, used to test the ends of the rounds as they are finished to size. Because the green rounds shrink as they dry, the shaving process requires a high level of skill and experience. The ends must be left slightly oversized—just so they remain a tight drive fit for the holes in the ladder sides. If this is not carefully attended to, the joint formed when the round is driven into the ladder sides will be loose, resulting in a ladder unfit for use. So great is Donald's skill that never once did he shave a round too small.

Donald was a laddermaker as well, and I was privileged to watch him make one upon a special bench set up beside his tool shed. The finished ladder is shown in illustrations 16 and 20. Illustration 21 shows a modern spade bit, specially altered for boring the holes that receive the ladder rounds. Earlier, Donald bored clear through the ladder's sides and drove small wooden wedges into the ends of the rounds to tighten the joints. By the time I visited him, however, he was boring to within a quarter inch of the outside face, leaving a weatherproof joint. He secured each joint with a nail driven through the top face of the ladder side.

In assembling a ladder, the rounds are first hammered into the holes bored to receive them in one of the ladder sides. The opposite ends are then painstakingly started into the holes in the remaining side. (Edward Clay of North Thetford, Vermont, told me about a trick used by an oldtime laddermaker in

East Lyme, New Hampshire, which made this operation easier. He made the two end rounds and the center round of his ladders longer by an eighth of an inch than the others. This trick greatly aided the insertion of the rounds into the ladder's second side.)

The second side is hammered home using a short, heavy sledge hammer against a waste block of wood to avoid marring the surface. Watching, one is again conscious of the care used in sizing the ends of the rounds. Each round went into its hole only grudgingly, yet the ends were not so much oversized as to split the sides. The result was a cleanly made, tight, safe ladder—a tribute to Donald's craft.

A small block plane puts a slight bevel on the four corners of each side, then the ladder is finished using a fifty/fifty mixture of boiled linseed oil and turpentine. "Painting a ladder locks in the water and starts rot," Donald told me. He often reinforced the ends and middle of his ladders using a device made of heavy galvanized sheet steel, cut to his own pattern. To prevent spreading in a long ladder, he bolted two or three threaded galvanized rods through its sides at the same locations as the galvanized reinforcements.

The following information concerning old-fashioned ladders comes from Edward Clay, a retired farmer in North Thetford, Vermont, William Godfrey of Blood Brook, West Fairlee, Vermont, and Carmine Guica of Cavendish, Vermont. These men were in their late seventies and eighties.

The side stringers of traditional, country-made ladders were of three kinds. The oldest and most primitive were made from small diameter spruce poles peeled and bored to receive the rounds. An example exists in the Unitarian church in Cavendish, Vermont. This ladder, which has through holes for the rounds, is used to reach the bell tower and dates to the building of the church in 1844.

The second type was made by snapping a chalkline, as a cutting guide, along a spruce pole of correct diameter and length and sawing it in two with a hand ripsaw. The sides were peeled of bark and left "as is," or cleaned up and flattened on the outside with a hand plane.

The third way was to select sound, knot-free spruce sides sawn at the local sawmill.

19. Shaving the round.

20. Testing the new ladder.

21. Bundle of finished rounds. The spade bit at bottom is specially altered for boring the ladder sides.

22. Orien Dunn beside his boring rig, which is called a "log horse." His left hand rests on the handle of the boring auger.

3

The Pump Log Maker

Orien Dunn
Victory, Vermont
The Northeast Kingdom

In a little cottage, a garden hard by,
    And an orchard of fruit-bearing trees;
A site, where no strife or profusion comes
nigh.
    With a glass of pure water to drink
when I'm dry,
I'd enjoy both my freedom and ease.
                Anonymous

The old trade of boring pump logs is closely allied to the even more ancient art of the water witch or dowser. The latter found the water spring, and the former made the wooden pipes that, when buried in the earth, conveyed the water to the pump or water tub at the house or farm site. Many villages in Vermont still have their dowsers who, with the aid of rods or a fork of apple or willow, can find underground springs and veins of water. Many can even ask the rod whether the water is potable, how deep it runs, and what the flow rate per minute is and receive true and accurate answers. Even so, few today have seen a dowser in action, and virtually none have witnessed pump logs being made—hence the following description and photographs.

In 1979 I wrote Orien Dunn, an oldtime pump log maker, to ask if he would be willing to show me how pump logs were made. As a boy, Mr. Dunn was taught how to make them by his father, Corrydon Dunn. There was a tradition of pump log making in this family, for an uncle also made them. Mr. Dunn kindly agreed to demonstrate the process for me, and on May 28, 1980, I drove up to the Northeast Kingdom to visit him at his home in Victory. I found Mr. Dunn, then seventy-eight-years old, to be a most impressive old gentleman. He possessed, in full measure, the innate courtesy and dignity so often found in elderly country people, a dignity that makes them seem at home anywhere. He had set up his equipment that morning, and he shortly began the demonstration.

The wood preferred by Mr. Dunn is fir balsam, possibly because of its resinous pitch that perhaps helps preserve the wood underground. The balsam sections averaged six to nine inches in diameter. They were bored in pairs—one piece being eight feet in length, the other nine. Mr. Dunn has seen ten-footers bored on occasion, but these required an extra long auger. Allowing for the joint connecting the two pieces, the overall length of the pair was one rod, that is, sixteen and one-half feet. The rod is an ancient unit of English measurement that was brought over and continued in use by the original settlers and those who followed, until very recent times. Jim Nott, an old farmer on Jericho Hill

23. An end view of Orien Dunn's house in Victory, Vermont.

24. Setting up for boring a pump log. Note the two U-shaped rests that keep the auger level with the center line of the log.

in Hartford, Vermont, once mentioned to me that he had grown up with the rod, but that during his manhood he had had to adapt to the yard. "We used the rod to measure land, lay out roads, and as a standard in putting together the frames of barns," he said.

Mr. Dunn recalls that when he was sixteen he and his father made two hundred rods of pump logs for one man at a price of forty cents a rod. That figures to 3300 running feet of a 1-1/2-inch diameter hole bored through solid wood for eighty dollars, or just under 2.4 cents a foot.

The auger used is called a "pod auger." It has a different kind of feed screw and lacks the side-cutting spurs of present-day auger bits. Modern bits will not bore a straight hole nor keep one on center, because they insist on following the grain of the wood—a slanting grain means a slanting hole. The old pod auger is made so that its cutting edge bores independently of the direction or twist of the grain. A form of pod auger is still in use today for making the bores of clarinets, recorders, and other musical instruments.

The foremost problem in making a pump log is boring the hole so that it is exactly centered in each end of the log. I was impressed by the condition of the tools and other equipment and by the care lavished on them. Mr. Dunn keeps his auger literally razor sharp and polished bright as silver. A wooden case fits over its end, and the long tool is carefully oiled after each use and stored on pegs set in a straight line to prevent its taking a set (becoming bent—see illustration 33). The auger is entered into the end of the log that was nearest the stump. In other words, he bores from the bottom to the top, though he has seen others do the opposite.

The boring is done on a "log horse" (see illustrations and figure 1) using the pod auger for the hole and a short "rimmer" (the old local name for a reamer), a device that cuts a funnel-shaped cavity in one end of each log to receive the tapered end of the next pump log in line as they are laid in the ground. The horse holds the log steady while it is bored and can be built in place or as a portable unit. Its top must be made to match the height of the operator's hips—a nice example of folk measurement. Levelness of the horse is of prime importance, lest the auger run crooked. Mr. Dunn enters the auger in the exact center of the end of the log and bores straight through until it comes out the other end.

To set up the process, the log is fixed upon the horse by tapping it sharply downward upon a sharpened steel point about 3/4-inches high. The point holds the log against the lateral thrust of the auger. At either side are hand-forged, iron "dogs"—sharpened, L-shaped hooks—fastened to the horse by big iron staples. They are driven into the log from each side to keep it from rolling during the boring process.

The difference in diameter between the two ends of the log is carefully calculated and split in half. The small end is then raised that much by means of a wedge. The line of the bored hole is thus kept in the same plane as that of the auger.

The auger is supported between two U-shaped steel pieces, not unlike an oarlock. These pieces are set in steel plates fastened to the top of the horse and are adjustable, up or down. The one nearest the operator is set exactly in line with

25. Close-up of auger ready to enter the log. This is a special, hand-forged spoon bit auger. Note the L-shaped "dog" (there are four in all) that holds the log steady. Also note (to the left of the log) the tapered reamer (rimmer) for making the female joint in the finished logs.

27. Boring the pump log—a view of the entire rig.

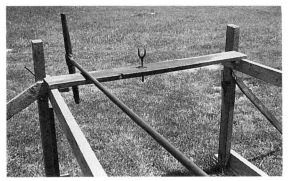

26. The auger and a U-shaped guide.

28. Note the crank on the end of the handle for extra leverage.

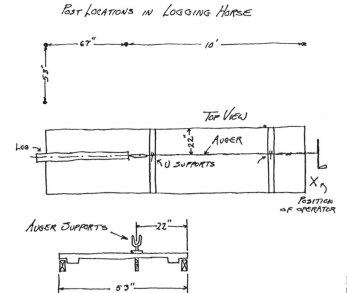

Post Locations in Logging Horse

Top View

Auger Supports

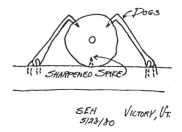

Fig. 1. Field sketch of some details of the boring process.

29. This view shows the auger almost through the pump log. Note that one U-shaped guide has been removed because it would be in the way at this stage.

30. Close-up of the sheepshead cutter, which is something like a giant pencil sharpener. This device cuts the male joint on one end of each pump log.

the center of the log. The second, placed about half-way to the log's end, floats so that the auger can maintain its center while the boring is done. Mr. Dunn tests an auger by laying it into the U supports and rotating its tip against a pine block temporarily nailed to the horse. Should the tip describe a circle, no matter how small, there is a bend in the auger shaft that must be straightened. The center line selected for the boring operation is twenty-two inches in from the right side of the horse (see sketch). This placement is important, for it allows room for the operator to be active to the left of the auger. The simple guideline exemplifies how the various steps in folk processes have been worked out and refined over long periods of time to eliminate wasteful motion and clumsiness.

Boring the hole commences with driving a small nail into the top surface of the log at the far end. This nail is centered on the log by eye. A string is tied to it and then stretched along the log and above the auger shaft and tied to the auger's handle, which is set vertically. By means of this string, the auger and the log are coaxed into an exact horizontal alignment to prevent running off center during the boring operation. If the auger point is off center vertically, it is aligned by screwing the U supports up or down as required.

The boring goes swiftly. Mr. Dunn stated that he used to be able to bore a log in just six minutes. He stood to the left of the auger, grasping the crank handle with his left hand, palm downward. The right hand reaches forward to bring the plain end of the handle around at each turn. After seven or eight revolutions have been made, the auger is backed out to clear the chips. In no time, the ground below the end of the log was littered with fresh, clean shavings. When the auger cut through at the opposite end, it had remained on dead center all the way. The length of the auger is lightly oiled, as are the bearing points of the U supports. Mr. Dunn also kept a light film of oil on his hands, stating, "The auger handle will take the skin off your hands if you don't oil them."

Once the boring of the logs is done, the ends have to be fitted so they will join tightly and not leak water. Now the "rimmer" is brought into play. With the log still fastened in the horse, the small end of the rimmer is inserted into the bored hole and turned in a clockwise direction. The tool's sharp, tapered edge quickly forms a tapered hole—the "female" part of the joint.

To make the "male" joint, the pump log is removed from the horse, and the unworked end is laid across the lower notch of a "three-legged horse," a primitive clamping device. This device held the log firmly, while Mr. Dunn used a sharp axe to trim the end to a rough taper. A rim approximately 3/4-inch wide was left around the bored hole. The log was then placed in the second notch, and a draw shave evened out the chopping facets left by the axe.

Finally, Mr. Dunn moved the log upward into the third notch of the three-legged horse and applied the "sheepshead" to the tapered end. This tool leaves a smooth taper, as on a freshly sharpened pencil, making a watertight fit. The sheepshead cuts a shoulder some four to five inches back from the point, allowing the logs to be driven tightly together. The tool requires very careful adjustment, because the taper it generates must mate perfectly with the tapered hole made by the rimmer.

During this whole time, the blackflies were out in force. Mr. Dunn said, "We can't have this." From a small cloth bag, he removed a few pieces of the fungi one finds growing on dead trees and stumps. The matter had been chopped into small pieces. He lit one with a match, and it gave off a pleasantly scented, pungent smoke that kept the flies off.

31. The finished hole—dead center. You can just see the auger's tip.

32. The "three-legged horse."

33. The auger has been wiped dry, oiled, and its points encased in a protective wooden case.

34. Ben Thresher, millman and blacksmith, West Barnet, Vermont.

4

Ben Thresher's Mill

West Barnet, Vermont

All these rely on their own hands, and each is skillful at his own craft. Without them a city would have no inhabitants; no settlers or travelers would come to it. . . . They maintain the fabric of this world and their prayers are about their daily work.
Ecclesiasticus 38:25–34
The New English Bible

In my travels throughout the rural countryside, while carrying out the fieldwork that is the basis of this book, I came one day to a lone, timeworn building huddled beside a small river. I parked my car and walked down the dirt track leading to a wide door, open to the sun. Traces of faded red paint clung to the trim, and a touch of dusty, orangey-tan color up under the eaves, showed to advantage against the rusty brown of the weathered clapboards. Only the rear wall retained its original color—a lovely faded yellow. The ancient building must once have been very handsome.

The main part of the structure was two stories plus an attic. At either end of the building was a small, one-story ell. To the one on my left, a long shed had once been attached. It had fallen in, and I could see the remains of a smashed rowboat, a couple of splintered wagons, and an old wheelbarrow under the wreckage. The narrow yard was littered with piles of planks. Rotted wagon and sled parts and wooden wheels lay everywhere. To each of them clung iron parts that could be scavenged and used again. Down beside the river, a rusted out turbine and several big silo hoops lay buried in the long grass, a trap for the unwary walker. Up beside the road, the cab of an old truck sat against the base of an electric pole. Beside it was a faded red Edsel and a much battered pickup truck.

As I drew closer, I heard the stacatto, high-pitched scream of lumber being planed. Peering through the door into the dimly lit interior, I saw a burly figure overseeing the passage of a wide pine plank through a thickness planer. A flurry of shavings attended its progress. When the end of the plank cleared the knives, the din stopped and was succeeded by the sound of the machine itself and the intermittent slapping of a pulley belt. The millman walked around, picked up the plank, and carried it over to a circular saw, and then he saw me standing just inside the door. He seized an iron wheel sticking up through the floor and began to turn it. Gradually the noise ceased entirely, and upon seeing my questioning glance, he said, "I just turned off the power. This mill runs on water you know." Then, "I'm Ben Thresher. What can I do for you?"

35. The mill building.

36. Upright wheel turns on or off the water turbine in the cellar. On the right of post is a Baxter thickness planer built in Lebanon, New Hampshire, ca. 1870.

37. Small woodworking bench near mill
entrance.

As it turned out, Ben was able to do quite a lot. For starters, over the next few years he showed me more about the operation and manufacturing processes of the oldtime water-powered mill than I ever knew existed. I spent days and weeks at the mill talking with Ben, watching him work, and taking photographs and measurements. His mill exemplifies nineteenth-century technology, a technology that was somewhere between that found in the colonial mills and the factory, much of which was used daily in this small corner of Vermont almost to the present day. Ben's mill is a living example of the once indissoluble linkages that existed among subsistence farming, village life, and small local mills.

Caught in a time warp between the mid-nineteenth- and early twentieth-centuries, Thresher's mill is an example of handcraft manufacturing methods carried over from the past two centuries. That they are still in use today, is, I think, due to three primary factors. First is the mill's location in an isolated community of scattered farms and tiny villages with which it has been in continuous contact since it was built. Second, the stable local situation has enabled the various owners of the mill to continue to meet community needs using old-fashioned tools and methods and outmoded water-powered machinery. There have been no large-scale disruptions of traditional life requiring, as elsewhere, a complete changeover to modern technological advances. The third factor has to do with the very traditional nature of Ben Thresher, a man who, in an altogether quiet manner, appreciates and holds onto the old ways of doing things. Over the years, many people have urged Ben to modernize and get the mill "up-to-date."

"Put in electric motors for the machines," they say. "Throw out that old stuff and get some modern machines in here, and you'll double your output."

Ben just smiles and, if pressed too hard, says, "Nope! I don't need to double my output. I guess I'll just stick to water power and what I know. It's always done the job."

Ben, however, is neither foolish nor stubborn enough to perform work that amounts to sheer drudgery simply for the sake of maintaining old ways. Though he maintains his blacksmith shop and works in it almost every day, there are certain things he cannot do at the anvil. For example, to perform welding work on truck frames and bodies, he put an arc welding outfit into the cab of the aforementioned derelict truck beside the electric pole. He uses a chain saw for cutting his firewood and for occasional logging instead of the old two-man crosscut saw and axe. Ben has even been known to use his chain saw in the mill to round off the end of sledge runners or to cut a heavy plank in two. And he now employs a heavy-duty, hand-held electric drill to bore deep holes in hardwood. Nevertheless, more than ninety percent of the work of the mill is accomplished by hand and with original, nineteenth-century machinery run by water power.

The left-hand ell was a working cider mill until about twenty years ago. The ell on the right contains the blacksmith shop. A wheelwright and wagon-making shop and a general woodworking shop fill the first floor of the main building. With the exception of the cider mill, each of these functions remains in operation. The mill is filled with machinery dating from the latter half of the

38. Antique bandsaw. Note the wooden working surface.

39. Antique table saw.

1800s, though a few pieces are dated even earlier. Each machine is belt-driven from line shafting and pulleys powered by the turbine. Some of them, notably a large woodturning lathe, a horizontal boring machine, and a rare copy lathe used to make wagon spokes, are mostly built of timber. Only the tool carriers and a few of the moving parts are made of metal. The time-honored babbitt or bronze sleeve bearing—oiled by hand or fed by a wick—was the available technology when this machinery was made, and I strongly doubt that there is a roller bearing in the place, and certainly the modern ball bearing is unknown here.

The balance of the machinery includes a thickness planer, a large jointer, a circular crosscutting saw and ripsaw, a large bandsaw, a threading machine, and a horizontal wood boring machine. Benches, vises, and old-fashioned hand tools line the walls. Patterns for sled runners, sleighs, and wagons hang from the blackened floor joists.

In a corner of the shop, a flight of stairs leads to a second floor. Here there are bending jigs, a wagon tire bender, and a steam box once supplied from a steam boiler in the cellar. These remain from the time when wagons, buggies, sleighs, and snow rollers were made here. Nailed to the wooden door trim are the brass nameplates of buggy makers who once worked in surrounding towns

40. Antique wooden hand-turning lathe.

41. Screw thread cutter. Note belt drive as with all machines in this mill.

and villages. A long bench in the paint shop is littered with cans of varnish and paints of wagon blue, fierce reds, and brilliant yellows. Other tins and colors line the wall beneath. In a cupboard are old brushes and a booklet or two of gold leaf for striping and ornamentation. A white plaster wall carries a long rainbow of colored paint brushings where workers cleaned their brushes. One, in bright blue, depicts an Indian with a single feather in his hair. At the front of the room, a heavy wooden swiveling crane sits beside large double doors opening to the outside, through which vehicles were hoisted up for painting.

Downstairs, bins full of outmoded iron hardware are scattered along plastered walls hung with snowshoes, tools, and more patterns for sledge runners and ox yokes. Littered benches line the windows along the front wall facing the road. Against the rear wall is a machine used for threading the ends of the round iron rods used for water tub hoops. The shop is not long enough to accommodate this process, and someone a long time ago bored a hole straight through the end of the mill exactly in line with the center of the machine. When threading hoop stock, one end of the rod is thrust through the worn hole, and anyone walking round the end of the mill would see it turning slowly round and round. On this side, too, are windows with a spectacular view of the millpond spilling over the whole length of the wooden dam.

42. Old calendars on smithy door.

Time has changed very little in this place. On the floor leading into the blacksmith shop hangs an early 1900s calendar, partially obscured by an up-to-date one bearing the likeness of a well-endowed, scantily clad, pinup beauty. In the gloom of the smithy, a water-driven trip hammer stands like an iron troll. Used for the rough forging of heavy stock, this machine shakes the very floor when in operation. Its small brother, an anvil on a solid oaken block, occupies a position by the forge. Nearby is a fat iron sow (swage block) for hammering and shaping glowing red iron into a variety of cross-sectional shapes. A stout post vise and a machinists vise adorn a littered bench under the window.

Hand tools lie everywhere; they clutter the anvil block, rest on the bench, and hang from the walls. Among them is a series of loop-ended, sharp-pointed iron rods in graduated sizes. These are used for aligning or enlarging holes bored into the wooden parts of sledges, wagons, and so forth. Tire shrinkers—devices to decrease the size of an iron tire for a wooden wheel that has shrunk—hang from a wall. The earlier of the two is built mostly of timber; the later one is made of iron and steel. The walls and open timbers of the roof are thickly coated with years of soot from the innumerable fires of soft coal burned in the forge. From the stone foundation below the smithy a line shaft protrudes. Once it carried a large grindstone upon which farmers sharpened their scythes and axes.

The mill's machinery is powered by a hydraulic system consisting of the following: The mill seat, that is, the actual mill site and the immediate environs necessary to its functioning, is a long narrow strip of land lining both sides of the stream. The mill seat dates to an earlier time when mills relied upon wooden water wheels driving the machinery of the mill through the weight of water running from a headrace (a long wooden or stone trough) into the wheel's buckets. The headrace was tailored to meet the exigencies of individual mill sites and was often located well upstream of the mill building. This original configuration survives in the size and shape of Ben Thresher's mill lot.

Located at the foot of a drop in the stream, Ben's mill has been powered by a water turbine since about 1848. (There is some difference of opinion as to just when the present mill was built. Ben says 1848, and I am content to rely on the local folk wisdom from whence he extracts this date.) The near end of the dam, located on a line even with the upstream end of the mill building, is framed into the mill structure. The waters of the mill pond flow through a wooden trash rack (trapping floating debris that could clog the wheel) into a deep, square wooden box (the forebay), and from thence, into a penstock connected to the turbine in the cellar of the mill. The initial segment of the penstock is a short section of iron boiler plate, five feet in diameter. To it is attached a wooden penstock built by Ben many years ago. Water is admitted to the turbine from a gate operated by a shaft and control wheel on the first floor. When asked why he did not replace the original wooden penstock with one of iron, Ben replied, "Bad for working in the winter. An iron penstock will freeze up much worse than a wooden one. One winter that five-foot iron section froze till there was just a six-inch hole through the ice in it. At the same time, the wooden one, which is thirty-nine inches in diameter, kept an eighteen-inch hole open through the ice in it."

The turbine is a very rare example of the horizontal type. A horizontal shaft, carrying a huge wooden pulley, is belted to the main shaft of the mill. This shaft runs in bearings fastened underneath the first floor. Above, on the first floor, individual machines are driven by belts from pulleys fixed to the main shaft. All this is clearly shown in the drawings and photographs accompanying the text.

Ben Thresher is the sustaining link between this mill and the scattered population of the surrounding countryside. Since his apprenticeship as a young man in the 1940s, he has mastered all phases of the work. For his customers, he makes an almost endless range of traditional devices and other artifacts. In making these things, his fine craftsmanship and Yankee inventiveness are employed to their fullest extent. Ben is one of the very few, increasingly rare people who still carries in his head a complete pattern of the traditional folk knowledge and wisdom necessary to operate a water-powered mill of this kind. One or two examples will suffice to illustrate this statement.

One day, I watched Ben fashioning a pair of runners for a local pattern of

43. "Sow" or swage block in smithy. Used in forming hot iron and steel.

44. Smithy forge. Handle beside chimney operates water-powered blower.

logging sled. He made each runner from a six-inch-thick "turn" or plank, which in the living tree had grown in a natural curve just suited to a sled runner. As he worked away shaping the heavy piece, he looked up, grinning, and said, "Bet you didn't know there's another way to make these."

I didn't and said so.

"Well," he said, "you see that big bending form over there in the corner?" I looked and saw a heavily built rectangular form with a pronounced curve at its top.

"That's a steam bending rig. That curve at the top is the curve of your runner. What you do is take a good sound ash piece the right size for your runner. It's straight, so you've got to bend the end. First, you figure out where the base of the bend is going to come along on the runner, and you mark it. Then you saw in with the bandsaw or a handsaw. Make a series of parallel cuts up to that point. You make 'em about half an inch apart and you stack 'em up from the bottom edge of the runner to the top of it. Then you shove that section into the steam box and steam her in good shape.

"When she comes out, you stick that end into the top of this big bending jig and pull the straight part right down against the body of it. You push big dowels through these holes in the jig here to hold the straight part down while the curved end dries. Then you've got your runner, with just the bend you want. But she's apt to straighten out, and she's not very strong yet. That comes when you 'iron it'—when you put on the steel runners and bring 'em right up and back around the curved end and fasten them.

"First, of course, you have to do something to lock that steamed curve into the runner so's it won't ever flatten out. Way you do that is you trim out a square oak pin, knock off the corners with a hatchet, and drive it down through a hole in an iron plate to round it. Take a jackknife and raise a few little chips along the length of it so's it won't come out. Then you bore a hole, just undersize, into the undercurve of your runner and drive that pin right through. That locks it for good."

Ben's work includes not only the many things he builds for his customers, but also the intricacies of keeping the mill and its equipment operable. He has, as mentioned, built the penstock new from beginning to end. He does each phase of dam maintenance himself, from flushing away the silt that builds up behind it each year to replacing supports and planking after washouts caused by spring flooding.

Ben Thresher is the other water tub maker left in Vermont. Besides tubs, he still makes cow stanchions, logging sleds, and carries out wagon and wheel repairs. He spends a great deal of time in the smithy, where he repairs logging chains and shapes the hooks of cant dogs and pulp hooks to exactly the shape that grabs the logs best. He can measure, make, and set an iron tire for a wagon wheel or shoe a horse or an ox. And Ben is constantly called upon to perform jobs that he has never tried before. He makes picnic tables for summer folks and forges antique hardware for them. He has even converted a silage fork to a sod lifter for the local gravedigger. Ben's Yankee ways and repartee often bring a smile from his customers. Not infrequently, they are awed by the self-sufficiency of this man and his mill and show a respect for the craft and industry of the past. His list of satisfied customers is endless.

During the past thirty or forty years, the way of life Ben Thresher represents has almost totally disappeared from the Yankee Highlands. Only in a few backcountry villages are its patterns still faintly to be seen. As the small mills were abandoned, they fell rapidly into a state of disrepair. The dams were breached to reduce taxes. Their equipment, priceless relics of our industrial history, was left to rust away or be sold at auction. The organic relationships that pertained among the tools and machinery, the men and what they made, were broken up. Only through the pitifully few survivors, like Ben Thresher and his mill, can we study and understand what were once complex functioning entities, the technological base of regional folklife.

In 1978 I was instrumental in getting the Historic American Engineering Record (HAER) to undertake a survey of Ben Thresher's mill, with support from Laurance S. Rockefeller who had purchased it. (The mill was later gifted back to Ben Thresher after a decision was made not to dismantle and re-erect it at the Billings Farm & 1890 Museum in Woodstock, Vermont.) The HAER project included portions of an engineering survey of the mill carried out in 1976 by Earl MacHarg and Arthur Nadeau, teachers at the Hartford Vocational High School in White River Junction, Vermont. That survey had been done under the aegis of the Vermont Folklife Research Project of the Woodstock Foundation.

The HAER study began during the summer of 1979, when a team of architects, a photographer, and an historian worked fulltime to record the mill's many details. That their work was thorough is vouched for by Ben himself. He told me that one day a young architect was drawing a circular saw rig fastened to the front of the mill that Ben used to saw firewood for heating the mill in winter. When the crew broke for lunch, Ben went out and counted the teeth around the circumference of the saw. Then he went into the mill and counted how many teeth the chap had shown on the drawing. Ben was mightily impressed when he found that the totals were exactly the same.

The photographs here are my own. The seven magnificent drawings of the mill were done by the HAER group. Though I do not expect Ben's mill, in the long run, to survive, these drawings make that sad fact somewhat more bearable. A little study, even by one unused to reading such drawings, gives one a clear impression of what this old mill is like. And for the immediate future, at least, anyone motoring through this part of Vermont can go and see the mill for themselves.

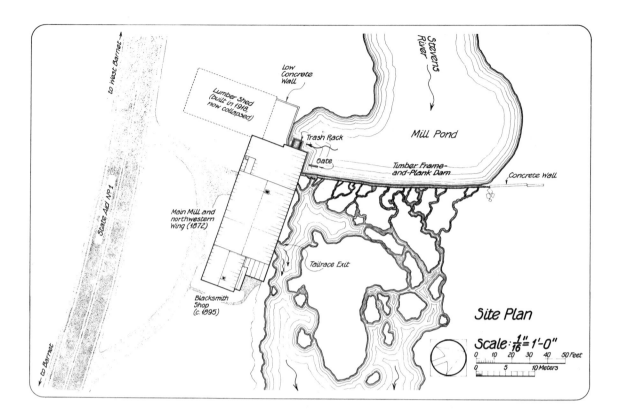

Site Plan

Scale: $\frac{1}{16}'' = 1'-0''$

to West Barnet →

Stevens River

Low Concrete Wall

Lumber Shed (built in 1918, now collapsed)

Trash Rack

Gate

Mill Pond

Timber Frame-and-Plank Dam

Concrete Wall

State Aid Nº1

Main Mill and northwestern Wing (1872)

Tailrace Exit

Blacksmith Shop (c. 1895)

← to Barnet

0 10 20 30 40 50 Feet
0 5 10 Meters

Fig. 2.

Reinforcement Wall (installation date unknown)

Site Section
looking West

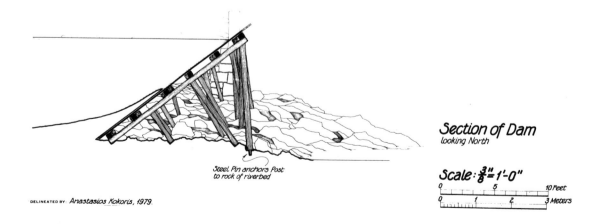

Steel Pin anchors Post to rock of riverbed

Section of Dam
looking North

Scale: $\frac{3}{8}'' = 1'-0''$

0 5 10 Feet
0 1 2 3 Meters

DELINEATED BY: Anastasios Kokoris, 1979.

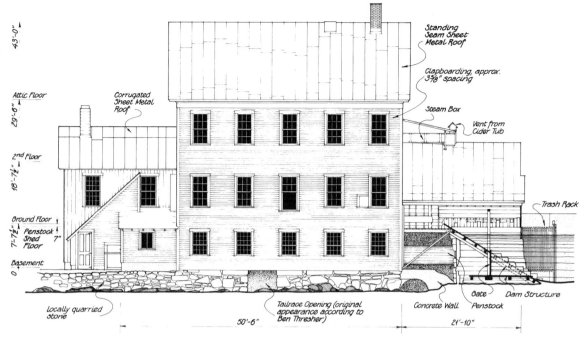

Rear (northeast) Elevation

43'-0"

Attic Floor
29'-6½"

2nd Floor
18'-7½"

Ground Floor
7'-7½"
Penstock
Shed
Floor 7"

Basement
0

Corrugated
Sheet Metal
Roof

Standing
Seam Sheet
Metal Roof

Clapboarding, approx.
3⅜" spacing

Steam Box

Vent from
Cider Tub

Trash Rack

Gate

Dam Structure

Concrete Wall

Penstock

locally quarried
stone

Tailrace Opening (original
appearance according to
Ben Thresher)

50'-6"

21'-10"

NOTE!
Building shown with floors level
and walls plumb; varying degrees
of settlement and deterioration
not shown. See HAER record
photographs for present (1979)
condition.

Paint Scheme (1979):

Clapboards – (rear elevation of
Main Mill only) – yellow ochre
– all other sides – unpainted

Window + Door Frames – dark red

Window Sashes – white

Roof – Cider Mill and Blacksmith
Shop – dark red
– Main Mill – unpainted (new)

Drawings based in part on field
notes made in 1976 by E. MacHarg
for the Woodstock Foundation.

Porch attached to front of
Blacksmith Shop is completely
deteriorated; original appearance
undetermined.

Fig. 3.

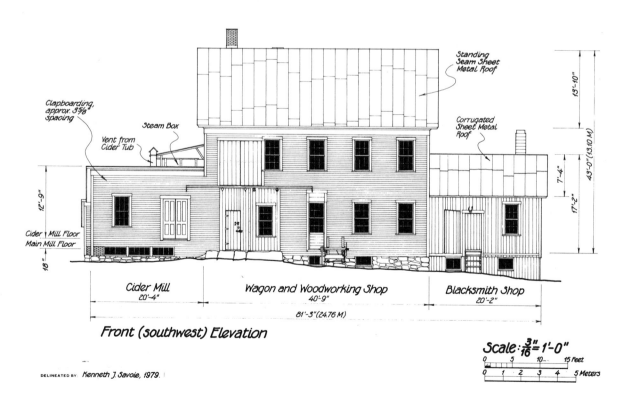

Front (southwest) Elevation

Clapboarding,
approx. 3⅜"
spacing

Steam Box

Vent from
Cider Tub

Standing
Seam Sheet
Metal Roof

Corrugated
Sheet Metal
Roof

13'-10"

43'-0" (13.10 M)

7'-4"

17'-2"

12'-9"

Cider Mill Floor
Main Mill Floor

18"

Cider Mill
20'-4"

Wagon and Woodworking Shop
40'-9"

Blacksmith Shop
20'-2"

81'-3" (24.76 M)

Scale: 3/16" = 1'-0"

0   5   10   15 Feet
0 1 2 3 4 5 Meters

DELINEATED BY: Kenneth J. Savoie, 1979.

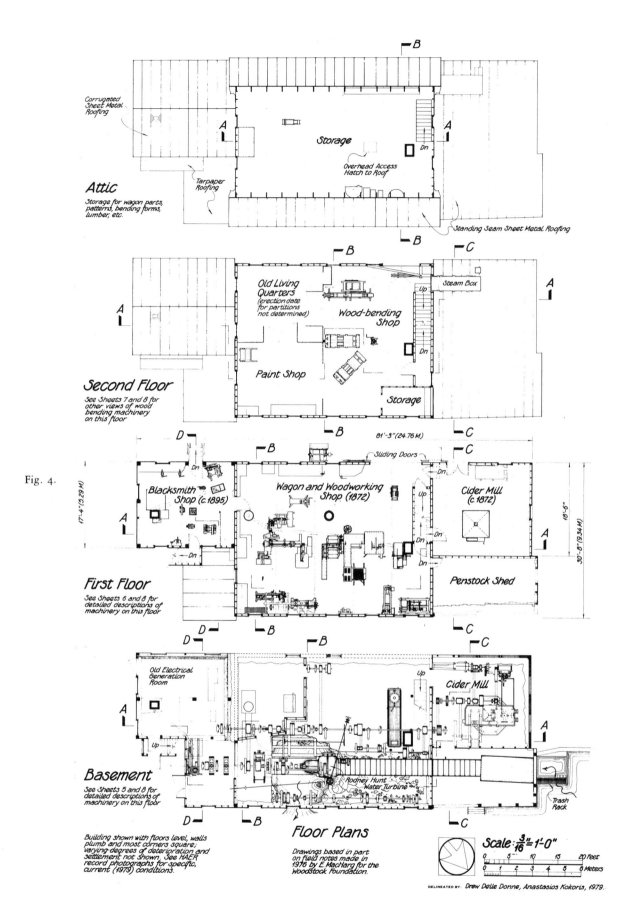

Fig. 4.

Attic

Storage for wagon parts, patterns, bending forms, lumber, etc.

Corrugated Sheet Metal Roofing

Tarpaper Roofing

Storage

Overhead Access Hatch to Roof

Standing Seam Sheet Metal Roofing

Second Floor

See Sheets 7 and 8 for other views of wood bending machinery on this floor

Old Living Quarters (erection date for partitions not determined)

Wood-bending Shop

Steam Box

Paint Shop

Storage

81'-3" (24.76 M)

First Floor

See Sheets 6 and 8 for detailed descriptions of machinery on this floor

Blacksmith Shop (c.1895)

Wagon and Woodworking Shop (1872)

Sliding Doors

Cider Mill (c.1872)

Penstock Shed

17'-4" (5.29 M)

18'-6"

30'-8" (9.34 M)

Basement

See Sheets 5 and 8 for detailed descriptions of machinery on this floor

Old Electrical Generation Room

Cider Mill

Rodney Hunt Water Turbine

Trash Rack

Building shown with floors level, walls plumb and most corners square; varying degrees of deterioration and settlement not shown. See HAER record photographs for specific, current (1979) conditions.

Floor Plans

Drawings based in part on field notes made in 1976 by E. MacHarg for the Woodstock Foundation.

Scale: 3/16" = 1'-0"

0   5   10   15   20 Feet
0 1 2 3 4 5 6 Meters

DELINEATED BY: *Drew Delle Donne, Anastasios Kokoris, 1979.*

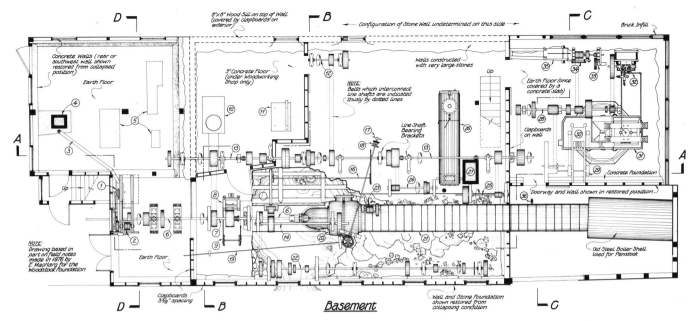
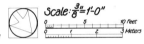

Basement

Labels within drawing:
- D
- 8"x8" Wood Sill on top of Wall (covered by clapboards on exterior)
- B
- ← Configuration of Stone Wall undetermined on this side →
- C
- Brick Infill
- Concrete Walls (rear or southwest wall shown restored from collapsed position)
- Earth Floor
- 3" Concrete Floor (under Woodworking Shop only)
- Walls constructed with very large stones
- Up
- Earth Floor (once covered by a concrete slab)
- NOTE: Belts which interconnect line shafts are indicated thusly by dotted lines
- Line Shaft Bearing Brackets
- Clapboards on wall
- A ... A
- Concrete Foundation
- Up
- Doorway and Wall shown in restored position
- Old Steel Boiler Shell used for Penstock
- Earth Floor
- NOTE: Drawing based in part on field notes made in 1976 by E. MacHarg for the Woodstock Foundation
- Clapboards 3⅝" spacing
- D
- B
- Wall and Stone Foundation shown restored from collapsing condition
- C

Numbered legend:

1. Forge Blower: mfd by Canedy-Otto Manufacturing Co, Chicago Heights, Ill.; presently driven by electric motor via belt
2. Belt drive countershaft for Forge Blower; used when power was taken from line shaft
3. Air duct from Blower to Forge
4. Chimney Base
5. Concrete foundations for electrical generation equipment installed in 1911 and 1913 by Don Judkins
6. Main Shaft (connected directly to Turbine)
7. Countershaft transmitting power from Main Shaft to Line Shaft (#13)
8. Belt Tensioner: acts as clutch engaging Main Shaft to Line Shaft (#13) by tightening belt with idler pulley mounted in hinged frame
9. Belt Tensioner control linkage mounted on ceiling
10. Furnace: maker unknown
11. Concrete Foundation Block: use unknown
12. Countershaft for Cordwood Saw
13. Line Shaft powering (from east to west) Trip Hammer, Post Drill, Wood Lathe, Grinder, Horizontal Boring Machine, Bandsaw, Cordwood Saw, Cross Cut Saw, Rip Saw, Jointer-Planer, and Cider Mill Line Shaft
14. Countershaft transmitting power from Main Shaft to Planer
15. Belt Tensioner: (see #8)
16. Belt Tensioner control linkage mounted on ceiling (Control Lever next to Planer)
17. Alternate Turbine Control Handle for use in basement
18. Shaft to Main Turbine Control Handwheel on first floor
19. Unused turbine control shaft; perhaps used during period Mill generated electricity for community (attached to a governor?)
20. Water Turbine: #4967 Hunt turbine (left-hand rotation) mfd in 1911 by Rodney Hunt Machine Co, Orange, Mass.; 18" water wheel delivers about 30 hp under 16 feet of head
21. Penstock: constructed in 1911 by Fenton Judkins; rebuilt c. 1949 by Ben Thresher; made of wooden staves bound together by steel hoop tie rods; boiler shell at end
22. Line Shaft powering (from east to west) Engine Lathe, Power Threader, Belt Sander, and Copy Lathe
23. Unused countershaft
24. Countershaft transmitting power from Line Shaft (#13) to Rip Saw
25. Countershaft transmitting power from Line Shaft (#13) to Jointer-Planer
26. Boiler: mfd by Ames Iron Works, Oswego, NY, installed c. 1915, probably in used condition; provides steam for steam box and cider evaporator tank, probably at about 15 psi
27. Chimney
28. Line Shaft driving Cider Mill machinery; shaft driven from Line Shaft (#13)
29. Countershaft transmitting power from Cider Mill Line Shaft (#28) to Apple Grinder
30. Apple Grinder: located under hopper in scales on first floor above; mfd by Boomer & Boschert Press Co, Syracuse, NY, pat'd April 13, 1881 and May 16, 1881; probably installed c. 1915 by Fenton Judkins
31. Cider Press: mfd by Boomer & Boschert Press Co, Syracuse, NY, no patent date; probably purchased in used condition; installed c. 1915 by Fenton Judkins
32. Hydraulic Pump for Cider Press; shop made
33. Cider Pump: shop made, pump apparatus made from bicycle tire pump; pumps fresh cider from collection pan under Cider Press to Cider Tank on first floor
34. Countershaft transmitting power from Cider Mill Line Shaft (#28) to Cider Pump
35. Cider Evaporating Tank for making cider jelly; installed c. 1915 by Fenton Judkins
36. Spigot for Hose used for washing down Cider Mill floor and equipment after making cider

Scale: ⅜" = 1'-0"

0   5   10 Feet
0 1 2 3 Meters

Fig. 5.

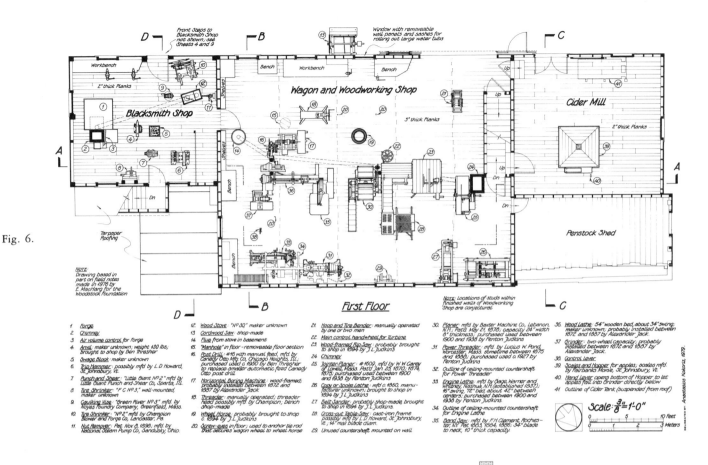

Fig. 6.

Blacksmith Shop · Wagon and Woodworking Shop · Cider Mill · Penstock Shed

First Floor

Front Steps to Blacksmith Shop not shown, see sheets 4 and 9

Window with removeable wall panels and sashes for rolling out large water tubs

NOTE: Drawing based in part on field notes made in 1976 by E. MacHarg for the Woodstock Foundation.

NOTE: Locations of studs within finished walls of Woodworking Shop are conjectural.

1. Forge
2. Chimney
3. Air volume control for forge
4. Anvil, maker unknown, weight 430 lbs., brought to shop by Ben Thresher
5. Swage Block, maker unknown
6. Trip Hammer, possibly mfd by L.D. Howard, St. Johnsbury, Vt.
7. Punch and Shear: "Little Giant No 2" mfd by Little Giant Punch and Shear Co., Sparta, Ill.
8. Tire Shrinker: "F C No.3", wall-mounted, maker unknown
9. Caulking Vise: "Green River No 3" mfd by Noyes Foundry Company, Greenfield, Mass.
10. Tire Shrinker: "No 2" mfd by Champion Blower and Forge Co, Lancaster, Pa.
11. Nut Remover, Pat. Nov. 8, 1898, mfd by National Steam Pump Co, Sandusky, Ohio.

12. Wood Stove: "No 30" maker unknown
13. Cordwood Saw: shop-made
14. Flue from stove in basement
15. "Manhole" in floor - removeable floor section
16. Post Drill: #16 with manual feed, mfd by Canedy Otto Mfg Co, Chicago Heights, Ill., purchased used c.1950 by Ben Thresher to replace smaller automatic feed Canedy Otto post drill.
17. Horizontal Boring Machine: wood-framed, probably installed between 1872 and 1887 by Alexander Jack.
18. Threader: manually operated; threader head possibly mfd by Champion, bench shop-made.
19. Wheel Horse: probably brought to shop c.1894 by J.L. Judkins.
20. Screw-eyes in floor, used to anchor tie rod that secures wagon wheel to wheel horse.

21. Hoop and Tire Bender: manually operated by one or two men
22. Main control handwheel for Turbine
23. Wood-framed Rip-Saw: probably brought to shop in 1894 by J.L. Judkins.
24. Chimney
25. Jointer-Planer: #1609, mfd by W.W. Carey of Lowell, Mass. Pat'd Jan 25, 1870, 1874, 1876; purchased used between 1900 and 1938 by Fenton Judkins.
26. Copy or Spoke Lathe: mfd c.1860, manufacturer unknown, brought to shop in 1894 by J.L. Judkins.
27. Belt Sander: probably shop-made, brought to shop in 1894 by J.L. Judkins.
28. Cross-cut Table Saw: cast-iron frame possibly mfd by L.D. Howard, St. Johnsbury, Vt., 14" mal blade diam.
29. Unused countershaft mounted on wall.

30. Planer: mfd by Baxter Machine Co, Lebanon, N.H., Pat'd May 21, 1878; capacity 24" width 6" thickness, purchased used between 1900 and 1938 by Fenton Judkins
31. Power Threader: mfd. by Lucius W. Pond, Worcester, Mass. sometime between 1875 and 1889; purchased used a 1927 by Fenton Judkins
32. Outline of ceiling-mounted countershaft for Power Threader
33. Engine Lathe: mfd by Gage, Warner and Whitney, Nashua, N.H. (established 1837); 16" swing, 72" bed; about 42" between centers; purchased between 1900 and 1938 by Fenton Judkins.
34. Outline of ceiling-mounted countershaft for Engine Lathe
35. Band Saw: mfd by F.H. Clement, Rochester, N.Y. Pat. 1863, 1864, 1866; 34" blade to neck, 10" width capacity.

36. Wood Lathe: 54" wooden bed, about 34" swing; maker unknown; probably installed between 1872 and 1887 by Alexander Jack.
37. Wood Lathe: smaller capacity; probably installed between 1872 and 1887 by Alexander Jack.
38. Control Lever.
39. Scales and Hopper for apples; scales mfd. by Fairbanks Morse, St. Johnsbury, Vt.
40. Hand Lever opens bottom of Hopper to let apples fall into Grinder directly below
41. Outline of Cider Tank (suspended from roof)

Scale: 3/8" = 1'-0"

DELINEATED BY: Anastasios Kokoris, 1979.

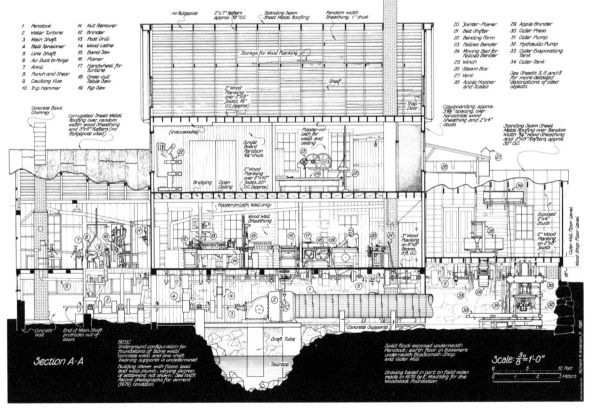

Fig. 7.

1. Penstock
2. Water Turbine
3. Main Shaft
4. Belt Tensioner
5. Line Shaft
6. Air Duct to Forge
7. Anvil
8. Punch and Shear
9. Caulking Vise
10. Trip Hammer
11. Nut Remover
12. Grinder
13. Post Drill
14. Wood Lathe
15. Band Saw
16. Planer
17. Handwheel for Turbine
18. Cross-cut Table Saw
19. Rip Saw

20. Jointer-Planer
21. Belt Shifter
22. Bending Form
23. Felloes Bender
24. Moving Bed for Felloes Bender
25. Winch
26. Steam Box
27. Apple Hopper and Scales

29. Apple Grinder
30. Cider Press
31. Cider Pump
32. Hydraulic Pump
33. Cider Evaporating Tank
34. Cider Tank

See Sheets 5, 6 and 8 for more detailed descriptions of cited objects.

Section A-A

NOTE! Underground configuration for foundations of stone walls, concrete walls and line shaft bearing supports is undetermined. Building shown with floors level and walls plumb; varying degrees of settlement not shown. See HAER Record photographs for current (1979) condition.

Drawing based in part on field notes made in 1976 by E. MacHarg for the Woodstock Foundation.

Scale: 3/8" = 1'-0"

DELINEATED BY: Richard A. Anderson, Jr., 1981.

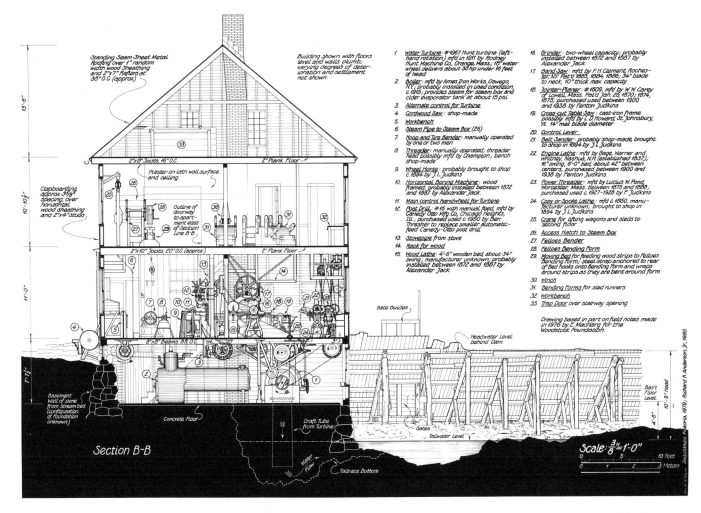

Standing Seam Sheet Metal Roofing over 1" random width wood Sheathing and 2"x7" Rafters at 38" O.C. (approx.)

Building shown with floors level and walls plumb; varying degrees of deterioration and settlement not shown.

Clapboarding approx. 3⅝" spacing over horizontal wood sheathing and 2"x4" studs

Plaster on-lath wall surface and ceiling

Outline of doorway to apartment east of Section Line B-B

2"x8" Joists, 16" O.C.

2" Plank Floor

2"x10" Joists, 20" O.C. (approx.)

2" Plank Floor

8"x8" Beams, 8 ft. O.C.

Basement Wall of stone from stream bed (configuration of foundation unknown)

Concrete Floor

Section B-B

Water Flow

Draft Tube from Turbine

Tailrace Bottom

Gate Guides

Headwater Level behind Dam

Gates

Tailwater Level

Bas't Floor Level

10'-9" Head

4'-3"

13'-6"

10'-10½"

11'-0"

7'-1"

1. *Water Turbine*: #1967 Hunt turbine (left-hand rotation) mfd in 1911 by Rodney Hunt Machine Co, Orange, Mass.; 15" water wheel delivers about 30 hp under 16 feet of head

2. *Boiler*: mfd by Ames Iron Works, Oswego, NY; probably installed in used condition, c.1915; provides steam for steam box and cider evaporator tank at about 15 psi

3. *Alternate control for Turbine*

4. *Cordwood Saw*: shop-made

5. *Workbench*

6. *Steam Pipe to Steam Box* (26)

7. *Hoop and Tire Bender*: manually operated by one or two men

8. *Threader*: manually operated; threader head possibly mfd by Champion; bench shop-made

9. *Wheel Horse*: probably brought to shop c.1894 by J.L. Judkins

10. *Horizontal Boring Machine*: wood framed; probably installed between 1872 and 1887 by Alexander Jack

11. *Main control handwheel for Turbine*

12. *Post Drill*: #16 with manual feed, mfd by Canedy Otto Mfg Co, Chicago Heights, Ill.; purchased used c.1950 by Ben Thresher to replace smaller automatic-feed Canedy-Otto post drill

13. *Stovepipe from stove*

14. *Rack for wood*

15. *Wood Lathe*: 4'-6" wooden bed about 34" swing; manufacturer unknown; probably installed between 1872 and 1887 by Alexander Jack

16. *Grinder*: two-wheel capacity; probably installed between 1872 and 1887 by Alexander Jack

17. *Band Saw*: mfd by F.H. Clement, Rochester, NY. Pat'd 1883, 1884, 1886; 34" blade to neck, 10" thick max. capacity

18. *Jointer-Planer*: #1609, mfd by W.W. Carey of Lowell, Mass. Pat'd Jan. 26, 1870; 1874, 1875; purchased used between 1900 and 1938 by Fenton Judkins

19. *Cross-cut Table Saw*: cast-iron frame possibly mfd by L.D. Howard, St. Johnsbury, Vt. 14" max blade diameter

20. *Control Lever*

21. *Belt Sander*: probably shop-made, brought to shop in 1894 by J.L. Judkins

22. *Engine Lathe*: mfd by Gage, Warner and Whitney, Nashua, N.H. (established 1837); 16" swing, 6'-0" bed, about 42" between centers; purchased between 1900 and 1938 by Fenton Judkins

23. *Power Threader*: mfd by Lucius W. Pond, Worcester, Mass. between 1875 and 1888; purchased used c.1927-1928 by F. Judkins

24. *Copy or Spoke Lathe*: mfd c.1850, manufacturer unknown; brought to shop in 1894 by J.L. Judkins

25. *Crane for lifting wagons and sleds to second floor*

26. *Access Hatch to Steam Box*

27. *Felloes Bender*

28. *Felloes Bending Form*

29. *Moving Bed* for feeding wood strips to Felloes Bending Form; steel strap anchored to rear of Bed hooks onto Bending Form and wraps around strips as they are bent around form

30. *Winch*

31. *Bending Forms* for sled runners

32. *Workbench*

33. *Trap Door* over stairway opening

Drawing based in part on field notes made in 1976 by E. MacHarg for the Woodstock Foundation.

Scale: 3/8" = 1'-0"

0   5   10 feet

0   1   2   3 Meters

Fig. 8.

45. Harris Scott, a bateauman, logger, and blacksmith, from West Milan, New Hampshire. The log scale in his hands was used to figure board footage in a log.

5

The North Country Log Drive Bateau

At times, the bow was high in air,
    And next the stern was lifted there.
So thus it tumbled, tossed, and rolled,
    And shipped enough to fill the hold,
Till more than once it seemed as though
    To feed the fish they all must go.

The Brownies' Voyage,
Palmer Cox, 1887

In all likelihood, we must look to the Canadian French for the origins of this rowing boat. Certainly the name is French. During the long French and Indian Wars, it was of inestimable use in ferrying troops and supplies to and from ships and along the shores and rivers around Lake Champlain. An old drawing I once saw showed French bateaux drawn up on shore. As with all later bateaux, the stern as well as the bow was sharply pointed, making it a double-ended boat. Overall, however (and even making allowances for the artist), the lines of the craft depicted seem to differ sharply from those of the almost delicately graceful American bateau.

In another book (*Goodbye Highland Yankee,* 1988), I have told how, as a boy, I built a Maine logging skiff. The impetus was my paternal grandfather's stories of his days on the Connecticut River long log drives. Gramp was a first-class bateau man, and he told me stories about how he and another young daredevil would take bateaux over the sluiceways of the dams they met along the drive so that the men would not have to hand carry ("forage") them around the end of the dam. In illustration 46, two men in a bateau have just ridden over the dam at Guildhall, Vermont, while working the tail of the Connecticut River log drive of 1909.

Illustration 47 shows two bateaux at Horseshoe Curve on the Deerfield River in southern Vermont. The two women in the further boat are having the ride of their lives. In the near boat are three drivers, two oarsmen, the steersman with his paddle, and the captain standing on a ledge. The job for these men, at the tail of the drive, is to get the stranded logs back into the main channel.

In illustration 48, we see a typical bateau underway somewhere on the Connecticut River in 1912, just three years before the last of the long log drives. The water here is shallow, and the craft is being poled.

Illustrations 49 and 50 appear to have been taken from a bridge. The locale is White River Junction, Vermont, and West Lebanon, New Hampshire, and the event is the 1912 log drive down the Connecticut. A lot of detail can be seen in these two pictures. In illustration 49, we see four teams on a horse raft with a

46. Riding a bateau over the dam at Guildhall, Vermont, 1909.

47. Bateaux at Horseshoe Curve on the Deerfield River.

48. The Connecticut River, 1912.

41

49. A horse raft, at White River Junction, Vermont.

50. Cook shack raft.

bateau moored ready for use. Note the hay. Each team is harnessed with whiffle trees for twitching stranded logs off the shores and meadows. The bateau in the foreground is loaded with bedrolls.

In illustration 50, we see a cook shack on a raft. The rivermen called this a Mary Ann. In the second boat can be seen a portable forge and an anvil for shoeing the drive horses. The bateau in the foreground holds a steering paddle. Illustration 51 shows rivermen in a bateau near West Lebanon, New Hampshire, taken about 1912.

In the autumn of 1972, while talking about the log drives with a friend, I suddenly realized that there probably weren't many bateaux left. The Connecticut River drive, the biggest and longest drive of all, brought logs up to sixty-feet long down from the upper Connecticut to Mt. Tom in Massachusetts. The last of these drives occurred in 1915. After that, though there were still some small log drives across northern New England, the drives were mostly of four-foot pulp for the paper mills.

It might be of some importance, I thought, to find a bateau, take off its lines, and note the details of its construction. Having a few free days, I decided to spend them on this effort. Earl MacHarg, a friend of mine who was born in Groveton, New Hampshire in the heart of the north country, owned a small travel trailer with a couple of bunks and was eager to go. We set off early on a clear October day.

Three days of combing the north country as far east as the Maine border elicited no bateaux. We visited West Stewartstown, the depot town for George Van Dyke's Connecticut Valley Lumber Company, and we went to the Brown Paper Company offices in Berlin, New Hampshire. We hit all the towns in between and round about. We tracked down pervasive rumors of a logging museum that was to be built—always four or five towns over. Everyone we spoke to was interested in helping, and they racked their brains trying to recall the whereabouts of a bateau.

My impression was that the bateau, once a commonplace of northern life, had disappeared with dramatic suddenness. Almost everyone we asked immediately remembered a good many bateaux that were still around. But as they thought about it, certainty gradually turned to bemusement, then to alarm. "There were six stored in so-and-so's barn. Come to think of it though, the roof fell in under the snow last winter and smashed 'em. But there must still be one or two somewhere up in this country. I'll keep thinking, and I sure hope you find one. Be a shame for 'em just to vanish."

There probably were, and maybe still are, a few bateaux left, but we couldn't find them and our time was getting short. Finally, one day early in the morning, we were driving through Errol, New Hampshire. I noticed a big garage with a couple of huge logging trucks parked outside. Somehow, as had occasionally happened in the past, I knew this was it. "Stop here Earl," I said. "I think we've struck paydirt."

Inside we found Robert Moody of Wilson Mills, Maine, and Leonard Jordan of Errol. Not only did both men know a great deal about bateaux, but they were also able to tell us where to find one. "It's on Aker's Pond. 'Bout a mile

51. Bateaumen near West Lebanon, New Hampshire.

out of Errol, on the road to Dixville Notch. There's a bateau right there on the shore. Local sportsman's club bought it and put it there. There's a chain across the road, but you can get permission to measure the boat if you ask at Clifford Lane's. Green house—you can't miss it."

Mr. Lane was delighted that someone was interested enough to take photographs and measurements of the boat.

"She's pretty well grown up with brush. You'll have to chop it out before you can see much, but go to it," he said.

We took down the chain across the road, hooked it back up behind us, and drove down the narrow dirt road to a small sparkling pond. Sure enough, in a clump of small trees by the shore we were just able to discern the outline of a large structure.

We had a sharp axe and a little bowsaw with us. In no time we had the site brushed out, and there before us lay the object of our search. Illustration 52 shows the bateau from the stern. The craft was by no means in first-class condition, but it was sound enough for us to be able to take thorough measurements.

52. The bateau found along the shore of Aker's Pond, Errol, New Hampshire.

Illustration 53 shows the stern in some detail. The half-moon-shaped pieces held the sternsman's seat. Illustration 54 shows a bateau oar, which are considerably longer than those for an ordinary rowboat.

We spent the balance of that day and all the next one taking off the lines and measurements of the bateau, photographing it, and noting the details of its construction. The information is given here in figure 9. From this information, the various steps in constructing a bateau can be derived.

Rodney Webb of Thetford, Vermont, worked for the Brown Paper Company during the 1950s. He told me that this company was still using bateaux then, but that they were not new ones. The craft is sturdy and ruggedly built and does not easily wear out. The ones he experienced had been in operation for a considerable time. At that time, they were cutting a lot of pulp, some of which was corded in the woods near a big manmade lake. Splash boards on the dam

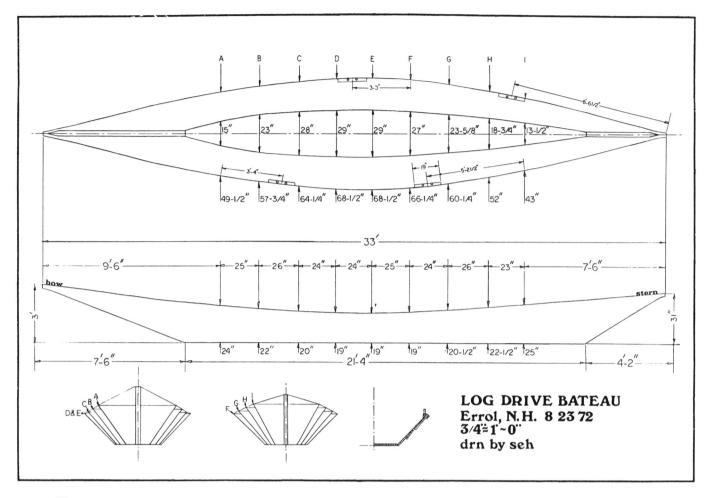

LOG DRIVE BATEAU
Errol, N.H. 8 23 72
3/4"=1'-0"
drn by seh

Fig. 9. A scale drawing of the lines and measurements of the Aker's Pond bateau.

53. Stern detail of Aker's Pond bateau, Errol, New Hampshire.

were used to raise the water level before the spring drive. The men then poled bateaux into the flooded woods and waded in the cold water to load the pulp. A bateau could carry out half a cord at a time. During this same period, a few small log drives and pulp drives continued in New Hampshire along the Androscoggin and on some rivers in Maine. Mr. Webb believes that the bateaux used for these drives were used ones, too. It is probably safe to estimate that new bateaux have not been built, at least in any numbers, since the 1930s, and perhaps even earlier.

There may be a few old men who remember how the boats were made, and an effort should be made to find and record what they can tell us. In the meantime, I do not think the following description is off by very much.

The bateau is such a large, heavy boat that it seems safe to assume that generally they were built close beside the rivers on which they were to be used. The craft could have been built by independent contractors or by employees of the logging companies. I suspect, though, that both were involved, with by far the larger number being made by company employees. I say this because the bateau is largely a product of hand labor. The carpentry, though somewhat demanding, is of a very practical nature and well within the reach of most of the jack-of-all-trades working for the companies in their depot towns.

The local sawmill would cut the necessary boards and plane them to thickness. A local woodworking mill would own the power machinery required to tongue and groove the boards for the bottom, as well as a large bandsaw on which to cut the ribs to shape. Beyond this, all that was required were common hand tools and a blacksmith to forge the small amount of ironwork required. During the heyday of the log drive, the capability to build new bateaux quickly and in reasonable numbers would have been imperative. The bateaux were fastened throughout using common round wire nails, and their daily work subjected them to severe strains and abuse. Though they lasted a long time, accidents and hard use eventually took their toll. Wherever possible, therefore, builders would have made patterns to avoid unnecessary work in laying out parts that were the same in every bateau.

An obvious example is the bateau bottom. It would be time consuming and foolish to set up and carefully lay out the curvature of identical new bottoms on an individual basis. Instead, a master pattern could be carefully fabricated out of seasoned, half-inch pine and hung on the wall. Each new bateau bottom would then be fabricated as a slightly oversized rectangle of wide, inch-thick, tongue and groove white pine boards, temporarily held together with wooden cleats nailed to its undersurface. (There was only one bottom seam in the bateau we measured. It was 17-1/2 inches from the left side facing forward.) A center line would then be snapped end to end along the top surface with a chalkline. The pattern would then be aligned at each of its ends with the chalked line, and its outline traced in heavy pencil. Once the waste wood was taken off with a ripsaw, the frames were nailed on.

The spacing of the frames is shown on the figure with the letters "A" through "I". The frames were mostly of ash, though a few were maple. They were sawn to shape on a bandsaw and nailed to the bottom using one nail at the end and one at the curve where the frame rises to the planking. The outside surface to which the planking was nailed was perfectly smooth with no notching to accommodate the planking. Instead, a wedge-shaped piece of hardwood filled each space between the planks and frames. They were held in place by the planking nails. The top of each frame was fastened to the planking and gunwale (see figure 10). After the frames were attached to the bottom, the whole thing was turned upside-down and fastened to a jig. The edges of the bottom were then planed fair to the frames in preparation for planking.

The 3/4-inch planking was laid on lapstreak, that is, each succeeding plank (there were three to a side) overlapped the edge of the one below it. Planks were nailed to the frames using 2-1/4-inch nails spaced one inch on center. The planks overlapped one inch in the center of the boat, gradually increasing to about 1-3/4 inches at the ends. The overlap was fastened together by nails driven from the inside. Each nail protruded from the outside plank, where it was bent to a U-shape using a hammer and clinching bar. The curved end of the nail was then driven tightly into the plank, clinching it.

The lower planks went on first and overlapped the bottom, to which they were fastened by nails driven every 2-1/2 inches. Planking was not feathered into the stems at either bow or stern. Instead, the full thickness of each plank

54. A bateau oar owned by Harris Scott, West Milan, New Hampshire.

was carried onto the face of the stem and fastened by two rows of nails. The nails in the outside row were close to the plank ends and spaced nine inches apart. The inner row, set back six or seven inches from the ends, entered the thickness of the stem and were spaced on two-inch centers. Because of the lack of feathering the profile of both bow and stern show three shallow "steps." The plan shows the ends of all three planks on one side cut off flush in line with the slanted surface of the stem. The ends of the three opposite planks were brought out even with this cut and trimmed at a right angle. A heavy iron band, made and fitted by the smith, was nailed into the stem and continued several inches back along the bottom to provide protection from boulders and ledges.

INCIDENTAL DETAIL:

Stems—White pine, 3-3/4 inches at thickest part. Inside length of bow stem ninety inches (5/8-inch manila rope through one inch hole bored through top of bow). Inside length of stern stem sixty-one-inches (3 1/2-inch ring of 3/8-inch round iron rod fastened to stern by 3/8 by 1-inch iron staple).

Gunwales—White pine, 7/8 by 1-3/4 inches. Each was spliced (see figure). Fastened from inside using nails on nine-inch centers clinched into outside surface.

Fig. 10. A sheet of field drawings of bateau details.

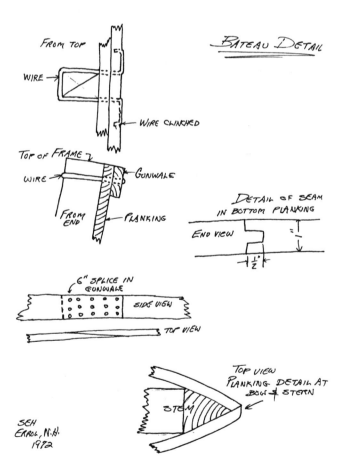

Seat rail—Spruce, 7/8 by 1-11/16 inches. Fastened using one nail per frame. The rail is twelve inches above bottom. Extends from frame "K" to frame "A".

Rowing—The bateau was rowed by four men who often stood. 7 by 1-1/8-inch thole pins of oak trimmed to shape with an axe were fitted into a beveled piece of ash nailed to the edge of the top plank. The oversized oars were machine made of spruce.

Steering—Bateaux were steered by a sternsman using a paddle. A captain, also equipped with a paddle, rode in the bow where he could spot stone snags and other hazards in time for the sternsman to steer around them.

Stem irons—Each stem had a piece of strap iron 1/8 by 7/8 inches nailed to it for protection. These were nailed on nine-inch centers. Each extended twelve inches onto the bottom, but the bow iron was thirty-seven inches short of reaching the stem top and the stern iron lacked by twenty-four inches.

Pitching and painting—Seams were caulked, then pitched using a mixture of lard and pine tar melted by a paddle-shaped pitching iron heated red-hot. This was done each year, and some bateaux were pitched all over on the outside. This bateau was once painted gray inside. Harris Scott of West Milan, New Hampshire, recalls that some were painted a dark, almost purple, blue outside. And Rodney Webb recalls the bateaux he used as being an all-over brownish color.

Fastenings—Nails used throughout, the common round wire nails being carefully matched to the size and thickness of the timbers. Plank laps nailed using 6d nails (2 inches). Frames to bottom planks using 10d nails (3 inches). Bottom planks into frames using 10d nails (3 inches). Seat rails to frames using 8d nails (2-1/2 inches). Thole pin blocks from outside through gunwales using 10d nails (3 inches). Planks to frames using 7d nails (2-1/4 inches).

55. Sawmill worker, 1937.

6

Sawmilling

See you our little mill that clacks,
So busy by the brook?
She has ground her corn and paid her tax
Ever since Domesday Book.
From *Puck's Song,*
by Rudyard Kipling

THE PITSAW MEN

The water-driven grist mills that ground good English grain into flour so seized Kipling's imagination that in *Puck's Song* he names them as one of the immemorially old and characteristic features of the English landscape. The first verse of this poem reads:

> See you the ferny ride that steals
> Into the oak-woods far?
> O that was where they hewed the keels
> That rolled to Trafalgar.

It is significant that in the first verse of this poem Kipling speaks of shipbuilding, for the building of wooden ships includes a trade almost as ancient as the miller's: that of the pitsaw men. Hewing was all very well for shaping the keel and ribs of a ship, but it was not an efficient means of making the planking that covered it. Hewing is a simple process involving the removal of the rounded portions of a large log, shaping it into a squared, or rectangular, cross section. The diagonals of the end of the finished timber are then roughly equal to the original diameter of the small end of the log.

The width of a plank or board, however, greatly exceeds its thickness. Moreover, either one is used for such a variety of purposes that it must be available in a large number of different widths and thicknesses. Planks cannot easily be hewn from a log; they have either to be split out or sawn. It is difficult if not impossible to control dimensions closely when splitting logs, however, nor can wide stock be made. The method is wasteful and labor intensive, and its use was confined to a few traditional crafts that used only narrow pieces. Such pieces could then be smoothed with the drawknife and shaving horse, the method used by the ladder round maker, the bucket maker, and the makers of fence rails and sheep hurdles.

Sawing was the only means of producing the long, wide boards and planks required by many trades. For centuries, this work was accomplished by hand, the log being sawn lengthwise by means of a long, flexible ripsaw with a tiller

49

56. Original 1795 up and down sawmill on Blood Brook. A view from stream level, showing the remains of a press box, which held a turbine.

(crossways) handle at the top end and a removable "box" handle at the other. This device was called a whipsaw, and it was kept sharp and carefully oiled against rust. In England and America, it was employed by teams of two itinerant men who walked the countryside carrying the saw and its handles from job to job. Besides the saw, the tools of their trade were few enough: a canvas sack to hold the great blade, a chalkline, files and a swaging block and hammer to sharpen and set the saw's teeth. These sawyers had a fixed itinerary to cover every year. Their visits took them to the workyards of wagon makers and carpenters. Shipyards and other large-scale, wooden industries in the population centers employed full-time sawyers living in fixed abodes. In either case, the work was arduous and ill paid, ranking toward the bottom of the social caste system among the hand trades. It was thirsty work, too, and at day's end, the men repaired to a pub for a drench of good brown ale or something stronger.

In pitsawing, a log was debarked and rolled onto trestles laid above a dug pit. An approximation of square-edged boards could be had by flattening two opposite faces of the log with a broadaxe. The finished boards were faintly wedge-shaped because one end of the log was smaller than the other. These tapered boards are sometimes seen in very old, wide-board flooring in New England homes. The log was secured with log dogs, L-shaped iron hooks driven into the log and one of the trestles. With a line soaked in soot, the sawyers snapped lines from one end of the log to the other, laying out the thicknesses of the planks and boards to be cut. The pitman dropped down a short ladder into the pit, while the top sawyer stood on the log and lowered the narrow end of the saw to him. The top man followed the line and raised the saw at the end of each stroke. The pitman pulled down on the saw for its cutting stroke. Against the itching sawdust, he might wear a broad-brimmed hat and a scarf knotted around his face and neck.

When, with the passage of time, various kinds of machines developed, it became commonplace to transmute the rotary motion of a gear or wheel to a straight-line reciprocating motion using a strong wooden rod as the connecting mechanism. Not surprisingly, someone noticed the resemblance of this to the motion of the pitman's shoulder joints and arms as he pulled at the saw. Thus the term pitman rod became an ineradicable part of engineering jargon.

THE SASH MILL OR UP AND DOWN SAW

The sash mill was essentially a larger version of the pit sawyer's whipsaw. The saw blade was fastened top and bottom to the center of a stout wooden frame made like a window sash, hence the name sash mill. The frame, riding up and down in vertical ways greased with a mixture of lard and pine pitch, was driven by a heavy iron crank connected by wooden gearing to a water wheel. Some sash mills had one end of a strong, limber pole fastened to the top bar of the sash. Its other end was anchored in the roof beams. The pole acted as a spring and helped return the sash frame to the top after each cutting stroke. The alternative name, up and down sawmill, comes from the fact that the saw strokes traveled up and down in a straight-line motion.

The path taken by the saw teeth was clearly visible as a characteristic pattern of closely spaced, straight striations on the face of the sawn boards, at right angles to their length. Each mark indicated one downstroke of the saw. The handsawn boards cut by pit sawyers carried the same markings, but they were finer and ran at an angle to the board's length, since the top sawyer advanced ahead of the pitman so that the saw ran at a slant. Sawmarks on boards used in furniture, house trim, wagons, and so on were removed by hand using a roughing plane: a jack plane whose blade had been ground into a shallow arc. This planing was sometimes, but not invariably, followed by a smoothing plane. Parts of old furniture that are hidden from sight—drawer bottoms, for example—often retain the wide grooves left by the roughing plane. A water-powered sash mill from the Royalton, Vermont, area, saved and rebuilt at the Shelburne Museum in Shelburne, Vermont, has a primitive, powered board planer. It consists of a broad circular disk with three steel cutters on the circumference, running in a horizontal plane. This is a far cry from the modern thickness planer, but it must have been a great advance over the laborious work of removing sawmill marks by hand planing.

Saw logs were "dogged down" (fastened) to the carriage and fed into the saw either by hand with a lever or by means of a cable mechanism. Each revolution of the crank shaft caused a dog to engage a ratchet wheel bolted to a large wooden wheel beneath the mill floor. This advanced the log carriage into the saw just as the downstroke began. Since the saw blade widened from bottom to top, each descending tooth cut a little farther into the log. Sash saws were dreadfully slow but were a considerable advance over the pitsaw method of making lumber. The sash saw cut through the entire length of log, except for the last two or three inches, which would have carried the blade into the saw carriage itself. This last, uncut bit was split with a hand axe, freeing the board from the log. For the carriage return, the ratchet dog kicked out, and the operator raised a gate, turning the water onto a small wheel that ran the carriage and log back for the next cut. The output of a sash mill averaged 500 to 1500 board feet a day, depending upon how much water was available.

Illustrations 56, 57, and 58 show the remains of a sash mill built on Blood Brook in West Fairlee, Vermont, in 1795. It was built on an original sawmill grant carrying fifty acres. About 1895, the mill was converted into a circular saw rig. The overshot wheel was removed, and a turbine, supplied by a wooden penstock carrying water from the millpond, was installed in a press box built of staves. The function of the press box was to confine the water supplied by the penstock and feed it through the turbine.

Mill work was always hard and often dangerous. Besides the obvious risks of working close to whirling machinery and open belting, there was always an element of the unexpected. The story of a narrow escape was related to me by Harold Day of Sharon, Vermont. Mr. Day, now deceased, was seventy-four at the time I interviewed him in 1970. His family had built and run mills on Quation Brook since the late 1700s. His own turbine-powered sawmill, designed and built by him in the 1940s, was the last in a series of three mills built by his family. His great, great grandfather, "Big" Orin Day, was a soldier in the Revolutionary War. The sobriquet was used to distinguish him from his son,

57. View of press box, gearing, and sawmill pulley from above. A wooden penstock supplied water from a nearby pond.

58. Detail of the wooden pulley. Note how the pieces were joined using "butterflies." Note also the wedging of the pulley to the shaft.

59. Original up and down saw blade on the mill floor.

60. Close-up of the teeth.

"Little" Orin (there were no Juniors in those times). Big Orin built the first of the Day mills—an up and down sawmill.

Little Orin's son Edwin was a cooper. He built the second of the Day mills. It drew its water from a small pond well upstream by means of a wooden penstock built by Edwin and Harold's father, Herbert. Herbert learned the cooper and miller trades from his father, in whose mill he worked as a young man. One day, after his "nooning," Herbert went back to work early to tinker with the turbine but neglected to tell his father Edwin. Climbing down into the press box, he began his work. Edwin Day also returned early to work. Stopping at the dam, he seized the gate pole and opened it. Herbert, luckily, heard the rattle of the chain and managed to climb out of the press box just as the water came roaring in.

That particular mill had been gone sixty-five years before my interview with Harold Day, but he showed me the remains of the dam—a large "tole log" in the brook bottom with a few pieces of planking still attached. The penstock came out a foot or two below, as shown by a circle of planks still sticking out of the bank. Well below lay the stone foundations of the mill with the remnants of the press box beside it, three-quarter-inch iron anchor rods sprouting from each corner. From it ran the tailrace, a ditch ten feet wide and five feet deep.

In 1896, Harold's father built a mortared stone dam at the head of Quation Brook. He sold water from it to a mill in Sharon Village, some two and one-half miles downstream. Every morning at five o'clock, he took a lantern and went to the dam to open the gate. Two hours later, the water arrived at the Sharon mill in time for the day's work. At three o'clock, he shut the dam gate, allowing enough water for the mill to operate until five. For the labor of opening and shutting the gate and for the supply of water, Herbert Day received one dollar a day.

Harold asked me once if I knew the word "punona." When I'd given up guessing, he told me it was a word made up and used by his grandfather Edwin. The old gentleman had made it a lifelong practice to fulfill his customers' needs "punona" (upon honor).

The following is a brief description of the workings of an "old up and down mill" by an eyewitness, Harris Scott of West Milan, New Hampshire.

"On the old up and down saw the teeth had an awful hook in them. There was an old up and down mill in my grandfather's blacksmith shop in Milan. My father and grandfather used to saw sled turns [sledge runners cut from a tree section that grew with a natural crook in it] in that saw because you could set your curved log up and saw right down through your sled turn. It was big enough to do that. Then you could put it down and either work it out by hand or with a big bandsaw they had in there too. My grandfather kept that up and down saw there on purpose to saw out sled wood. He could go to the woods and get a natural turn of wood for a sled runner and saw out any thickness you wanted. That damn saw, I think, took pretty near half an inch of wood each time it went down [on the cutting stroke] because it was pretty stiff [thick]. And I think there was a dog on the side, and there was a long lever. And you fed by hand. Fed that ratchet by hand, yeah! They run it by steam power. Had an old boiler down in the cellar. I was about fourteen or fifteen years old then. I have wished a thousand times since then that I had taken that old mill and moved it over here and set it up. 'Cause every bit of it was there.

"It had to have quite a pit under it too, because you had as much of your saw frame underneath as you had on top. And you had these big wooden posts, big ones with the riggings for your belting to run on bolted to them. And they always had a can of lard setting there to grease the slides up and down because it wouldn't heat enough but that it would stay there pretty good. Oil would heat enough so it would run off."

STEAM SAWMILLS

During the last quarter of the 1800s, logging intensified, especially in the northeastern parts of Vermont and in northern New Hampshire. Sometimes timber was too far from rivers to be sent down on the log drives. Often it was easier to saw the logs into lumber close by the logging area rather than haul them out to a sawmill. It became fairly common for timber operators to erect portable steam sawmills within the perimeter of their logging effort. These rigs were, of course, circular sawmills, and my own father worked in one when he was not much more than a boy. I once asked him what it was like, and the following, in his own words, is his response to that question.

61. Wide pine board sawn in this 1795 up and down mill. Note that the last few inches were split out using an axe because these saws could not cut to the end without cutting into the saw frame.

62. In the 1890s, the up and down saw was replaced by a four-foot diameter circular saw. It was then that the turbine was put in. The original mill was powered by an overshot water wheel.

"This was in the fall of 1918. I was fourteen in January, and I went to work for them that fall. They sold their lumber down in Manchester, New Hampshire, to be shipped all over the country. There was a lot of woods between Groton and North Ryegate, Vermont, that'd never been logged out—full of old growth pine, some of it two and a half feet through on the stump. Pine and hemlock and some hardwoods. We took it all. Some they cut square edged. Some they left round edged and sawed an inch and a quarter thick. I think that went for crutches and heel stock. It all had to be sorted as to kind and dimension, and that was my first job.

"It was a portable mill. When I got there, they put me down in the pit, the millway, the place where the boards come out off the saw onto a platform. You kept your round-edged white birch in one pile, and your hemlock in one pile, and your pine in another, and still another for the spruce. The teamster pulled up with a wagon, and the driver helped with the load. Then he carted it out to the yard where there was a man sticking lumber, and they piled it into big stacks to dry. Every layer had an inch of waste lumber go between it and the next one to let the air circulate through the pile. And so's the boards wouldn't warp. That was something new. Other mills stacked lumber as high as the men could reach, say fifteen feet. These people stacked maybe seven or eight feet high and about five feet wide. It dried out so much faster that way.

"I worked there a week, and then they needed another teamster in the woods. They hired a team from Windy Williams who had a little farm. He used to farm and rent horses, and this team had a reputation. Bill Yetton, the boss, went with me down to William's farm to get the team. They were flea bitten grays—one mare and a gelding. Flea bitten gray is a special color. They have little brown flecks all through the gray and they look like flea bites. Only way you could get a harness on the gelding was put a twister around his nose. Williams had two pulley blocks hitched to a beam, and he strung the harness up on that. After he got the collar on, if we were lucky, about the third shot we could drop the harness on him and get the straps fastened to hold it on him. Then he was all right. None of the regular teamsters would drive them: they knew what they were.

"I pulled into the pit with them, loaded up, and made a trip all right. Old Acey Duncan, he was a local character that stood about six feet, five inches—just whalebone. He told me, 'If you have any trouble, I'll help you out.'

"Well, there was this fellow from Manchester, New Hampshire, name of Smitty. He was driving the other team, stacking, and he wouldn't climb onto the load unless he had a whip or a club in his hand. He was a good teamster, but he didn't hesitate to use the whip either. On my second load, the horses balked. I got down and went and gave them each a cigarette to eat, then sat down in front of them where they could see me. I had a smoke. Smitty come tearing down and grabbed his club right off quick to start in on my team. 'Fore he could hit them, I grabbed a stake off the wagon and headed him off. He was a lot bigger than I was, so I grabbed the stake. You could hear him holler for a mile. He was going to show me how to team, but that was the trouble—they'd been abused too much, see? Old Acey came down and picked him up in one hand and

63. Hauling logs with a single sled, 1940. The dragging logs act as a brake on hills.

shook him just like a rat. Threw him onto his wagon and told him to go along to the mill. Says to me, 'What are you going to do now?'

"I says, 'I think they'll go now. They've had a little breather and a cigarette.'

"He went back to the mill. I put the stake back in, got up onto the load, and picked up the reins. The horses took right off. They forgot all about being balky. Three or four times a day I'd stop and feed them cigarettes whether they balked or not. Never had any trouble with them, and I drove them about a month. Then they had that lot cleaned up on top of the mountain, and they moved the rig down to Moore brothers' farm. That was when I went into the mill as handyman. I learned everything. Tried to anyway.

"My first job was cutting sticking for piling lumber. I had a little saw there by the table, and I sawed my stickings out of waste, anything you could get an inch piece out of. When I got a bunch piled up, the teamsters had to take them out to the yard. Then I'd go inside, and there was this old fireman named Tar Box. All he'd done all his life was run a steam engine. He worked for those people. He showed me how to pile lumber. And he showed me how to run the steam engine, too. If you don't think it's tricky keeping steam up! We had a board sawyer by the name of Bill Hubbard; probably the best board sawyer in New England. He was fast, and he would get down there a half hour early and go all over his saw. It had inserted teeth. He kept them in good condition. He'd file them and specially watch out for frozen hemlock which would shell saw teeth. They'd fly out and go into the pit beneath the saw like so many bullets.

"If Tar Box was sick or wanted a day off, I'd go in and fire. Bill Hubbard would come down and say, 'Now you're going to earn your money today, because I'm going to "steam you" in an hour.'

"Steaming meant they'd have to shut down the mill 'cause the boiler was out of steam. But Tar Box had showed me a lot of tricks on it. Like, when you get these old growth hemlock slabs [slabs are the waste pieces cut from the first and last face of the log] with bark on them an inch and a half, two inches thick, you'd set it to one side. Then when the steam begins to go down, you'd throw in a couple. Keep 'em in the bottom and then throw your pine and the other stuff on top of it. Boy, there were days you'd burn slabs just as fast as you'd make them.

"The boiler set down about six feet below the bed of the mill, and they'd cut those slabs three feet long and throw them down. There were days it was thirty below zero with the wind blowing. Always a battle between Hubbard and I. Once in awhile, he'd catch me. Man how he'd chuckle! But he wouldn't waste any time. He'd go to work on the saw, and the boys got logs down and ready. Ten minutes, I had steam up again and away we went.

"You ran your boiler water as low as you could because it heated much faster. Used to run it a third to half on the glass gauge on the boiler. One time the water we were using was awful muddy—full of clay. Tar Box took the day off, and I didn't know about the clay. It was a miserable day to fire, everything wringing wet and the slabs dripping water after they'd been in the boiler room awhile. Long about ten o'clock, the Moore brothers—t'was their farm, they had eleven hundred acres—came by to look things over. Bill was having one of his jamming days, but I had a lot of good hemlock from the top of the mountain and plenty of it saved and I got ahead of Bill. The safety valve blew off with a roar. You'd swear there were soap suds in the boiler that day! There was a bloom of suds sixty feet in the air and about four feet across. The Moore brothers we didn't see again for a week. Last we saw of them they were running across the fields.

"I was scared. Bill ran down as I pulled open the firebox door to let cold air in onto the fire. For a month there, with that clay water, it happened once or twice a day. I was just a kid, and I was trying to make it blow. Thought it was fun!

"How big was the steam engine? It was huge. Had a big flywheel, probably six feet and maybe two feet wide. It was weighted so it would stop off center. If it stopped dead center you had to take the belt off and pry it around so's it could start again. It ran the pulley on the board saw. That one was probably ten inches or a foot in diameter and two feet wide. It was made all of little pieces of wood glued together. We had one blowup one day. Talk about a mess! Just like a corn popper popping corn.

"Nope! The belt wasn't guarded. If a man fell into it, it was all up with him. It was made of thick leather spliced together. That splice was tapered thick to thin, and it was a good foot long as I remember. Factory pressed and glued. No lacing in it at all, an endless belt. They put belt dressing on it three or four times a day for adhesion, and they had an adjustment where you could jack the engine with big bolts if the belt needed tightening. Once it had done stretching

64. Everett Jones, Sharon, Vermont, filing a mill saw.

it was O.K. When it broke, they put on a new one and sent it to be fixed if it was worth it.

"The guy who takes away [sawn lumber] from the board sawyer had a gauge and a big black crayon to mark how many feet were in the board—right on top of it. Each board was marked. When that lumber was sold, it was tallied, then and there, using that number. It was loaded into boxcars. There was a man there named Art that did nothing but haul lumber and load it into the cars. He had three or four guys with anywhere from eight to sixteen horses. They all made a living, summer and winter, hauling lumber. In the winter, they rolled the snow and hauled on it. Used to wear Johnson wool pants and a four-buckle overshoe over felt boots.

"The board saw had a friction drive. You had a big handle stick up there. To bring the saw carriage back with the log on it, you'd pull back on that stick. To make the log go ahead, you'd push it. Friction was worn down, but Bill Hubbard was a big guy in fighting trim and he could make it go! One day he had a tremendous log on the carriage. He got it all squared up, and he wanted to go over and have a cup of coffee with the Finnish choppers in their tents. So he hollered to me and said, 'I want this thing all sawed up by the time I get back.'

"I got my courage up, and I was going pretty good. I bet I took twenty boards off it, and I'd go a little faster on each one.

"Well, you had what they called a 'jack,' and when the carriage came back you had to click it twice to saw off an inch-thick board. And they had a 'turner.' He was a fellow that turned the logs on the carriage. He clicked the jack end and set the dogs—you set the dogs on the heading. That dog clamped down on a ratchet like a wedge, and they bit into the top and bottom of the log like a hammer blow to hold it steady. Well, I got speeding and showing off, and I went too far. I jumped on the lever and didn't have enough lead in my pants to stop it. I put the whole log right out through the end of the mill! Right off the carriage and the track it run on. I bet it was out there ten feet from the mill.

"Bill Hubbard come back, and he stopped there and looked around. 'What the hell happened?' he said.

"I said, 'I got to showing off and missed the end.'

"He said, 'You will know better next time.'

"The men got a big pole and some blocks and blocked it up; then you could slide it right back onto the saw carriage. Bill got quite a kick out of that.

"They needed more teams to get the logs down off the mountain to the mill. One of the local men had just had quite a lot of money left to him. He went out West with one of the local horse dealers and bought a bunch of work horses; got 'em mostly in Iowa, Ohio, out through that section. So I was using one of the new teams one day, and Rob, he was the boss, told me, 'When you get up there those boys will load the logs. Don't you touch a thing, and when they say you've got a load, you just come on back down here.'

"Well there was one place there, about halfway down the mountain, where you had a wild curve. It was so steep that the four horses had to dig to get that bobsled up over it on the way up. And coming down, you take four horses and a bobsled and a couple of big logs sixty, seventy-feet long behind you, you've got quite an outfit to get round the corner. [The bobsled, in this instance, was just the front set of runners to keep the front end of the log off the ground.] Well, they chained 'em down, and I went down through and began unloading at the mill.

"When I got back up there a fella named Dave Gatley was being loaded. They finished him and began to chain the logs, and he said, 'What are you stopping for? You're not loading that kid now. I'm a teamster! I'll tell you when to stop!' He had them pile up those logs like it was a load of hay.

"'You'll never make it,' I told him.

"'Don't you worry about it,' he said.

"He started out, and when he got almost down to that wild corner two men were putting on chains. And they wanted to unload some of the logs before he went down and around.

"'You haven't got chains enough to hold that load,' they told him.

"'You put 'em on, and I'll get down and around,' responded Dave.

"He never even made the corner. It was ninety-feet down over the bank, and he went right off the logging road and down over. And that load of logs and that bobsled are still there today along with part of his harness. The only things he had when he come up out of there was his bridles and collars. But no horses! I think what he done, he jumped off. He claimed he rode it down, but I know better. He jumped or got thrown off. Nobody could figure out how his horses lived through it. Last time I saw him, he had his team on a rope and he was leading them home.

"One time they moved the mill right in against the foot of a cliff, oh, maybe ninety-feet high. They rolled the logs over it onto a pile at the bottom. I had one horse then, and my job was to go into that mess and skid the logs out onto a rollway so the men could roll them out to the board sawyer. That was quite a busy job.

"I'd run the chain under the log and hook Jim up. When you got it to the rollway, you just unhitched the chain, and Jim pulled it out from under the log. You'd hang onto the chain, and he'd go right back up there for another log by himself.

"We were putting down a lot of Norway pine. It's very smooth, and when it's frozen you'd swear it had been greased. They had a big log up there at the top, and the horse was young and pretty nervous and the log got away from him. Jim and I had just got the chain unhitched from a log and were headed toward the barn when they hollered. I grabbed a cant dog and walloped him across the butt, and he lit out. And the boys in the mill piled out of both ends. That log came down and went right straight through the mill and out the other end. Never did any damage at all—just took out four or five posts holding up the roof and let it down onto the board saw. Sawed a hole right through the roof. Tar Box stayed behind and shut the boiler valve before he took off."

65. Earl Hood, Topsham, Vermont, cidermaker, storyteller, and all-round Yankee.

7

The Cider Men

Pat Willey and Will Chandless
Topsham, Vermont

Here's to thee, old apple tree,
    Whence thou may'st bud
And whence thou may'st blow
    And whence thou may'st bear apples
enow;
Hats full and caps full,
    Bushels full and sacks full,
And our pockets full too . . .
                                Mother Goose

One warm day in August of 1971, when I was searching for water mills along the Tabor Branch between East Corinth and Topsham Four Corners, a small red double barn on a farm beside the road attracted me. A few minutes later, I found myself telling its owner that I had stopped because I felt sure this was some kind of old mill. He raised his eyebrows, grinned, and took a key from his pocket. "Come on," he said, "I'll show you," and he walked over and unlocked the door.

It took a few seconds for my eyes to adjust to the dusky interior, but then I was very glad I'd stopped. In the center of the single room was a cyclopean structure built of huge sawn timbers. Two vertical, twelve-inch square posts rose from each side of a wooden platform flanking a square, heavily built, slatted, wooden box set in the platform's center. Double tenons had been cut at each end of a twelve-inch by twenty-inch horizontal beam and morticed straight through the top of each post. Stout hardwood wedges had been driven through mortices cut in the projecting ends of the tenons and bore tightly against the outer face of each vertical post. Four iron rods were bolted through the base of the press, and the top beam locked the structure together and helped take the strain off the wooden frame when cider was being pressed. Two massive iron pressing screws ran through the top beam. The screws told me immediately that this was an old-fashioned, country-made cider press. It was one of a legion of such devices in Vermont that had pressed the aromatic juices of untold millions of apples: Baldwins, Sops of Wine, Rhode Island Greenings, Snows, William's Favorite, McIntosh Reds, Bethels, and a whole spectrum of wild varieties no longer identifiable by name. What I did not know then was that the square, slatted box indicated I was in the presence of an archaic, oat-straw cider press.

The owner knew little about the history of the mill or how it worked. He put me in touch with Earle Hood, an East Topsham man in his mid-seventies who had once worked there making cider. Earle and Joe Quinn, a Hancock, New Hampshire, cidermaker of eighty, told me in their fine local speech how cider was made in such a mill.

66. Slatted wooden pressing tub with apple grinder hanging above. Heavy posts are the side frame and reinforcing rods of the press frame.

This small mill had ceased operations a little more than twenty years earlier. Pressing the cider took place on the first floor. Before they were pressed, the apples were wet down outside the mill and carried in big, brown-ash baskets up a cleated ramp in a corner of the room to storage bins on the second floor, where they were allowed to sweat.

Through a square hole cut in the second floor, a patent apple grinder sat above the pressing tub. The grinder was simply an open wooden box with wide, flaring sides, looking much like a square funnel. In its bottom revolved a fat, belt-driven iron cylinder thickly studded with sharp, raised teeth—like those on a hand cheese grater only much coarser. The apples were shoveled into the grinder, which instantly reduced them to a fine pulp called pomace, or "pummice" as it is pronounced locally. The grinder was kept unclogged by a paddle-shaped board in the funnel box. It was fastened to one end of a long beam pivoted in the middle. The beam's other end rode an eccentric fastened to the face of a pulley, making the paddle move up and down in the grinder opening. When it was down, no apples could enter the grinder; when it was up, apples were again free to fall downward into the grinder's sharp teeth.

From the grinder, the pomace ran down a chute into the pressing box where it was layered six to ten inches deep by a hoe. A thick pad of clean oat or rye straw was laid on top of each layer of pomace, and boards were laid on the straw. The process was repeated until the box was full of alternating layers of boards and pomace, much like the strata of an archaeological site. A heavy plank cover was then laid on the uppermost layer of straw. Thick lengths of wooden blocking went on top to distribute the force of the press screws. The screws were activated by stout wooden levers thrust into holes in ratchet mechanisms in the lower ends of heavy bulbous castings.

The screws were roughly thirty-six inches long. After they had been turned down as far as they could go, the screws were raised and another layer of blocking was placed underneath. The screws were turned down again, and more cider was pressed. The process was repeated until all the juice was squeezed from the pomace. A wooden tub placed in a well below the press caught the cider that flowed from a notch cut into the rim of the platform. The liquid was dipped from the tub into the customer's own barrels.

The purpose of the straw and board layers was twofold. First, it brought equal pressure to bear on all the pomace at once. Without them, the pomace would simply have been an unwieldly mass of uncontrollable slop, incapable of being pressed. Second, the straw afforded a network of tiny channels through which the apple juice could escape between the slats in the tub's four sides. The mass of layered straw and pomace was called a "cheese," possibly because of the similarities between pressing cider and cheese curd. In modern cidermaking, the layers of pomace, still called a "cheese," are individually wrapped in textile sheets separated by slatted wooden racks instead of straw and boards.

The mill dam, which had washed away during high water several years earlier (a few neighbors muttered darkly that it had had some help), was of timber, the usual dam type on Tabor Branch. Its "tole log," that is, the massive log lying in a trench cut in the streambed and to which the upstream portion of

67. The Pat Willey and Will Chandless oat-straw cider mill, Topsham, Vermont.

the dam was secured, had been put in place by Earle Hood's grandmother's uncle, Tate Avery. Mr. Hood was uncertain of the date, but his grandmother died in 1894 at the age of sixty-four, so it was a long time ago. In all likelihood, an older mill once stood on this mill seat before the cider mill was built in about 1909 by a man named Pat Willey. Willey moved a wool carding mill here from East Topsham, after marrying the granddaughter of the owner. He installed the carding mill in the upstream building and the cider mill in the downstream section.

The way in which the dam and "power" of this small mill were arranged is interesting and illustrative of the endless ingenuity of a populace well accustomed to doing things with their hands. The end of the dam opposite the mill was anchored to the bank by an abutment built of heavy timbering. Its other end abutted the mill foundation itself, a dry-laid stone wall several feet thick. Into the inside face of one of the stones, someone long ago had carved the initials "W. H. C." (perhaps for Will Chandless, former owner). Wooden sheathing lined the outside surface of the foundation, making it watertight and thus preventing water from entering the mill cellar. Marks on the foundation indicated that the dam had been eight feet in height.

A planked opening in the foundation let the waters of the mill pond into a stoutly timbered pen. From there it was fed into a square wooden penstock, which carried it several feet downward over a ledge and into the casing of a small turbine. A gate at the turbine entrance, controlled by a wheel on the first floor of the mill, let water into the turbine or shut it off, as required. The turbine's vertical power shaft terminated in a cast-iron gear, which meshed with another gear with replaceable wooden teeth. This was a common practice since it made for quieter operation and reduced the wear and tear of two iron gears running together. Homemade wooden pulleys and leather belting transmitted power to the grinder on the second floor. The turbine, sitting on a bed of flat stone, shot the water out into a tailrace that reentered the Tabor Branch twenty or more feet downstream. Mr. Hood described the turbine as being more than a hundred years old. It was, he thought, built in Taftsville, Vermont. There's a good probability that this origin is correct, for Joseph Hathaway of Taftsville invented two "improved" types of turbine (with patent numbers 81,362, September 1, 1868, and 94,821, September 14, 1869) that appear markedly similar to the old cider mill turbine on Tabor Branch.

Perhaps it was the presence of tool marks and other evidences of hand construction everywhere about that made the ghosts of the past seem so very close at hand in this small mill.

Hard cider is a drink on the dry side. Although it has great authority in its natural state, it can be sweetened somewhat and its proof raised even higher by adding sugar to it during fermentation. It can be distilled into a powerful brandy by using a copper jacket and worm fitted to an iron kettle, and it often was. Another stout drink was applejack, made out of barreled hard cider exposed to temperatures below freezing. The local winters, during which the thermometer sometimes registers thirty or more below zero, are ideal for the conversion process. As the cider froze, its water content changed to slush ice. The alcohol gathered near the bung in the center of the barrel, where it could be drained off and jugged.

JOSEPH QUINN SPEAKS ON HARD CIDER

"Cider is better from ripe apples—like Early Macs, or Mackintosh, when they first pick 'em. Can't make good cider out of Baldwins in October; they're O.K. in November—late November is best. And Northern Spies too. Overripe apples make cider that turns faster, goes into alcohol faster. Some used to put wild apples in with the orchard variety, but I didn't like the taste, though it does make a stronger vinegar. If you want to add something to apples to make a good cider, put in a bushel of pears. 'Nother thing that improves the taste and looks of cider is a couple of garden beets. Pull 'em when they're three or four inches in diameter, wash them, and put them right into a pressing. It will darken the color and improve the flavor. This is specially good for the pale cider you get if you start the season too early, using green apples.

"You turned the press screws by hand with a bar . . . turn 'em down pretty tight, then let it rest for an hour. Then squeeze it some more. The juice ran down into a big vat, and it had a lot of sediment in it. Didn't affect the quality 'cause they was making it for hard cider, not sweet cider. Keg it right up, sediment and all, and never leave the bung out of the barrel. It'd be good for years and years. When it got too hard, they'd use it for vinegar.

"With that kind of press it took all day to make a pressing. Back in those days, we'd get two and a half, three gallons of cider to a hundred pounds of apples. Today, with the hydraulic press, which gives, say, twenty tons of pressure, you get seven gallons.

"We never used any keg less than five gallons. Anybody that just wanted some cider to drink sweet, and leave the rest for vinegar, used the five gallon keg. Wood kegs make the best vinegar. But the biggest ones was about two-hundred gallons. They were hogsheads used for molasses. Father made good hard cider, and he always kept a barrel of it down cellar. Company used to stop by, and he'd put a red-hot poker into a pitcher of it, and they'd have a chat. I recall one fellow. He had a habit of making little rhymes. One spring he come and said to Father, 'I'd like a pitcher of cider, William.' So Father sent me down to get it. Father turned him out a little glass, and he drank it and smacked his lips. He kept looking into the empty glass, but Father didn't say nothing. So finally the man, he says,

> 'I had a little hen and she had a wooden leg,
> That same little hen, she laid a wooden egg.
> 'Twas the nicest little hen we had upon the farm,
> I don't think another drink would do me any harm.'

"Hard cider had an awful wallop to it, and a little went a long way. I never really got out of the custom of cider all my life. Neither did Father. When he was a young man he worked for an old farmer in the neighborhood. He liked Father pretty well, and one day he told him, 'From now on, William, we'll have tea with our noon meal.' So he'd put on the teapot and boil it all day, or until it run out of water. Then he'd put in some water and throw in more tea.

"Well, one day they turned out the tea into the cups, and a feather come out. 'Oh dear,' he says, 'another hen has fallen in the well and got drowned.' So he says, 'William, I tell you what you do.' He says, 'you go down cellar to the cider barrel and draw a pitcher of cider.' He says, 'No hen falling in there that I know of.' So Father went down, drawed a pitcher of cider, and tasted of it. Boy, that was better than any tea that they had had for a long time.

"Father, he didn't have much education, but he learned fast. After a few days, he'd go down and draw a pitcher of cider, and then he'd put it to his head and drink it. And then he'd draw the pitcher full again and take it up for their lunches. It really created a sort of habit, or a custom, and after, when we got to having apples at the old farm, Father always had a barrel of cider down cellar.

"In later years, when I was about fifty, I traded trucks. The fellows come to get my truck, and they had a drink or two of cider and started off. 'Well,' I thought, 'I'll go down to town to try out my new truck.' When I got along a ways, I see my old truck sitting aside the road in a gravel pit. I swung in, and they was both in the cab sound asleep. I woke 'em up and said, 'Are you in trouble?' 'No, no,' says the driver, 'no trouble, but the road got narrow. We thought we'd stay here till it widened out.'"

EARLE HOOD SPEAKS ABOUT EARLY DAYS IN TOPSHAM

"During early days a blacksmith shop stood on the south side of the cider mill. Later it was moved down to East Corinth where it still stands. A man named Will Chandless owned the mills after Willey. Chandless was a good mechanic. He made carriages and wagons, shod horses and oxen, made cider, and carded wool. His son Will helped him, and he was a young devil. Once when there was a National Guard muster in the village, he and his mates bought a load of straw to sleep on. When the muster was over, they gave it to a poor old man who loaded it onto his hayrack. The old man got up on the load, and just as he drove away, young Will run up and touched a match to the straw. The old man got away with his life and saved the oxen, but the straw and the hayrack burned up.

"They was lots of other mills, specially along the Powderspring. They made coffins, chair stock and chairs, clothes pins, carriages, and other things. Flour was ground in a grist mill two houses below where the store is now. My grandfather caught the miller taking second tole, an' he picked him up and shook him like a woodchuck.

"One time a local man had a colt that wouldn't break to halter; all he'd do was just pull and pull. He give him to a horsebreaker to see what he could do. The man drove a stout post into the ground beside the millpond and tied the colt to it. Well, he begun to rear back, and soon as he pulled the rope tight, the breaker cut it. The colt went right over backward into the pond. That cured him!

"My grandfather met his death in this pond by drownding. He'd been to the store to buy shoes for his little children, and on his way home he carried a sack of grist into the mill to be ground. The night was dark and rainy, and when he come out onto the walkway over the pond he got turned 'round. He stepped off into the deepest part of the pond, right next to the dam. They found him there next morning. He still had the shoes clutched in his hands, and the bag of meal was hanging round his neck where it dragged him under the water.

"They was Indians here way back. They come and lived in tents in the summer. One young boy, my grandfather told me, shot coppers right out of people's hands with a bow and arrow, to pick up a little money.

"Well, I'll tell you how they buried the paupers down in the back part of the graveyard here. It was pretty wet in there, and when the grave was dug it filled right up with water. They used to put a couple men on top of the coffin to ride it down and sink it while the hole was filled up with dirt."

Edward Godfrey—Cidermaker
Blood Brook Road
West Fairlee, Vermont

At about the same time I found the old oat-straw cider mill in Topsham, I discovered Edward Godfrey's small mill on the Blood Brook Road in West Fairlee, Vermont. There are some remarkable similarities between the two mills. For instance, in Edward Godfrey's mill, the cider is still pressed by hand. The apples are still ground in the same way. In two respects, though, the Godfrey mill is based on an even older technology. The grinding head is handmade rather than factory manufactured, and the pressing screws lack the ratchet feature of the screws in the Willey mill. But the Godfrey mill is more modern than the Willey mill in that the grinder is driven by a small gasoline

68. Edward Godfrey standing by the cider press. Cider tub is in front; pomace box is to the right.

engine. The internal combustion engine and electric motor rendered the old wooden dams and turbines in common use obsolete.

Edward Godfrey was not working the press at the time of my visit, and I was able to talk with him at some length about his mill. Part of his equipment, the press screws for instance, may be even older than like items in the Willey cider mill. Mr. Godfrey expressed himself so well concerning his cider operation that the transcripts of his tape, with the photographs of the equipment, will give a clear picture of how these old mills worked and of their place in the rural scheme of things.

"This mill," said Edward Godfrey, "came from old Sheldon Miller's [a man then in his eighties] farm up here in Blood Brook; his grandfather had it. It's a very old mill. Father used to make cider down here—he got the screws in 1921. Sheldon's grandfather lived to be 104. So this mill goes away back into the 1800s."

Illustration 68 shows Edward Godfrey standing in front of the cider press. Note the pressing platform at knee level. The cider, as it is pressed, runs into the wooden tub. The heavy timber, just beneath the two pressing screws, runs loose. It applies pressure to blocking placed on top of the cheese and rides in an open groove along each of the two vertical posts. Metal pins inserted under it through holes in the side posts hold it up out of the way while a pressing is being readied. (Note one of the pins just above the rack of drinking cups on the left-hand post.) The base of each post is securely fastened to a big beam (the left end of which can be seen) that passes beneath the pressing platform. The pressing screws hang from a large, fixed beam at the top. These screws lack the ratchet arrangement of those in the Willey mill, where the operator merely inserted a wooden bar into the ratchet hole and worked it back and forth to lower the screw. In this mill, to turn the screws down upon the cheese, an iron bar must be inserted, turned, removed, and reinserted into the holes that show at the ends of the screws. Each turn of the bar rotates the screw slightly less than half a turn. The pomace tub, which holds the pomace used to make the individual cheeses, shows at the lower right-hand corner of the illustration.

"This is the original frame of the press. All I ever done was put in this new piece to hold the screws. The old one got pretty weak, and I was afraid she might go through the roof.

"Just hand power to turn the screws—that old five-foot bar back there. Everybody wants me to put in hydraulics, but I ain't going to. Everybody tells me it makes better cider, but I don't know as I agree. You get a very slow squeeze out of this press. It was cold last Sunday, as you remember, and the cider run thicker than hell. I filled up three milk cans for a fella, and there was still some to come. Told him, 'Let it stay right here and run in the afternoon. I'll bring it over to you tonight.' Well, it set there in the afternoon, and it run out seven gallons, just setting there dripping. So, I don't know but I like this way pretty well, though it is hard work when you get on that old bar."

69. Apple grinder is emplaced in the structure, atop the right end of the pomace box.

Illustration 69 shows the pomace box and the grinder mounted on the top of the structure. Against the wall at the left-hand side, one can just see the pulley and belt that drive the grinder.

"This is the grinder. All those little teeth are just nails driven into a wooden drum. Fellow owned it before I did, run the old one till it went to hell. Then he went to the woods, cut a white birch just that size, trimmed it up, and made himself a new drum. It's been going—well, I've had it nineteen or twenty years.

"The apples go right in just like a food grinder. Breaks them up just like mincemeat, you know. I run it with a little gasoline engine. It'll take a good bushel and a half of apples at a time, any kind of apples, all mixed together. Dump them in and let 'em go. Comes right out in this big box here, as pomace. The deer like it, but mostly I bury it. Tried some on my garden a couple of years ago. Pretty near ruined it—too much acid, I guess. Didn't get nothing last year."

70. Racks and bransacking for making up the "cheeses."

"My two boys and my wife work here with me. Once I start grinding, they start 'laying it up' right away. You take that open frame over there and lay it on the platform. Then you take one of those bransack sheets off the wall and lay it over the top of it. Fill it full of pomace and level it off. Fold the corners right across the top, and you've got your cheese started. Then you take the frame off and lay one of those slatted racks on top. Lay the frame on again and do it over. I can put on a big enough cheese to take off almost two barrels of cider at one time, around 180 gallons. That's what makes it hard; somebody will come along and want a bushel or two pressed. I can't do it in less than four. Four's the smallest. It really should have five bushels to make a good cheese.

"Have to be careful lining your racks up, to get them all square. They can break up if you're not. I've run this set about eight years. Birdall, the fellow who had this outfit when I got it off him, he had a set go twenty years."

Illustration 71 is a closeup of one of the pressing screws, showing the holes for the turning bar. The iron block under the screw protects the wooden piece by distributing the pressure of the screw. Note the heavy, square screw threads and the thick "nut" attached to the underside of the fixed beam above.

71. Detail of one of the pressing screws shown in illustration 68.

"See, when your cheese is built, you've got all this space between it and the screws to fill up with blocking so the screws'll come to bear. You put your blocking on the racks to protect them. Then you pull these pins and let the beam come down on it. For blocking, you start with three planks this way, then three more at right angles, and so on as you go down, to keep it all filled in so's the screws will bite. The blocking takes the pressure of your screws and works it out, so it comes over the whole cheese. Gotta put these iron blocks, one under each screw, else they'll tear the beam to pieces—put holes right into it.

"Had a trailer load of apples come in one night from Newbury. They left 'em right under those trees, and the leaves drifted down and got into the apples. Made the cider awful bitter.

"We strain the cider as we jug it. Use white cloth for a jug and bransacking for a barrel. Macs are the worst to strain—fill the strainer right up. Don't fill the jugs too full, and leave the cap just barely loose to let the gas work out. Hard to get glass jugs anymore. The plastic ones make the cider taste; it's not a neutral material like glass is.

"Learned to make cider watching it made for Dad. He always had four to six barrels in the cellar. Went with him every fall when he picked apples for cider. Grew up knowing how.

"Oat-straw? I've never used it, but my nephew's niece runs an oat-straw press up in Warren. Just a little one, but they say the cider's a lot nicer. I've never had a drink of it, so I don't know if it is or not. My brother-in-law tried his damndest to get me going with straw you know.

"You say that old cider mill up in Topsham had ratchets on the screws? I wish mine did; be a lot easier to turn down. These screws are much older, more old-fashioned. When they get going hard, you have to go back a little bit.

"Had a young couple here last year from Buffalo, New York. Get lots of people come here, and they all say this is the cleanest cider mill they was ever in. Years ago, mister, there was nothing clean about them."

72. Draft horse farmer, 1941.

Part II

FARMING CRAFT

73. Farmers in town with box-body sled,
1940.

8

Farm-Built Sleds and Sledges

Jim Nott
Jericho Hill
West Hartford, Vermont

Eight joiners in joiners hall,
Working with their tools and all,
Mother Goose

To the making of wooden wagons and carts went a long list of highly skilled, tool-intensive operations. In fabricating wheels, frames, and bodies, no fewer than six trades were required: woodman, sawyer, wainwright, wheelwright, blacksmith, and painter each played a part. During preindustrial times, up to perhaps the 1830s and 1840s, such trades were passed down from master to apprentice. The work was done almost entirely through hand tools and hand manufacture, a tedious, laborious, time-consuming process. In fact, until well into the nineteenth century, wheeled vehicles were far from being as numerous as is commonly supposed. On both sides of the Atlantic, wagons and carriages were most commonly found in heavily populated areas. Large farms, stage lines, freighting companies, and the privileged classes were the only societal entities able to support their use.

In rough rural districts, then much of Europe and almost all of America, roads were poor or nonexistent. In regions that remained isolated, this situation persisted. For example, a Boston lady who had taught in a mountain settlement school in the southern Appalachians in 1910 told me that, to get to a railhead to go home for Christmas, she had to ride forty miles on horseback along the beds of mountain creeks. There were no roads at all in the region. The mountain people, she said, rode miles to reach a mill, with their grist in a sack slung behind the saddle. And they still relied on the wooden sledge for moving heavy loads. This cheap, easily made device was an imperative for hauling loads heavier than a man or packhorse could tote over the rough, grassy meadows, along the mountain tracks, and through the forests of rural countrysides. The wooden runnered sledge, and its counterpart the dray, had been in use in Europe for centuries. Their European provenance is indicated by their names: sledge is derived from the Middle Dutch "sleedse," whilst dray comes from the Anglo-Saxon "draege." Either is a low, strongly made wooden frame, fastened to a set of wood-shod runners. A box body was often added to the sledge to give a larger load capacity. In New England, a sledge with a box body was often called a pung, from the old term "tom pung," which is derived from the Indian word tobbogan.

74. Unloading firewood from a small double-runner with box body, 1940.

73

75. Farm couple in town to sell butter, 1940. The vehicle is a pung.

Built with timber and by peasants and small farmers using few and simple tools, such vehicles were drawn by one or more yoke of oxen, the traditional draft animal of the lower orders since time out of mind, or, more rarely, by horses. With them, rural folk were able to haul sacked grain, logs, and other heavy loads across the trackless wastes in which they lived. Pungs and drays could penetrate into places where a wagon, even had they had one, could not go.

This ancient pattern of rural transport came to the eastern United States as part of the cultural baggage carried by the earliest settlers. Because of the primitive conditions pertaining in frontier settlements, the sledge and dray continued in widespread use until well into the nineteenth century. They continued, in fact, to be used in rough, isolated regions such as the Ozarks, the southern Appalachians, and northern new England long after the large-scale production of wooden wheels and wagons in the shops and mills of the late 1800s. In the region covered in this book the wooden dray, sledge, and a few derivative forms remained in use until within the lifetimes of currently living men—indeed are still occasionally used in maple sugaring and logging.

As elsewhere, good roads were built only in response to the increasing numbers of automobiles and trucks in the 1920s and 1930s. It is now forgotten how isolated many parts of the region were due to the primitive conditions of travel. My father, as a salesman in the upper Connecticut Valley region of Vermont and New Hampshire in the early 1930s, sometimes encountered corduroy roads (roads made of brush with poles and small logs laid across at right angles to the roadbed) in swampy sections of the back districts.

Ox-drawn, wheelless transport thus continued in use in this northern region long after wagons and ox carts were more readily at hand. So useful was this mode, that specialized types developed in response to unusual conditions. For example, the stone boat (a heavy plank, tobbogan-like device) was made for carting stone off a plowed field. Using a wagon for this task was more difficult, sometimes impossible, in soft or boggy ground.

Another kind of woods sled was derived, in part, from the invention of the two-man crosscut saw late in the nineteenth century. This implement replaced the axe as the primary tool for felling trees and bucking the prostrate trunks into sawlog lengths. Its use, together with increases in the production of pulp or pulpwood (soft wood cut into four-foot lengths for the paper industry) and the cutting of cordwood, led to a considerable growth in the timber harvest. In response to the increased activity in logging, a new form of wooden sled developed for use in snow-filled forests. Variously known as double-runners, bobsleds, and traverse sleds, they differed somewhat in details of construction, but each, in essence, consisted of two short sleds, one at either end of a long body. Stout but higher and more lightly built than the sledge, double-runnered sleds relied upon steel-shod runners and iron braces and fastenings to strengthen them against the rigorous strains of heavy loads. The two sleds were connected, front to rear, by a reach: a heavy, strong timber often made adjustable to accommodate longer or shorter log lengths.

The logging dray was a simple handmade rig that worked alongside the logging sled. The dray had a single sled at the front. To this was fastened a V-shaped arrangement of two thick dray poles connected by pinned crosspieces.

76. Stacking a sledge load of manure, 1940.

The apex of the V pivoted on an iron pin set into the heavy, central crossbunk of the sled. It was possible to take a dray deep into snow-filled woods over the roughest terrain where nothing else could go and bring out a load of sawlogs securely chained to the sled and the dray poles. The ends of the poles dragged on the ground, lending stability to the load. On steep, icy hills, they slowed the load, a superior brake to that on the double-runner logging sled.

These forms of folk transport, along with the technology for making them by hand, have been passed along for centuries. There is every likelihood that such artifacts have been in use ever since primitive farmers first produced a surplus that required to be hauled and stored for the winter season.

It is perhaps not altogether curious that, in the past, the forging and shaping of cold, grey iron has been a mysterious, indeed magical, process. In ancient times, the knowledge of how to work iron was the exclusive possession of arcane cults; traditionally, small groups of initiates working for priesthoods and warrior-kings as the only segments of society able to afford the technology.

In the description that follows, it will be noted that very little iron was used in the folk construction of wooden sledges and drays by Jim Nott, a Vermonter in his early eighties (since deceased). Indeed, he makes specific reference to its scarcity. In folk realms, iron continued to be a scarce material and hence was always considered valuable. Steel was reserved for the cutting edges of tools and implements. For example, the head of an axe was forged of iron, then split at the working edge to receive a cutting bit of steel welded in by the smith.

When working with wood, early craftsmen developed a corpus of knowledge by which they were able either to eliminate the use of iron almost entirely or, at the least, to reserve its use to essential stress points and fastenings. This ancient technic was firmly rooted in the subsistence farming life of this region. An economy of scarcity meant that it was imperative for people to make and repair as much as they could for themselves. Most farmers, and many village folk, were jacks-of-all-trades.

Only after iron and steel came more readily to hand, after the mating of the first coke-fired blast furnace with a steel rolling mill in 1859, did local blacksmiths and wagon makers begin to substitute iron for parts formerly made of wood. Despite its availability, many of the hill folk in the Yankee Highlands stubbornly persisted in using only a modicum of iron. They held strongly to age-old patterns and construction methods well into the twentieth century.

Different kinds of wood can be selected, cut, and joined so that the union works as a functioning whole, a vehicle equal to the strains put upon it. Jim Nott, the farmer-craftsman whose words follow, continued throughout his long working life to make wooden farm sleds and to shoe the runners with wooden strips secured by split and wedged wooden pegs. He made the different woods serve in the place of iron wherever possible.

MERTON "JIM" NOTT ON FARM-BUILT SLEDS AND SLEDGES

I first interviewed Jim Nott in 1973. He had worked the old family sidehill farm for most of a lifetime. He showed me a series of small wooden models of the different kinds of farm sleds he had been taught to make as a boy by his grandfather and father. Ten years later, Jim had retired from farming and was living in Burlington, Vermont. One day, he called to say that he'd like to give me something. When I drove up to see him and his charming wife Rosemary, he had the models lined up on a table. "I want you to have them," he said. "I'll tell you how we made them, and you can put it in your book." After a delicious lunch, we spent the afternoon discussing how he was taught and the many sleds he had built himself. Here, in part, is what he told me.

"The two-horse scoot we built and used for rough roads and the hills and mountains. It was very low, so it was easy to load it with big logs. We made it with one cross beam set with iron spikes to keep the logs from rolling. It was indestructible. We made it so's to take it apart for storage. They weren't a deep snow outfit, but we got around with it O.K., and it handled big stuff and a lot of it. It was used mostly to haul logs out of the woods and down to the sawmill.

77. A two-horse scoot.

"In those days, when sawmills set at the foot of the hill, we went up and drew the logs downhill to the mill. After the logs went through the mill, we had to get the lumber to the railroad station and load it into the (box)cars. There used to be quite a sawmill down there in what we always called Sucker City. I remember when I was a kid old enough to drive a pair of horses, we'd go down with three or four teams together and load a freight car. I remember one time we ran into some oak timber four inches by eighteen feet. It was long stuff; all two men could do to lift one and pile it in. If we hurried, sometimes we could make two trips a day, but usually there was just time for one. At the time, we were carting it three miles, all downhill. This was back about 1915. We were just beginning, now and then, to use trucks to cart some lumber.

"But the scoot was about all you needed. It didn't steer worth a hoot—made that way special. If 'twas going to slew, it'd slew one way or t'other. Horses hitched up to the front end of it, but that's all. Worked very well. It'd go over ledges and around stones; seemed to be able to go most anywhere.

"The runners were all wood-shod. Everybody had their own idea what type of timber they'd use to shoe the runners with. We always used leverwood to shoe the runners. Dewey Lyman used to use maple, but it was anything you wanted. They'd wear out, and you'd replace 'em.

"Used 'em most of the time in the woods and in the spring, during mud season. A wood-shod sled will go very easily through the mud—you can't do that with a steel-shod sled, strange as it seems. We'd wear off three inches of runner in the spring gathering sap and everything else.

"To reshoe, we'd turn the scoot bottom side up and get another rod and whittle it down with an axe, the way you wanted it, and set it with wooden pins. We wedged the pins, but we did it a little differently than a greenhorn might think. After we bored the hole for it, we 'cracked' [split] the end of the pin a little and started a wedge in it. Then we put that end down into the hole and tapped it in tight with a hammer. That's how we did the job, and it worked. Saw the pegs flush where they stuck up above the runner and flatten it off a little bit. We knocked a peg through the bunks too.

78. Two-horse handy sled with box body.

"Usually you could find trees in the woods growing with a natural crook. That's where the old fellas would head. They'd cut 'em and try to save eight or ten ahead for making new runners.

"The handy sled—that's a wood-shod sled, and we put it together with wooden pins, too. Dad came in one afternoon with two birch planks. We took them into the workshop next morning and began to saw them out for runners using a handsaw. I can remember, along towards noon I could have sworn you could hear my elbow squeak. We turned the old sled over, pried out the pins and took off the old runners, put on the new runners, and put in the new pins.

"Funny thing about making a runner, you'd think it had to be perfectly flat and straight from one end to the other. That's not the way you made them. The old fellas always cut 'em convex so's the center would be a half inch lower. That way the runners only touched in the middle. They always froze down after they'd set a spell while you loaded 'em. We always made 'em that way because the old fellas did. They'd rock a little so the horses could break them loose and start 'em. We put in that slight curve with a drawshave—tricks of the trade.

"The handy sled with box body was for all uses: manure or woods use. It was a short sled but longer than ord'nary. We'd go to mill with it quite a lot. The stuff we ground for cattle we took to mill with it. My grandfather's diary showed, and it was my father's pet grain, one bag of oats and two bags of corn was mixed during the grinding. Might add a little cottonseed to go along with it. That was high producing [milk] stuff. Grown right there on the farm.

"That handy sled was prob'ly six to eight feet long. 'Bout standard width—the width of two horses. We used oxen too. I learned to drive oxen getting in hay. Dad said, 'You can either drag the bull rake or drive the oxen.' Didn't take me long to make up my mind. We carted hay in the handy sled. We ran the handy sled from October, November, clear through till March, and used it to draw about anything.

"The dray? Well, there was another mountain thing. Could put on, oh, half, three quarters of a cord and come down off the mountain with it. And we had some real mountains where we did that. That would slew one way and the other. We'd draw the front end, and then we'd begin to edge around the corners.

79. A two-horse logging dray.

It would come round the corner back of us and be a little free and easy. You loaded on the front end, and this tail end was dragging on the ground. That's sled-length wood. We kept a 'bunter' on the front so they wouldn't get by you. Natural brakes. We used the dray on what we had to, and then we changed sleds and put on a conventional one. You couldn't pile as much on a dray, but you could run through the rough stuff with it. My old dray hung on the back of my barn for fifty years till somebody come along and wanted to buy it. My dad built it in two or three hours. It's the hind part that's the dray you know.

80. A two-horse, single-beam sled.

"The first part's the bobsled. That would take a big log out. Sometimes we could use a horse so as to roll the log up onto it. We never did anything by hand, you know, that we could get a horse to do.

"The two-horse, single-beam sled and the two-horse, three-beam sled, they're made differently. The beams [bunks] are made so they'll give going over rough ground, and the runners tip up more. Also, the front runners have a fifth wheel for the body to swivel on, so the horse can go right around, you see. There's chains by the runners you can unhook to go under them, for braking coming down a steep hill. The two-horse, single-beam sled has a drawbar, a draw end, you can let out. It might go, oh, fifteen, twenty feet—make a long sled. See this little hitch? That's where you could put your skid pole so's to roll a log up. One of 'em on either side. One use for the two-horse, three-beam sled and the two-horse single sled was for hauling sawed lumber. The two-horse, single-beam sled carried the biggest load because it had heavy steel runners. The three-beam one wasn't ironed quite so heavy. It'd carry a pretty fair load though.

81. A two-horse, three-beam sled.

"My dad used to say that anybody with an axe and something to bore a hole with, they could put together a sled. And it prob'ly wouldn't cost more than fifteen or twenty dollars to have it ironed by the blacksmith. This heavier one would take twice as much iron as it would have if they'd kept it all wood.

"It was considered an advantage on this three-beam sled that it was cheaper to build because it wasn't ironed so heavy. The three-beam, light one was most common on the hill neighborhood here. My dad built two or three to sell to the boys. And his father made three or four and sold to the boys, too.

"The patterns and the sizes—where did they come from? Well, they came down from my father and his father. In fact, I've got my father's full-size patterns. Lined it off a sled and sawed it out of half-inch stuff. They built the first sleds down in the southern parts here and in Massachusetts and maybe New Hampshire. They built stone drags [stone boats], too.

"They used to move a whole house with the woman in it. Take two big logs and point the ends some. Hitch three or four ox teams onto the two front corners, and away they'd go. Houses weren't so big in those days. It's funny to see one going down across the field.

"Most of what we used to build sleds was oak and ash, some white birch. Used soft woods where we could because it was so easy to work. Red oak here. Little white oak. Used red oak for everything from fence posts to sled poles. Pretty strong stuff, and it would spring and bend rather than break. Ash was a very good material to use, but you never knew what you had. You'd take a log down to the mill and get it cut out to just what you wanted and get it home and it wasn't good for anything. It was just 'brash.' It was chancy. Prob'ly wouldn't be more than one in ten or a dozen or fifteen that'd be bad, but you wanted to look out for them. Used yellow birch some. Didn't look for it though. Very strong though and hard to split. Usually had it sawed to boards.

"Only thing you really needed to build a wooden-shod sled was an adze [Mr. Nott pronounced it 'aidze'], axe, and a T-auger. Used wood for everything. An old cuss we knew could hew all the parts out with an axe. But I want to tell you his tools were pretty damned sharp. Any bolts went in, we got from the blacksmith. Dad always saved every piece of iron he found. He'd pick over the ashes of a house that'd burned down, or a barn, for the iron he could find. Iron was fairly scarce and expensive. Most of the farmers were pretty good smiths. When a blacksmith 'ironed' a job, he'd write down a few notes and save them. Then he'd know what to do when you came in again.

"These vehicles were commonly painted blue with black trimming. My dad, just about the first snowfall, would have his sled all painted up good. He'd start off and say, 'Well, I'll see you later.' Then about dark he'd pull in with something he could just ride on. He'd sold his sled. So he'd go out in the woods and make another one. He made one most every winter. It was something he could do during stormy weather. He filed saws, too. That was a little pick-up job that he had lined up. All kinds of saws from circular to two-man crosscuts. Good at it.

"I used to saw one to two hundred cords of wood every year with a gasoline power saw rig. That was something I could make big money at—a dollar an hour. I got so I could file saws pretty good after a few sarcastic remarks from Dad. Had wheels under the saw rig in the summer and a sled in the winter. Took it around the neighborhood and did sawing. Thankful I came out of it as good as I did. I never got hurt on a crosscut saw or a circular saw, and I never got hit with a tree.

"The old blue farm paint, well, we bought it. Painting a barn, we'd get some red ocher and linseed oil.

"I started making sleds and driving team when I was about sixteen years old, and I let the last of the horses go 1940, '45.

"Joining the body to the runners? Blacksmith helped. Moccasin and half-moccasin runners? That's what we called the stick we used to flatten out for the green runner. The moccasin was rounded on the bottom. We were apt to put that on flat. Some people thought the moccasin was better, that it worked good in snow. But it didn't work any better than anything else that I could ever see. The term half-moccasin doesn't ring a bell.

"The reason I made these models is that in working with the Grange I got around the state a lot. I found that folks didn't know what a sled was anymore, or how it was used or the names. They didn't know the names of the parts: runner, shoes, cross beams. Even the body had the stakes, the bunter [small framework on the front], and the raves. When you took the body off, you'd run into those heavy timbers called bunks, sled bunks—lots of times four by eights. We used elm quite a lot on the bunks, because elm was one wood that would twist a lot and still come back. 'Twouldn't break, just twist. Even better than oak. So I said to myself, I'm going to build a sled or two, and that'll be my contribution to history."

THE TOOLS USED

T-augers	Several sizes for boring the holes
Bucksaw, Two-man crosscut, Hand Saw	All three used for shaping and cutting
Light sledge hammer	Setting the pieces
Carpenter's hammer	Driving pegs
Axe, Adze	Both used in shaping, trimming, fitting, and hewing
Jack plane	Fitting, smoothing, knocking off sharp edges, and trimming as desired
Smithy	Forging any iron parts

82. Edward Clay holding a braided trace
of Indian seed corn in front of his corn
barn.

9

Indian Corn

Edward Clay
North Thetford, Vermont

How smart a hand-cut cornfield stands,
    The stookums all one size and height!
Their tops turned down inside the bands,
The bands composed of two good strands
    Of wheatstraw, special-thrashed and bright;
That's farming—work laid out and done,
    I call it agronomic skill,
It shows why grandpa used a "horse"
    And father "set round the hill."

Rhymes of Vermont Rural Life
by Daniel L. Cady, 1919

The lines quoted above are from Daniel L. Cady's book, *Rhymes of Rural Vermont Life.* They contain a surprising amount of information about oldtime ways of cutting Indian, or flint, corn, a traditional regional crop. The first fact is that corn was still cut by hand, using tools and methods commonly used well before the Civil War. Second, the stalks were carefully stacked in wigwam-shaped piles called, by Cady, "the stookums," an interesting rural diminutive of the term "stook." Stook, from the Middle English "stouke," refers to a stack of small bundles of cut grain tied together in sheaves. The grain can be wheat, oats, rye, or corn. Shock (Middle English "shocke") was the name commonly used for a corn stack along the New Hampshire side of the Connecticut River around West Lebanon and Plainfield. Even today, in my own mind, I associate shock with corn and stook with the smaller grains, but the terms were, to some extent, used interchangeably up and down both sides of the river.

In conjunction with "the stookums all one size and height," "smart" indicates the intense pride some men took in the uniform appearance of the long lines of corn stooks filling their fields at harvest time. The small bundles from which the stook was built were individually tied using "two good strands of wheatstraw, special-thrashed and bright," which means that the wheat was threshed out by hand with the flail. This process, unlike machine-threshed wheat, saved the structural integrity of the straw so that it could be used in place of string—braided into hats and other items. When wheat disappeared as a crop, coarse brown twine replaced it for tying the bundles of corn.

Finally, we are left with some peculiar terms in the rhyme: grandpa used a "horse" and "father 'set round the hill.' " Each refers to special ways of piling the bundles of tied corn stalks when forming the stook or shock. It was imperative to make stooks that would stand securely in the field while they dried. "Cutting round the horse" is shown in the accompanying illustrations. This is the way Edward Clay's grandfather cut his corn both before and after the Civil War. The method was continued in use on the Clay farm until the end of the 1930s.

"Cutting round the hill," as was done by Edward's father, is not shown here, but Ed described how it was done. It was a method he, himself, did not favor, preferring the way he had learned from his grandfather. Either method resulted in harvested fields filled with long, straight lines of rustling brown, conical stooks, with the bright orange pumpkins that were grown amongst the corn scattered around their bases. Big fields of stooks along the Connecticut, and smaller ones lying back in the mountains, were a common sight when I was a boy.

While conducting the field research for the Billings Farm & 1890 Museum, I stopped one day to photograph a fine barn in North Thetford and fell into conversation with Arthur Palmer, its owner. Arthur helped me in many ways. He answered my questions, explained a great deal about the farm equipment used by his father and grandfather that rested, covered in dust and cobwebs in spare corners of the barn and sheds, and introduced me to several farm families in back areas I might not have found on my own. One day, he said, "You know, if you want to talk with a man who really knows the old ways you ought to visit Ed Clay on the next ridge over from here."

I promptly did, driving into his yard that very morning. A spare, straight, mustached man dressed in work clothes and sneakers came outside, and we fell into easy conversation there in the yard. Later, over a cup of tea in his kitchen, Ed offered to demonstrate his grandfather's corn-cutting tools, which I had been photographing. There was a stand of corn near the barn. We gathered the tools together, and he began. This was field corn, not the traditional Indian corn which by then had not been grown on this farm for two decades or more, but it served quite well for showing how the work was done. The demonstration exemplified the extensive and variegated patchwork of independent know-how carried in the minds of these rural folk not so very long ago.

83. The "stooking horse."

As Ed and I gathered the stooking horse, the sharpened hoe, and the other things he needed, he nodded his head toward a dusty wooden machine in a corner.

"That's my old Eclipse corn planter," he said. "Used to take a little while to set it up to plant as it ought. You know, we used to plant Indian corn by hand to an old rhyme. Went like this:

> One for the blackbird,
> One for the crow,
> One for the cutworm,
> And four to grow.

84. The corn cutter. This is a sharpened hoe in use since the time of Edward Clay's grandfather.

"What that rhyme means is that we used to plant Indian corn the way the Indians did—in hills of seven kernels set three feet apart, both ways. Had a wooden bar with three sharpened stakes set three-feet apart, with a set of shafts on it for a horse. Drew it both ways across the corn piece, and planted on the intersections. Carried a pail of fertilizer, and a pail of seed corn, and a hoe to cover it. Put seven kernels in a hill; figured three of them would be destroyed before maturity. So they got four, four stalks of corn. And years ago—I've heard

85. The stooking horse in use. Bundles of corn are cut and tied, then placed around the quadrants formed by a stout pin thrust through the hole in the stooking horse. When the stook is formed, the pin is withdrawn and the horse moved along the rows for the next stook.

this many a time—had a fellow who couldn't count. And to make it easier for him, they'd take a T.D. pipe, you know, one of those clay pipes. And they'd put some butternut leaves down the bottom of the bowl so it would hold just seven kernels. Just scoop up the bowl full of corn and drop it. Move on to the next place. Man comes along with a hoe and covers it.

"Planted in hills so's to hoe around it and keep the weeds down. We very often planted beans and pumpkins in amongst the hills. Beans'd climb the stalks, and the pumpkins helped smother out weeds. Succotash and pumpkin pie right in the same field. [Succotash, an Indian dish, has always been a favorite New England dish. It is made of corn and dried shell beans cooked together.]

" 'Course the corn planter did the counting and spacing for you. We'd put Stanley's Crow Repellent on the seed. Put it on the corn in a wooden box and stirred it well. Then if the crows pulled the seed, it burned 'em from gizzard to tail—kinda discouraged them. You know we had to adjust the planter to throw just the seven grains of seed corn before we used it. Took about a pint of seed 'fore we'd get it right. Used untreated corn out in the yard. Then the chickens could eat it up so it wouldn't be wasted. Waste a kernel of corn, you know, and you'll come to want.

"We raised our own seed corn. Saved out the best ears each year and traced 'em. Hung them up where the rats couldn't get them, and then shelled 'em out and planted the seed."

CUTTING AND STOOKING

"There was thousands of bushels of Indian corn raised in this part of the country. Everything was all hand labor. Very early days, the corn was planted by

86. Cutting and laying out the bundles.

hand and cultivated with a horse and walking cultivator or hoed by hand. It was cut and tied in stooks by hand. It was husked and shelled by hand, then ground in the grist mill into cornmeal.

"We cut round the horse. That was a longish piece of wood with two legs at one end. Just back of them was a hole with a loose pin stuck through it. That's where you built your stook.

"The corn was ready to cut when the first three or four kernels on the bottom of the ear were seared. And the corn was nice and green. There'd be enough juice in the stalks to ripen off the grain. You set the stooking horse between two rows of corn and you cut two rows on each side. You followed one row of corn. If 'twas straight, your row of stooks would be straight. Just as straight as though you'd surveyed it.

"I always cut with a hand hoe and a short handle. It was my grandfather's before me. Keep it sharpened up just like a razor. Take half a dozen stalks, and shave 'em off right tight to the ground. Lay them crossways, right across the row. Tied them with a bit of string. You set 'em up, one at a time, in the four quadrants formed by the pin. Jam the butts in the ground slanted out, so they make a circle and won't fall over. That lets ground moisture travel up the stalk to ripen the grain. Then you tie around the top so it'll stand up and shed rain, pull the pin out, and slide the horse along to cut the next stook.

"How big were the stooks? We made them small enough so we could pick 'em up with a pitchfork and pitch them onto a wagon. We often left them in the field till after it snowed so's they'd be good and dry.

"Cutting around the hill? Well, my dad liked to cut corn that way, but I never did. You didn't use the stooking horse. You cut right on a row. What you done was take a hill where the stook was to be and leave two or three stalks standing. Then you stacked around them, and they supported the stook. When you came to take the stooks off the field, you had to carry a corn sickle and cut those two or three standing stalks inside the stook before you could lift it up. Lots of folks cut that way though.

"On a crop of good heavy flint corn, the stooks would be about eight feet apart. It was an all-purpose grain really. We had it ground at mill for table use, and we husked it and fed it out to cattle. With oxen you could feed it right on the cob. They'd eat it cob and all. When we fed it to the stock, we husked it and put it in that crib there. Let it dry, and then, by golly, we'd fill a bag up with corn and put in all the oats we could get down between the ears. Take it to the

87. The tying strings.

88. A tied bundle showing the knot used.

89. Building up the corn stook around the horse.

90. Tying the finished stook near the top, stooking horse still in place.

91. Edward Clay and the finished stook.

grist mill and have it ground, cobs and all. It made a pretty good feed. Wasn't as high in protein and digestible nutrients as what you have today, but you just didn't have this stuff then. As the old saying goes, make do or do without.

" 'Course we shelled it off the cob and got it ground into cornmeal for our own consumption. You could use a corn sheller, but we often did it by hand. Used a cob against the ear, and it worked pretty well. Then we winnowed it. Put a sack in the bottom of a washtub so the kernels wouldn't bounce out, then poured the kernels down into it while the breeze was blowing to take out the chaff and clean it. Worked very well.

"When I was eighteen, right after the Depression, and things began to straighten out a little bit, we raised ten hundred and fifty bushels of grain here. Oats, wheat, and corn, and we filled our silo. We had four horses and a yoke of oxen, and we kept them all busy. I was a little younger then than I am now. I've plowed all day with a three-horse team in years gone by, and then go in on the barn floor, by golly, and husk corn all night.

"Cornmeal was mighty good eating. Put some of it into Indian pudding. And I love johnnycake. Take fresh johnnycake out of the oven in the wintertime, by golly. Cut out a good slab and put some butter on it and some maple syrup and make a whole meal. Just with lots of butter."

92. Shelling Indian corn by hand using an empty cob as sheller.

93. Hand-shelling.

94. Preparing to winnow the shelled corn. The bransack is placed in the bottom of one tub to keep the kernels from jumping out as the corn is winnowed.

95. Winnowing the corn. A light breeze blows the chaff away as the corn is poured into the lower tub.

96. Sam Alexander, stone mason, 1937.

10

Building Wall

Earl Hood
Topsham, Vermont

Edward Clay
North Thetford, Vermont

Jim Billings was raised on a hill farm in Rochester, Vermont. He told me the farm was so stony, his father, a God-fearing man who never used profanity, refused to do the plowing because it couldn't be done without swearing. He got his brother, who had no such compunctions, to do it for him. Jim used to hide under the bushes at the field edge and listen to his uncle curse as he followed the plow among the rocks. Lying quiet under the leaves, he picked up many a salty phrase to help him through life.

During the years I was engaged in fieldwork, I talked at length with elderly men who knew a great deal about working stone and building wall. If you were a farmer during the days of horse- and ox-drawn farm equipment—right up through the 1920s and 1930s—it was impossible to avoid learning a considerable amount about these skills. Stones, big and little, were everywhere, and no matter how carefully they were picked off a field, the next year was sure to bring up a new crop. There is a story about an old man hoeing corn on a hot day. Along came two city men in a car, and they stopped to ask directions. One man noticed the stones among the corn shoots and, thinking he'd have a little fun, said, "My, there's a lot of stone in this state."

"Yeah, there is. 'Bout three stun to every clod."

"Where did they all come from?" asked the city man.

The farmer glanced at him from under the brim of his hat and grunted, "Glacier brought 'em a long time back."

"That so," said the man, nudging his friend. "Where'd the glacier go?"

The farmer peered out from under his hat and grinned. "Went back after more stun."

I have referred elsewhere to the network of stone walls cobwebbing these hills. Most people know that they marked the edges of farm fields now lost to the woods. Stone walls, in combination with hedgerows, outline the shapes of early fields, telling us who settled there. The Dutch to the west, the French in the north, and the Yankees from lower New England each used distinctive field shapes, the origins of which were cultural.

Though the grueling labor associated with such work can easily lead one to believe otherwise, invariably there was a surprising body of skills and folk knowledge necessary to work on the farm and in the woods. Working with stone was no exception, as is shown by the following material excerpted from field interviews.

"My grandfather was noted for his work with stone—building wall you know," explained Earl Hood. "The ones he couldn't lift himself, he'd use the oxen and a chain and roll them up. All alone, nobody with him or nothing. One time he was back over on the other side of the hill here. And he was on the underside, lower side, of a big stone, and it was almost too much for him but he 'hild' [held] it with his iron bar. If it'd gone over on him, it'd killed him. He was a big six footer in his stocking feet and bony and 'muscley.' They said he could call the stones right around with his iron bar and make them do what he wanted them to.

"He had two spruce poles he used to roll the stone up onto the wall. They had two-inch auger holes bored close to each end, and he'd put hardwood rungs across into the holes and have a kind of ladder, he called it—to roll the big stones up onto the wall.

"He laid his wall different than the most of the folks. He dug down to hardpan and put in some little stones. Most folks just rolled the big stones in there, and when the ground froze, they'd heave and the top stones would roll off. Well, he put them little stones in the bottom and then his big stone on top of 'em. Then when it did freeze, they'd roll around on them little stones and didn't roll enough to upset the wall. I wish you could see that wall over there in the pasture. It's a double wall. He and his brother made it when my father was a boy. Two walls filled in with smaller stones. Then they bring that wall up to the top.

"My father said he could lay a stone wall, but he said he'd have to move the stone or find one to fit. But my grandfather would look at the hole in the wall, and then he'd look at his stone to see what he'd got. He'd pick out just one stone that would just fit that place. When he laid it once, that was the end of it. He never rolled it and upturned it. He laid it just so. There was an old fella down here to the village used to come up here on Sundays and other days and visit with him. After Gramp died, he told me Gramp made every minute count. He never moved but what he knew what he was going to do."

SINGLE AND DOUBLE STONE WALLS

"To begin with," Ed Clay began, "stone was always laid just as it was gathered off the field—undressed. Double walls have a base as wide again as single walls. Both sides of a double wall slope in toward the top. The wall is squared on the top. They built "half walls" where stone was scarce. They were two and a half to three feet high with a rail fence along the top. They split thick slab posts out of old growth pine. Mortices were bored and chiseled out to take the rails. They buried the posts in the wall as the stone was laid up. Some of this type fence was built way back on this farm. Sheep, especially, were put inside this kind of fence. Any cloven-hooved animal will hesitate to cross a stone fence because its hooves are spread by the stones and it's painful to the animal.

"Double walls were sometimes built as much as five-feet high. All stone wall was built on a dug foundation. On dry, gravelly, or stony soil, these were dug five- to six-inches deep. On clay soils prone to heaving in a frost, they'd go one and a half feet deep. We dug foundations with a pick and shovel or by plowing down and digging out the loose earth. I always put big stone into these foundation trenches. Now and then a wall would run right across a ledge. If it

was sloped, holes were drilled on the down side and iron pins set in to level the first course. Kept the wall from tumbling. If a wall was against the downslant of a plowed field, the old one-way plow gradually worked the dirt in against it. 'Course the dirt washed in from the rains too. The uphill of a wall placed like that will eventually come to be two feet under the ground. You put livestock inside an old wall like that and you've got to add more stone to it.

"In a single wall there was no interior filling of stone. But the wall still had to be carefully built. Once you got above the base stones it could carry two or

97. Ancient stone wall and maples along a Vermont country road.

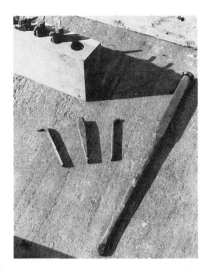

98. Old-fashioned stone drill on right. The piece in the center of the three small objects is a splitting wedge used in conjunction with the two "feathers" on each side.

99. Drilling the holes in order to split the end off the stone.

100. Spooning out the stone dust.

three series of stones laid side by side. You put in long stones crosswise to lock them. In laying any kind of stone wall you always lock your stone by laying a big one over two or three smaller stones and vicey versa. On a double wall you lay in stones long enough to go clear across—one side to the other. If they are scarce on the field you put 'em in as you find them. If plentiful, you lay them in two rows: one maybe a third of the way up and the other about two-thirds of the way.

"When you put the filling in a double wall, if the shape of your stone is right, you can lay them to shed water out of the wall so it won't gather and freeze in the winter. Also with a double wall, the ends, say at the opening for a gate, will be laid 'locking fashion' with long stones going back lengthways into the wall. If you had them handy, you capped off a double wall with flat stones.

"Stone gate posts were cut from a ledge using drills and wedges. You put them into a hole on a stone footing, then hung the gate from them. The gate hangers were made of hand-forged iron; the smith put barbs along the four corners pointing outward. They were sunk in drilled holes and filled in with melted lead.

"Two men building a double wall, with another two men drawing the stone to 'em, could lay a rod [16.5 feet] of wall about five-foot high in a good day's work.

"In my father's and grandfather's day, they sometimes built a stile into a fence. Travel between farms then, when people used to walk, was 'cross-lots.' A stile was about three feet wide and half the depth of the wall. Had stone steps laid up to it on both sides, and it had a little wooden gate."

PICKING STONE OFF THE FIELD

"All loose stone was picked off by hand. If it averaged a small size, it was thrown into an ox cart which held thirty bushel. Big stuff was levered onto a stone boat. We took the stone to the edge of the field to the men laying wall. People used oxen to haul stone. They were the choice for slow, heavy work, even though your big work horses began coming in after 1880. 'Course we had the Morgans, but they were just a little small for it.

"We moved a buried stone by digging 'round it and yanking it out with a chain fastened in a 'rolling hitch.' The chain led back over the stone so's to turn it when the oxen started. Large stones were loosened with a crowbar levered on a 'bait' [a stone fulcrum]. As we got the stone raised, we put more baits under it to hold our 'purchase' [the height gained by the bar]."

DISPOSING OF GREAT STONES AND LEDGE

"We had two ways. We buried the stone or blasted it. When the ground was soft in the spring, we dug a deep hole, put a rolling hitch on the stone, and dumped it in with whatever small stone was around. Then we covered it under two, two and a half feet of dirt. As a young fellow, I've spent many a night in spring digging holes beside big stones to bury 'em. And I've had the experience, after years of plowing by my folks, of plowing down to one of these big stones my ancestors buried.

"When I was a boy, they was still blasting such stones with black powder. I remember one time I went to the sawmill with my father. They had a huge pine log there, and the mill didn't have a topsaw so they couldn't cut it as it was. Well, by God, they bored a one-inch hole a foot deep into one end and packed it with black powder and a fuse in a newspaper tube. Touched it off, and that log split dead in two from end to end. Quite a sight! Then they could lay each half flat on the saw carriage and saw it into lumber.

"Black powder blew with more pressure than dynamite. The stone didn't shatter as much. But, as I say, I came in on the last end of it, and I've always used dynamite. Had a big 'blue rock' in the pasture once. That's the hardest local stone there is. It's very difficult to drill, but we wanted to blast it out so we had to drill it. Took two men. One held the stone drill and gave it a quarter or half turn after every strike of the sledge. It was an old-style drill—had two lips 'stead of four.

"This particular stone was three times as big as a kitchen table. We never did find out how deep it went. Anyway, Dad and I got tired of catching the plow point on it. First day, we used two stone drills and pounded away all day to get a hole one-foot deep. We bailed out the stone dust, then we took a stick of dynamite, broke it up into small balls, and packed the hole with it. Took a blasting cap, ran a fuse through it, and left an inch sticking out the bottom of it. The other end was prob'ly three-, four-foot long. Crimped the cap with my teeth and poked a little hole for the fuse down into the dynamite and molded it around the fuse. Then we took and piled a foot and a half of just plain mud on the top of the whole thing, with the fuse sticking out the side of the pile. See, the mud makes the blast go down into the stone. Even water, if you pour it over a stone just before you light the fuse, will help make the force go downward.

"Well, we touched her off. It broke it up some, but not all of it by any means. We didn't feel like drilling anymore, so we wrapped several sticks around one in the middle that had a fuse. Laid 'em on the stone and 'mudded' it. Then we filled up some bransacks with dirt and put them on too. (I tell you, it didn't take nothing to set off that blasting cap, and when we laid the stick down on top of the stone, we put down some sand first so she wouldn't roll off and explode and kill us.) We kept going till we had that damned stone lowered by two and a half feet. Filled the hole with dirt, and she never caught a plow point again.

"How'd we split out stone gate posts? We made them out of granite or slate up in the ledges or from a big boulder. You drilled a bunch of small holes, two inches apart. You followed the grain if you could. Put your holes right along a straight line. Then you put two 'feathers' in each hole. They were made of steel, tapered thin to thick top to bottom. They had little fingers bent over at the tops to keep them in place. Put a small steel wedge between each pair of feathers and start to tap them down with a stone hammer. Little bit at a time on each one. Pretty soon those wedges put more pressure on the stone than it could hold, and it split right in two. Just repeat it to square out the rest of the post."

101. Wedges and feathers in place. Stone mason Harvey Bumps is tapping down the wedges. Soon enough pressure will be built up to split the stone.

102. The end has been split off, showing the drill holes.

103. Farmer, team, and walking plow,
1937.

11

Plowing

Edward Clay
North Thetford, Vermont

My nose is downward; I go deep and dig into the ground; I move as the grey foe of the wood guides me, and my lord who goes stooping as guardian at my tail; he pushes me in the plain, bears and urges me, sows in my track. I hasten forth, brought from the grove, strongly bound, carried on the wagon, I have many wounds; on one side of me as I go there is green, on the other side my track is clear black. Driven through my back a cunning point hangs beneath; another on my head fixed and prone falls at my side, so that I tear with my teeth, if he who is my lord serves me rightly from behind.

Ancient English riddle in the
Exeter Book*

By the end of the nineteenth century, the New England swivel or sidehill plow (the terms are interchangeable) had been largely superseded in the American West by plows especially adapted for turning tough prairie sod. The sidehill plow, however, continued to be widely used on many farms in this region until shortly after World War II. As its name suggests, this plow was particularly handy for working steep, irregular, stony fields. It was, of course, a walking plow, which meant that the plowman walked behind it, holding onto the plow stilts to guide it. The mouldboard and plowshare hinged on a swivel. At furrow's end, a kick to a spring latch allowed them to swing to the opposite side and lock in place for the return furrow. This swivel action was a revolutionary advance over all previous plows. It enabled farmers to turn each new furrow against the one preceding it and thus plow back and forth across the field. Before, one had to plow around the field, a more clumsy and time-consuming method.

The sidehill plow was an interesting combination of ancient and modern technologies. In some respects, it bore a modest resemblance to the wooden plow of Neolithic times. But whereas the primitive plow merely scratched the earth, this one was capable of turning a deep furrow in soils more difficult to work than the prehistoric farmer could have imagined. The Neolithic plow is still used in many parts of the world, an example of technological overlap. Overlapping occurs for two basic reasons. It is often found among peoples who for cultural reasons and, at least in part, because of long isolation cling to ancestral ways. It can also occur, however, when a group, perhaps for economic or environmental reasons, is unable to make efficient use of new or improved tools and implements. In either case, archaic, outmoded tools and methods remain in daily use.

An example can be found in the early, nineteenth-century, one-way iron plow. This artifact continued to be used in the conservative folk world of the

* The answer is a plow. From George C. Homans, *English Villagers of the Thirteenth Century* (New York, 1960), p. 50.

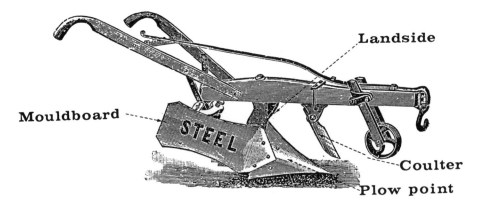

Landside

Mouldboard

STEEL

Coulter

Plow point

Fig. 11. A late nineteenth-century side-hill plow; made by Sargent, Osgood, and Roundy, Randolph, Vermont.

Yankee Highlands long after the more efficient sidehill plow became available later in the century. The immediate ancestor of the cast-iron, one-way plow was the wooden plow of colonial times. English restrictions on manufacturing and on producing iron and steel had greatly slowed the Industrial Revolution in the colonies. As late as 1810, plows were still being built of wood by village plow-wrights. Made completely by hand, these plows were comprised of "a strong wooden beam, wooden handles, and a wooden mould-board set at an angle, in an effort to tip the furrow as it was lifted from its bed. Another board was used as the landside."

The beam was a piece of strong timber (several decades later, it was often made of iron), by which the yoke of oxen drew the plow and to which was fastened the balance of the plow parts. The most important of these was the mouldboard, a large curved section at the base of the plow—often the first part one notices due to its complex shape. It was constructed using cut-and-try methods. If correctly made, the mouldboard turned the furrow slice. It some-times worked reasonably well—but often it did not. It was shod (faced) by the blacksmith with thin plates of iron or steel forged from worn-out scythe blades, old horseshoes, cast-off saws, and like pieces of metal.

The plow piece described in the riddle above as "another on my head fixed and prone falls at the side, so that I tear with my teeth" is, of course, the plowshare. A broad, hand-forged, knife-edged point at the front of the mouldboard, it cut the furrow slice from the edge of earth being plowed, that is, the furrow's "landside." The plow itself had a landside. This structure, located at its base, supported the mouldboard and plowshare. It took its name from its function of bearing against the "landside," the face of the earth being cut. Like the mouldboard it, too, was iron shod.

Another plow part, mentioned in the riddle above as "Driven through my back a cunning point hangs beneath," is the plow coulter. Known locally as the plow sword (later corrupted to plowsward), this was a thick, knifelike piece wedged into the beam just ahead of, and in line with, the plowshare. The coulter sliced the sod just ahead of the share, thus easing the work of the share and mouldboard. This helped the plowman keep a straight, properly turned furrow. The coulter, known in England since the eleventh century, was often but not invariably fitted to the wooden plow. During the later 1800s, it became a standard feature on walking plows.

The lag in the American manufacturing technic, so apparent in these ancient wooden plows, can perhaps be appreciated by reading the words of an astute observer who used one of them as a youth:

> Perhaps in no department of agriculture has greater improvement taken place than in plowing, and in the construction of plows. Formerly nothing could be more slovenly executed. A straight line was not to be seen. The land was not half turned over. . . . The plow itself, when in action, resembled very much a live animal, with a sort of grasshopper motion, which one man at the stilts and often two men riding upon the beam, were struggling to keep down, and like police officers, to prevent its escape. A man was always required . . . [for] the discouraging duty of raising again and turning over by main force, those furrow slices which, notwithstanding they had been raised by the plow, like a reluctant boy pulled out of bed in the morning, with his eyes half open, insists upon getting back again as soon as his master's back is turned. . . . I have looked back with dismay upon a long furrow-slice obstinately turning back into the furrow, after I had supposed it securely laid over. Somewhat of this experience may have been necessary, to enable me to estimate properly the excellence of English plowing, when the implement seemed to move through the ground with as much quietness, directness, ease—I might almost say grace—as a boat through the water.[1]

By the end of the eighteenth century, the infant American iron and steel industry began to supply these metals in increasing quantities. Perhaps it was not entirely coincidental that Thomas Jefferson, during this period, made a plow much ahead of its time. Its worth was recognized by Jethro Wood who, in 1819, patented an iron plow with its parts cast in sections. Wood's plow was a revolutionary advance, and it helped foster a burst of farm implement manufacturing that lasted throughout the rest of the century. After Wood's time, plows were made in large numbers in a multitude of small shops, actually incipient factories, instead of being made by hand one or two at a time by local plowwrights.

Henceforth, cast iron was used to make the mouldboard, landside, and plowshare. Parts for a given make of plow were interchangeable, allowing worn-out or broken pieces to be easily and quickly replaced. Of the great improvements in American plow making during the last half of the century, one man wrote in 1885,

> The young farmer, if possessed of any spirit, as he guides a well set, keen cutting American plow through the ground behind a spanking team, his implement answering promptly to his touch, shaving the roots, and covering all with the rushing furrow as it ripples from the polished mouldboard, feels an exhilarating interest in his work, akin to that of the sailor who plows the waves with a light, trim vessel under a spanking breeze. There is the same sort of mastery over the elements and a like freedom of action in

1. A. B. Allen, *Horticultural and Agricultural Implements and Tools* (New York, 1846), p. 6.

governing them. In my observation of foreign farming it seemed to me that the marked superiority of American farmers, was largely due to the finish and capacity of the agricultural implements in use in this country.[2]

Whether of English or American make, and whether built of wood or iron and steel, all of these early plows shared a common feature—they were one-way plows. With such plows, the plowman was unable to plow back alongside his last furrow. He was forced either to begin in the field's center and work outward or to plow opposite edges and work inward.

While collecting items for the Billings Farm & 1890 Museum, I combed the regional countryside. Often when going through old barns, I found ancient one-way plows off in a corner or stored overhead on the beams. There they were, despite the fact that the farmer himself used a sidehill plow or, perhaps, one drawn by a tractor. A few of the old plows had the iron-shod, wooden mouldboard of colonial times. The explanation for their continued existence is partly cultural: Yankees are savers. It has always been Yankee practice to save things used by one's forefathers; one never knew when those things might come in handy. But even more, these people held an affection for the old ways. Not surprisingly, I found that among the most difficult things to purchase were the smaller hand tools, whether of house or barn, such as scythes and plows or sewing and kitchen artifacts. During their working lives, men and women had spent countless, wearisome days using these items around the house and farmstead. They simply did not like to part with them.

During that time, I chanced to read George Homan's book, *English Villagers of the Thirteenth Century*. In it was an excellent description of medieval plowing taken from ancient manor rolls. Though heavier and more cumbersome, the medieval plow was the direct ancestor of the wooden, one-way plow of colonial times. The method of using it was the same: One began by entering the plow just to the left of the field's center line and plowing up and down the piece, working ever outward. The earth was turned toward the middle of the field, because the mouldboard of a one-way plow is invariably built on its right-hand side and therefore throws the furrow to the right. At the end of each furrow, the plow was laid over on its side and dragged by the draft team across the ends of the field to the far furrow. As plowing continued, this distance constantly increased so that, for the final furrows at the field's edges, the plow was being dragged across its entire width.

A second method reversed this order of plowing. The plow made the first furrow at the right edge of the field. It was then dragged across the end of the field to turn the second furrow along its left edge. Eventually, the two sets of furrows met in the center of the piece, and the plowing was done. Either method left a narrow, unplowed strip where the plow was dragged across the ends of the field. Anciently, these two strips were called the "headlands."

One day, soon after finishing Homan's book, I was having a cup of tea in the kitchen of Edward Clay, a seventy-year-old farmer in North Thetford, Vermont.

2. Robert L. Ardrey, *American Agricultural Implements* (Chicago, 1894; reprint, New York: Arno Press, Inc., 1972), p. 18.

On the off chance, I asked him if he knew anything about how the one-way plow was used. His answer is, I think, an impressive example both of how slowly some things change and of the esoteric information we can sometimes receive from the elder people of the region.

"Oh yes, I learned from my grandfather as a boy. I've got a couple of those old plows out in the shed right now. One of 'em's a Nourse Eagle plow, a very old make. Couldn't use 'em the same as a sidehill plow. You had to start the first furrow at the center of the field and plow down to the end. Then you came back up beside it on the right. That threw the first two furrows together, and after that you kept plowing round and round till you reached both edges and the field was done. You had to lay the plow over on its side and drag it across the ends of the field, 'cause your furrows kept getting farther and farther apart as you worked. Those ends weren't plowed a'tall."

"Did you have a name for them?" I asked.

"Oh yes," he answered, "we always called 'em the headlands."

Ed's account agreed with various other details of medieval plowing Homan wrote about. The farmer knew, for example, that entering the plow at the center of a piece eventually resulted in a ridge of earth along its middle, and that over the years this ridge could be flattened by plowing in from the edges. Conversely, plowing from the field edges inward dished the land. Leveling it was accomplished by plowing from the center for a few seasons.

Another use of the plow was for ditching—running a long furrow for drains (England) or burying a waterline of wooden pump logs (America) from a hillside spring to the farmsite.

In the nearby town of Bradford, I bought a collection of old plows. All had been used within a twenty- or thirty-mile radius. Two, made in early settlement times, were built of hardwood morticed and pegged together. Their mouldboards were shod with thin iron strips. Another, a direct descendant of these colonial wooden plows, was of iron cast in one piece. Two more were assembled from separate cast-iron pieces after Wood's method of manufacture, using interchangeable parts. A third type, by a local maker named Strickland, was a very early sidehill plow. Its iron and steel mouldboard swung from a hinge and could be turned over at furrow's end to plow back alongside the furrow just turned. A curious device secured the mouldboard after it had been turned over; it was nothing but a very heavy hook that dropped into a hole in the mouldboard. Like much of the rest of the ironwork on this plow, it had been forged by hand.

The whole range of early to late American plow types had thus been garnered from barns in one small locus. Moreover, in Edward Clay, there was a local man who still knew the exact details of how all these early examples were used. He told me that the old-fashioned, one-way plow he had been taught to use by his grandfather was in common use for a considerable period after the swivel plow became available—an example of a traditional culture stubbornly clinging to an implement hallowed by customary use. Though the sidehill plow did eventually replace the one-way plow, the process by which this occurred was far more uneven, and of a much later date, than is commonly realized.

104. Bucking logs with a two-man cross-cut saw, 1939.

12

The Tanbark Boy

Edward Clay
North Thetford, Vermont

The thirsty, leather-aproned wee man, working away at his trade in an Irish hedgerow, was, of course, a faerie cobbler. Few mortals have been privileged to drink the brew he supped from his piggin, but we may be sure that the leather of our shoes, like the leather he worked, was bark-tanned stuff made in a tanning pit. In Ireland, the tanning bark would have been stripped from the oak; in America, a lot of it came from the hemlock tree.

By the 1920s, Vermont bark was being shipped away to be ground, but shortly before that, when there were still local tanneries, the process was carried out in the villages where the bark was cut. After harvesting and drying, it was laid in a circular stoned trench in which ran a rough-edged millstone, turning on a horizontal wooden axle fixed to a post in the center. Just outside the trench, an ox hitched to the axle's end pulled the stone round and round, grinding the bark to bits.

The cutting of tanbark was a recognized folk trade everywhere in the preindustrial world. That world survived and prospered on a foundation of hundreds of similar small trades, the stuff of everyday life. In this chapter, Edward Clay, a farmer in North Thetford, Vermont, tells about cutting tanbark. During the summer of 1924 when he was twelve years old, his father took him into the woods to learn the trade. Tanbark was then one of a dwindling number of cash crops still available to hill farmers.

It is interesting to note that economic considerations often altered the daily life of a folk culture, just as they do at other levels of society. In this instance, Ed explains why the cutting of hemlock logs, ordinarily winter's work, had to be done in the summertime if you were harvesting the tree's bark.

"Tanbark! Sure, it was used in tanning leather to make shoes. We took it off red and white hemlock. Red oak is good, too, but there never was enough around here to bother with. You take old growth hemlock, the bark down on the stump runs one and a half to two inches thick. The sap stops running in August, depending on whether it's been a wet or a dry summer, and you can't peel the bark after that—it sticks tight. So you have to begin, oh, say in May, soon as you can twist the bark off a branch with your fingers.

"We worked the bark in four-foot lengths. We took off the first piece before we felled the tree, 'cause you can reach O.K. to do it and it's easier. You take your tree and cut through the bark right around the stump with a good sharp axe. Use a notch on your axe helve to measure by, and go up four feet and cut round again. Cut straight down from the top ring to the bottom one. Then you take a bark spud and peel that bark right off. You might make two downcuts and take it off in two pieces so's it'd pile handier.

"After that you fall the tree, limb it out, and buck it up into logs with a two-man crosscut saw. Set those logs up on bedsticks and start ringing right around every four feet. Go the length of the log, then turn it over on the bedsticks with a cant dog to get at the underside. Chop a gash between the rings, take a bark spud, and start spudding off the bark. A bark spud is a short iron shaft with a socket for a wooden handle on one end. The other end is forged out into a small flat shape a little bit like a thin-edged paddle, maybe two inches wide and a quarter inch thick. The shaft has just a little bend to it right where it joins, so's you can slip the paddle end under the bark and peel it easy without scraping your knuckles. Whole thing wa'nt but about two-foot long. You work the spud right down around both sides of the cut following the log. The bark comes loose in one big round piece. Split it down the other side with the axe to get your two pieces for the pile.

"We'd set three or four bedsticks on the ground and brace a post at each end. Pile the bark up between 'em in a cord measure. You piled it loose so it would dry during the rest of the summer. Bark side up, and put every piece on two pieces below it. Just like with stones in a wall. Leave the skinned logs right where they lay for the summer. You didn't want to skid 'em into landings, 'cause they'd get full of dirt and raise hell with the saw at the mill.

"Come winter and the snow, we'd go in with horses or oxen and skid the logs and take 'em out to the sawmill. The tanbark helped pay the saw bill. We'd pile it tight on a double-runner, say a cord at a time. Sometimes the sawmill would take it and sell it off. Other times we'd sled it into the railroad station at Ely. The buyer would have a boxcar spotted, and we'd load it in there. He'd tally the loads as we brought 'em in and pay us cash. The last of it, we was getting ten dollars a cord."

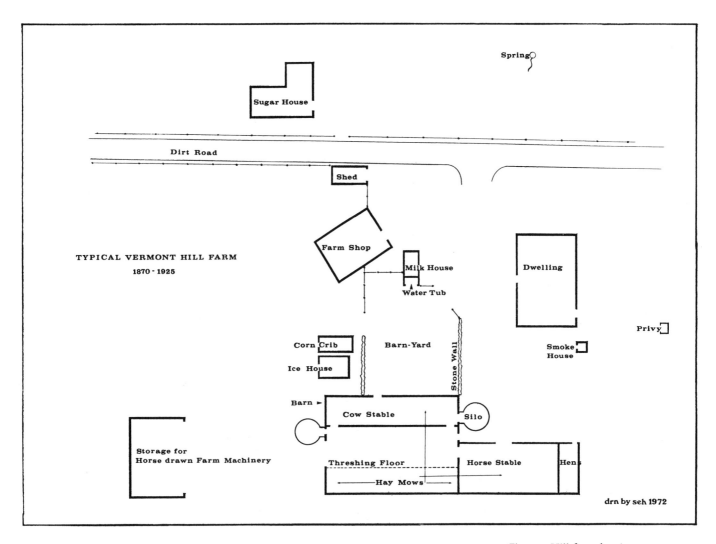

Fig. 12. Hill farm drawing.

105. Farm wife, 1937.

13

Recollections of a Farm Woman

Nettie Adams, Barnard, Vermont
Born 1889

The treadmill routine of work is: washing, baking, ironing, fixing dried fruit, airing clothes, sewing, cleaning, baking, and cleaning again. So it goes week after week. Eating and drinking, cooking and cleaning, scrubbing and scouring we go through life; and only lay down our implements on the verge of the grave! . . . You bake, and boil, and fry, and stew; worry and toil, just as if people's principal business in this world was to learn how much they could eat—and eat it.

Girls, do not scrub and cook and scour until you have no time left to plant a tree, or vine or flower
Letters to Country Girls 1853,
Jane G. Swissholm

There was a time when ladies knew nothing *beyond* their own family concerns; but in the present day there are many who know *nothing* about them. Each of these extremes should be avoided.
Family Receipts 1831,
H. L. Barnum[1]

"I'm very fond of nature, flowers and everything. I used to have a vegetable garden and sell vegetables in the summer. Didn't get much money, but it gave me a chance to have a lot of people. I like nature, and I like people. I've lived in this house fifty-seven years this spring [1976], but I grew up on the farm down the road.

"In the old houses, the kitchens took up about half the house—the kitchen and the pantry, which folks used to call the buttery. The buttery had a sink room with an iron sink and a place to set their milk in a water box. In the kitchen was an old wooden settee and a big stove. There was kerosene lamps for light.

"It was a hill farm, and Dad and Grandpa did all their work with oxen. Grandpa had several swarms of bees, and we had honey. Beautiful honey—nice, white, and clear. There was a little swamp back of the house, and bees always work best if there's water. And they made wonderful [maple] syrup and sugar. White sugar was never used for cooking. You had it only as a specialty, sometimes for a treat on Thanksgiving Day or Christmas. They had maple sugar on the table. It was kept in a wooden tub with wooden hoops. Grandmother took her chopping knife and put a piece of maple sugar in her chopping bowl. And she chopped round and round till it came fine, and she'd put that in a bowl on the table. They used to get the prizes [for honey and maple sugar at fairs] wherever we went. Didn't go too far, 'cause we didn't have any way to then.

"And we had an orchard with apples. He had pears and plums and cherry trees. The birds liked the cherries, so he had a bell hanging in the tree with a string into the window. Every little while, Grandmother would ring the bell and scare the birds out. I don't recall that any canning was ever done. The first canning I ever saw was when Mother took me to her mother's place in Bridgewater Corners, and she'd canned some peas. That was about seventy years ago. They had a big farm with two or three hired hands. And all that work was done by hand too. And that grandmother used to work outdoors a lot, especially in haying, anytime she was needed, and that was most of the time.

1. Heading quotes are taken from Helen Nearing, *Wise Words on the Good Life* (New York, 1980), pp. 124 and 122.

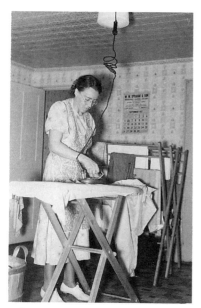

106. Hired girl ironing, 1937.

"That's the way I've always done. Mother always taught me to do my work well. She'd say, 'It isn't a matter of how much you do. It's how good you do it! If you learn to do your work well, it won't bother you to get a job when you're old enough to work out.'

"I went to work when I was a girl for Mrs. R. She was such a nice housekeeper you couldn't tell where you'd been. They used to have a skewer you put a white cloth over to get all around the mop boards and in the doors and in the little corners in the windows. You didn't want to skip one either. I was the only person that suited her to clean house. One year I couldn't help her, and she got someone else and the woman forgot her glasses. Mrs. R. got her a pair of hers and asked if she could see all right with them.

"'Oh yes,' said the woman, 'I can see the fly specks all up and down that corner.'

"Mrs. R. got mad and turned her out. There wasn't a fly speck in the house, nor a fly either.

"My grandparents on my mother's side used to keep about forty cows. Their house was built on a bank and 'twas an enormous great house. Years ago they had big houses and big rooms. My great grandmother lived with my grandfather the last of her days. She was a full-blooded Indian and an Indian doctor. She used to have herbs and roots and barks, and I don't know what in this big open upstairs chamber. All the rafters was hanging with things drying. She was always fixing up medicines for people. And I can remember very well of her steeping up strawberry leaves and making tea for when we'd have a tea party. I was probably seven or eight then, and she'd make the tea and we'd have lunch together. She came from out West. As a child, it didn't sink in like it does later, and I've no idea what tribe she was. And no way to find out now. Nothing was entered in records in those days like it is now.

"Boys always slept upstairs in the old houses. Up where it was never finished off. Sometimes there were cracks, and I've heard my dad tell how he'd wake up in the morning and the snow would be on his bed. They never had boys sleep in warm rooms. I don't know why, but they never did.

"There was an ell to the house, and out through there was a carriage shed and the wood shed divided into three bents. They filled them up year by year so the wood in one of them was always perfectly dry. It was all split up neatly in sixteen-inch lengths. And they took great care in piling it. Beyond these was the hog house, and it had different pens with a walk along the front. At the end of it was the old swill barrel. All the extra milk was put in there. Every morning and night it was dumped in and stirred up so it was always sour. Pigs do better on sour milk. We called it 'lobbered milk.' Same as when you're going to make old-fashioned Dutch cheese. And then out beyond was the outhouse, so every time Grandmother had to go to the outhouse she slopped the pigs a little bit with that sour milk. Then when she came back through the wood shed, she'd stop and fill her apron with wood. No wasted steps.

"This grandfather didn't have as many cows as my other one had—perhaps twenty but usually less than that. They was what they called native cows, and I've never been able to find out where they came from. They were bigger than

107. Petting the family pigs, 1939.

most any of the cows they have nowadays, and they was all different colors. There was one that was blue. Blue as could be. Some were spotted with some white. He had calves that some were half blue and half something else, and they were all mixed up. They were native cows, that's what we had. They was always big cows, and they had big calves. And when they were growing along, Grandpa used to pick two that went good together as far as size went and so on and perhaps their horns was kind of nice. And he'd raise them up as a pair of oxen.

"In the nineties, they were still making butter as their cash crop. Brought the milk into the house and strained it and put it into cans about nine inches through. There was a sunken box with spring water running through it, in the pantry. The cans of milk went down in there to cool, with wedges to keep them sunk down. The water ran from that into the sink and then out the drain. Usually there'd be three milkings in there. When they'd milk again, they'd skim those in the water. They'd take them out and skim the cream off with a long handled dipper into a big kettle. When you got the cream off, you took the skim milk and fed it to the calves, and the rest went into the barrel for the pigs.

"The cream you kept till it soured some, and when you had enough you churned it. We had an old-fashioned swing churn. Grandmother'd sit down with her knitting and push that with her foot. When she got tired, she'd rest and then she'd push it some more. But if Grandfather was around, he'd push it, only he'd do it by hand. I can remember sitting on top of the churn when Grandfather was pushing it. It was quite a lot of butter when it was done. That butter we boxed up in five-pound boxes. Put 'em in a thirty-pound crate and sent it to Boston. I think they shipped it once a week. Had to take it in the buggy into Woodstock to the train depot. If you had too much butter on hand, you had to pack it down in some brine in a crock to keep it. You'd use that yourself. Used to stamp the butter. I guess my folks stopped making butter, oh, about 1900 when the creameries came in. We had a separator then and sold the cream to the creamery, and they made the butter there.

"There was a place underneath the churn to draw off the buttermilk, and that went into the pigs' milk too. Grandma would save out some for cooking. It made the most delicious biscuits. Grandmother made potato yeast. Kept it in a quart jar and a big bowl. As she made bread, she'd dip out so much. When it got down to where there wasn't only a little left, she'd start a new mess and put some of the old into it to get it going. It would be foaming and make a yeast, you know. Sometimes it spoiled on you, so you'd go get some from a neighbor and start over.

"When she made biscuits, or doughnuts, or anything of the kind, she had a pan, a big pan. And she'd sift the flour into that, and then she'd make like a hen's nest in the middle. She always cooked with sour milk, never with sweet, and she always used soda. And she'd have the same bowl she always used. The old saying was that you'd cook in the same bowl on cooking day just as long as you could remember what you cooked in it last. You start in with making things that you didn't put in anything, for flavor, but what you could follow it with, see—in the same dish. If you made biscuits, you'd take your bowl and you have so much sour milk to put into it. She could tell to a spoonful how much to put in. Put in your soda and stir it up good. Wet the nest in the flour and start working the milk into it. Turn and turn your pan and keep your little chicken nest in there till it was thick enough. Then you take the dough out, rolled it, and cut it. She kept her pan and rolling pin and everything on top of the flour barrel. Cooked it right in the wood stove. One thing she always had in the house was lemon cake that she kept in a pail. It was funny, for she kept it under the couch in the sitting room. It made a good place to keep it; it was cool and out of the way.

"I never heard tell of coal when I was a little girl. It was always wood. Even all the stores burned wood. My grandfather used to sell wood. In the winter, all the extra time you had that you didn't have to do chores, you worked in the woods getting out wood to sell. And when you drew it to market, the sled had sides that held just a cord. It was piled in just as particular, and if any of it had bark on it, it was piled so it didn't show. One time the men decided to get the wood out together. They had a caravan of ox teams. When the first team went out of sight round the bend up there, the last team was just coming into sight way down at the lower end of the road.

"Oh yes, children helped with wood, too, according to the size of the

108. Hired man splitting firewood, 1941.

child. Everybody was brought up to do something. They weren't racing around like they are today, with cars and everything. American people, you know, waste more money when you get right around to it than it takes them to live.

"Furniture? I don't remember any overstuffed furniture. Plain wooden chairs and rockers. Feather beds laid on a straw tick on a rope bed. Every day you made the bed. You turned down the feather bed and stirred your mattress all up. Used to have corn husks for the mattress tick, too. It had a slit down the middle that you could button up after you put the stuffing in. Nice, warm, soft way to sleep. You settle into that old feather bed. A lot of them had goose feathers you know, picked off a live goose. You have to pick them when the time is right, I think it was at the full of the moon or something. You go out and get a goose by the neck, and you put a grain sack over your lap and sit right down. Turn the goose bottom side up right between your knees and lay the head right out there. The feathers come off the breast, just as easy. Didn't hurt them a bit. If you pull out one or two and they come a bit hard, you wait another day or two. Those are what you call live goose feathers. If you need feathers from a dead goose, they

109. Marjorie Nelson, age sixteen, driving a hay rake during the second haying on her father's farm, 1941.

weren't so lively to sleep on. I believe we picked them in the spring of the year. They needed that coat in the winter.

"The women made braided rugs in winter, and quilts, and a lot of them knit. My grandmother knit what they called double mittens. There'd be two strands of yarn. And when she got them done, they'd be striped; one stripe of blue and one of white. She'd send her wool away to be washed and made into what they call rolls. They'd be about as big through as my finger. And she spun them into yarn on her spinning wheel. I learned to spin. I weren't a good spinner, but I could do it. You fasten your yarn to that little spindle and measure off about this much. Then you set the wheel a turning. The secret is to do everything at just the right time. You've got to practice how; it's a science. She spun right through the early 1900s. She had an old trunk that she kept filled up with knitted things—mittens and stockings. If anybody around wanted a pair of mittens, they'd go to her. She got something like a dollar and a half a pair. And my great grandmothers on both sides used to weave—fancy tablecloths and towels and things. My mother never spun, but she made all our clothes. She was only thirty-seven when she died.

"Women were very, very neat. They brought their children up that way. To go visiting, you put on a white apron over your wrapper. Their children were taught to sew and darn and mend; and use a needle and a thimble before they was even old enough to go to school. My aunt cut out little squares of woolen cloth, and she taught her children to sew with them, to string them on a thread. They had a needle and thread and a little thimble. Little tiny thimbles for when you learn. I can't sew without a thimble even today. The little ones, every afternoon after they'd had their nap, they had to sit down and string those squares. That was their work. They was taught to work.

"I was taught to sew and braid a rug and to piece up a quilt. You took your square and turned the raw edge over like this. Then the other one was to go against it like that. Then you had to learn to sew it so that when you opened it out it was all smooth. It weren't too tight, and it weren't too loose. Then we'd baste them together so they stay flat and straight where they belonged. I sewed quite a lot of [quilt] blocks and took them to school. After your schoolwork was done, you got out your blocks and sewed a little. At home we would have small quilting parties with just a few neighbors sometimes.

"And we had husking parties too. When anybody had a big field of corn and got behind, they'd have a husking. You didn't go to have a good time; you went to work. In my day, everything was made to work to accomplish something, not for fun and play. Of course you could have fun. Enjoy you know, husking and telling stories and visit and this and that. You didn't have to sit there on a stool like a sober older person and not speak or anything. And they always had pumpkin pie for lunch at these huskings.

"Sometimes, after the husking, they'd have a dance. My father used to play the violin. You'd get out in the little back kitchen and dance. Never danced round dances as I remember. It was always quadrilles or a string dance or something. We called 'em kitchen tunks. I remember one of those houses had a beautiful old-fashioned fireplace. They used to bake brown bread and soft breads in it. Not white breads and raisin bread like we have today.

"People also used to have apple paring bees—pare apples and thread them on a string and hang them up to dry—in the evening. Sometimes the men run the hand-cranked apple parers and then passed the apples on to the women to core and quarter. And if the kids were old enough to understand, they'd string them. There'd be four hooks over the stove and two poles hung on them. The strings of apple slices were hung on those poles to dry.

"I was brought up as a child that a penny was a penny. I remember once I wanted a petticoat with some lace on it. And I wanted a hat with some posies on it. I weren't very old. So Grandmother got me a hat. You'd laugh if you could see it. It was a straight-around brim with a very small crown, and a little bunch of posies stuck up on one side. So I got my hat with the posies on it. I was pretty choice of it! Well, then she told me if I'd make the lace for my petticoat, she'd make me the petticoat. Well I knitted that lace out of just common ordinary thread. I've still got it. But it was more than a year before Mother got enough money saved up for the cloth to make that petticoat. But when you got something like that petticoat, then you really treasured it. Everything I had I was just as careful of it as if it was gold. And I'm the same today. If somebody bangs my dishes, it hurts me.

"All the knowledge I got I got right down there in that little old schoolhouse. If you had trouble with something, you stayed after school and the teacher drummed it into you. Or she'd help you noon hour or recess. All you had to do was ask her. Nowadays the teachers aren't teachers. I took taxes and algebra and quite a lot of things. I'm very good on figures. Anything under the sun you had to do we were taught to do it as near perfect as we could. We used to have a certain hour in school that we had to write in our writing book. You had printed copy in there, and you wrote it as nearly perfect as you could. The teacher was following right around watching to see you did, too.

"As many as sixty went there, and they learned. They didn't whisper. There was a horsewhip stood in the corner, and the teacher had no trouble with the children. They knew she was there for business and that they were too. Old-fashioned desks with two to a seat with a little partition in the middle. Ink wells, and if a boy sat behind you, he'd dip your hair in it if he could. You did your arithmetic on a little slate. Many children had to walk a mile and a half to school. You started at nine and quit at four. In winter it was dark by then. You started with first grade, and your mother was supposed to have taught you your letters and to count and to write your name. No grades at all. If you were good at arithmetic, or whatever, you buzzed right along and left the rest of them. Mostly you didn't go on to high school unless you were studying to be a doctor or something like that.

"I was good at arithmetics and diagramming sentences and at spelling. We used to have spelling bees, and I hardly ever got spelled down. They used to spell by the syllable and pronounce it as you went along. I used to have many oldtime words I used. Once a teacher and another friend came for supper, and I made a little better supper than I might have if I was alone. And I said, 'I mistrusted you might come.'

"And she flew mad and said there is no such word. But if you get an oldtime dictionary, you will find many of these old words. I try not to use them anymore though.

"Our plates were white. I can remember no colors, designs, or any raised parts. Very heavy ware. The cooking dishes was mostly tin. Frying pans and kettles were either cast iron or steel. They had a knife and a fork and some spoons, all silver, as I recall. My grandmother always ate with a steel knife. The real old tablecloths was linen, plain white. You put a knife and fork on the right side of the plate. The spoons were in a spoon holder set in the middle [of the table]. Just as plain as possible with no side dishes or anything you didn't need to have. You had a cup and saucer. The cup had no handle. I don't remember drinking coffee, it seems to me we had only tea back then. But Mother did make some kind of brown bread coffee that was awful good. You made steamed brown bread when you baked beans. Steamed it three hours on the stove and dried it off in the oven. Sometimes that made a crust on the bottom, and she saved it and dried it a little more in the oven. Then she poured hot water over it, and it had a nice kind of coffee flavor. But we always had tea to all the meals. The table was always set. The tin we had in those times was better than today; it was more sturdy.

"Later on when they sold white sugar it came in hundred-pound bags. They were nice and fine. Mother washed the bags and sewed them together to make tablecloths. Mother always bought a bolt of unbleached cotton cloth in the fall and made it up into sheets and pillow cases and what not.

"Always washed on Monday. My parents churned on Tuesday and Saturday. Wednesday, Thursday, and Friday were for things you could do—say sewing or extra housework or what not. Go to town or something. Saturday you had to do up your cooking for the next week, and wash things and churn again.

"On our farm we didn't get up quite so early in the morning, although we got up early enough. Do up the chores and have a kind of leisurely breakfast and visit a little, just kind of slow about it, and then do up your work in the house. Dad, of course, got the cattle fed up, some work out in the pasture, and so forth. And if he had an extra job, he'd do that and maybe cart the animals off somewhere. In a hard week, sometimes he'd come in and lay down on the floor and go to sleep. He was a great hand to do that.

"Sometimes we went visiting Sunday mornings. Had a special dinner Sunday afternoon. Sometimes an old-fashioned boiled dinner; a whole lot of vegetables cooked together. Make an Indian pudding to boil with it, and boil that about three hours. Have some cream and sugar on it. That was special. Delicious!

"Peddlers used to come 'round. We called them pack peddlers, and they usually had two packs—one strapped on their back and one in their hand like. They sold notions and trinkets, things like thread and thimbles, needles and scissors. Perhaps shirt-waist sets: embroidered ones, and you cut them out and make it yourself. Jake Livingston was one. He came to Woodstock and bought out a store. He came as a poor man. He was a Jew—a good old man and very honest. He started out as a pack peddler. Then he got an old horse and a long express wagon, and he had more things to sell. Finally he worked up to where he had the store and a house in town. He eventually had two other stores."

110. Canning beans in a farm kitchen,
1940.

Part III

A POTPOURRI FROM LIFE IN
THE YANKEE HIGHLANDS

111. Haying on the Clay farm, North
Thetford, Vermont, in the 1930s. Ed Clay
stands atop the wagon.

14

Miniatures

The literature of a people unaccustomed to setting pen to paper lies in oral tradition. Occasionally, as has happened during this century, traditional life undergoes vast and fundamental change. There is left, then, as a kind of residue, a last generation of older folk carrying in their minds the stories, anecdotes, and folk knowledge and wisdom that, together with an archaic vocabulary and outmoded patterns of speech, once gave meaning and coherency to their lives. All too often in such times, as Sēamus Ō Duilearga said, "the only archives of . . . oral tradition [are] the graveyards.[1]

Immediately obvious to a fieldworker in the Yankee Highlands were the shadings of local dialect and accent, often varying markedly among people only thirty or forty miles distant from one another. Their characteristic speech was larded with words in common use fifty and more years ago, but no longer heard. Less obvious was their reliance upon memory as the foundation for anecdote and story. Memory, of course, is the wellspring of oral tradition, and their command of it often startled those whose customary reliance is upon the written word.

Finally, I was struck by the speech patterns of informants as I worked with them. A majority evinced a seemingly unconscious skill in selecting words and phrases for maximum effect. Both men and women shared a capability to explain, clearly and simply, the many complex processes related to their daily lives on the farms and in the forests and mills, using a modicum of words. It gradually dawned on me that in their everyday discourse these people were natural storytellers. Their descriptions of even mundane events were stories— interesting and often sparkling with wit. Whether the tale was short or long made no difference; each one was complete in itself, with finely worked beginnings and natural endings.

This last portion of the book consists of excerpts from taped interviews. Most of the material was collected between the years 1968 and 1975, from people ranging in age from sixty-five to in their eighties. I do not believe it is

---

1. "Once Upon a Time," in *Studies in Folklife,* ed. Geraint Jenkins (London, 1969), p. 53.

possible to render their speech into the dialects in which they spoke; it has to be heard. To attempt to write out and capture its nuances would be a presumption on my part and would spoil the sense of what they say.

THE PANTRY

"Oh, it was probably twelve-feet long, maybe eight-feet wide. Had a window in it that looked out on the garden. It had a counter all around it covered with oil cloth. There were shelves underneath with gingham curtains to keep the dust and flies out. There were shelves all around above the counter, and they were curtained too. She kept all kinds of cookies there. She made thick molasses cookies and what she called a raisin cookie. And she made sour cream cookies. And when she made a cookie, she rolled out the dough, and cut them out round, and right in the center she'd make a mark with her thumb, an imprint, and she'd fill that with jelly, or a nut or raisins. The youngsters loved them. She made hermits. She always had caraway seed cookies and a big jar of doughnuts. She always put sugar in a brown paper bag and dropped in a few hot doughnuts as she took them out of the kettle. Shake the bag good, and you'd have sugared doughnuts.

"She made jelly rolls and lots of different kinds of cake. She baked every day. When she made bread, she'd boil a potato, mash it, and put it in. It made her loaves of bread that high!"

BREAKFAST

"She had her own hens. There was always bacon and eggs, fried eggs, fried potatoes, lots of hot oatmeal, and stacks of toast. Coffee. Sometimes she'd have pancakes and maple syrup. Sausage, her own sausage. Sometimes there'd be hash, or beans. Doughnuts, and she served pie if you wanted it.

112. Dinner at the farm, 1939.

"Farmers got up at four or five o'clock when they had to do all the work and the milking by hand. They'd go out and do two or three hours work in the barn. By the time they came in, they were ready for a meal. So they ate breakfast then, about eight o'clock.

"There was a big black cast-iron sink where the men washed up when they came in from the barn. You left your boots outside and ate in your stocking feet. There was a roller towel hanging beside the sink. There was a kind of carbolic soap for washing up—I think it was Lifebuoy. There was a cast-iron water pump on the end of the sink. Mom used a polish of some kind on the sink to make it shine, and it made the water bead on the surface. Her sink always shined. Iron fry pans, the same thing. Put some grease inside a new one and set in the stove till it smoked. Scrub it out with paper, and it was 'cured.' Stay shiny all its life."

GYPSIES

"I can remember Gypsies. When I was about four years old some Gypsies came through the little town of South Acworth, New Hampshire. I lived there at the time and had a twin brother. There was this Gypsie woman stopped at the house, and she had a high chair. She wanted to trade that chair to my mother for one of us boys. She didn't care which one. My mother didn't trade. I don't know which one of us she would have got rid of.

"About sixty years ago, I was living in West Springfield, Vermont. The Gypsies used to come to Springfield. They would camp just outside the village. They'd have, oh, four or five wagons, a pair of horses for each wagon. They were covered wagons; they had a canvas cover to them. I don't know if they ever did any harm, but the town was always stirred up when they came. Everything was locked up, and it was uneasy.

"I remember one time they stopped there. This one Gypsie bunch was supposed to be a bad one. I was about seven or eight years old and I went fishing. I came along to this old wooden bridge across the brook, and I saw this caravan of Gypsies coming. I was scared, so I got under the bridge and hid. I still remember how those old wheels rumbled when they was going across. I just knew they was going to stop to get water for their horses and they'd get me. I stayed there and shivered till they passed by. When I got nerve enough I came out from under the bridge and peeked and saw them going down the road. There was two little boys sitting on the back of the wagon, each one of them chewing on a loaf of bread. I knew they was going to stop for water and pick me up at the same time. They had tents they pitched and slept in nights. They just used to stay overnight and travel right through. On their way to somewhere."

TALLOW DIPS

"Yes, we burned candles when I was a kid. Used to make them ourselves. 'Course we had kerosene lamps, too. We never had electricity. All our lights were tallow dips or kerosene lamps. You had to fill them up with kerosene and keep the wicks clipped. And wash the chimneys. There was one on each end of the dining room table when we were eating. And some of them hung up and had a reflector on the back. But we had candles, and we burnt them in metal

113. Farm woman washing clothes, 1940.

candlesticks that had a little saucer built on the bottom to catch the hot tallow. Tallow made a good light.

"It was beef tallow. The only part of a beef that wasn't saved was the horns and hoofs. We heated the tallow to make the dips right on the stove. Had to be careful—you couldn't get it too hot. You had to keep dipping [the wicking] just enough so it would absorb and then let it harden and dip again. Seems as though we used to make them in the wintertime, or when it was cold. And I think after we dipped them we put them outdoors to cool. Then we could dip them faster. We got tallow at the butcher shop, too. They'd give it to you, glad to get rid of it.

"We'd have the wicking hung over light sticks so we could dip several at a time. Then hung the sticks between the backs of two chairs to harden. Had newspaper on the floor to catch the drippings. When they were done, and hardened, we laid them out in a wooden box to store them. That was so they could lay out flat and not become bent. I don't remember whether we put something on the outsides so they wouldn't stick to each other or not. Anyway, that's how we made them."

WASHING CLOTHES AND BLANKETS

"There was a folding washstand. It had a hand-cranked wringer in the center and a place on either side to hold washtubs. There was no hot water supply—you had to heat it and fill the tub by hand, using pails. And you scrubbed your clothes in there using a washboard and Fels Naptha soap. It was a strong yellow soap. Mixed with sugar, it made a very good poultice. First you fill a copper boiler on the stove and put in the soap. Then you put in your white clothes and let them boil. You had a forked stick to take them out and put them in the washtub to scrub them. Then they went into the other tub, which was rinse water. Then you had to wring them out, and they went into the clothes basket to be hung to dry. It took a woman with a family all day to do the wash.

"You didn't put colored clothes in the boiler. They went straight into the washtub for scrubbing by hand. Dad had a big iron kettle built into an arch, and he used it to scald hogs during butchering. We'd fill that with water and build a fire under it and wash the blankets in it. You'd put in enough cold water so it was just about warm."

BARN DANCES

"Dances in a barn. Especially if someone had built a new barn, they always dedicated them with a barn dance. Square dances. There was a spring to the floor. And on those old square dances, you had to keep in time to the music and everybody else. If you didn't, you were going down when they were coming up—you met the floor. There was a dance hall in Ryegate Corners that was made that way—with a spring floor in it. I'll bet the floor would spring two inches. And in the summertime they had dances at Barnet Pond. There was a lake and a pavilion, and you could go out in boats upon the water."

TRAMPS AND HIRED MEN

"You don't see too much of it nowadays, but there were tramps around back then. I remember them going along the roads here in Hartland [Vermont]. Sometimes they'd stop and ask for something to eat—offer to cut wood or something to pay for it. Depression days and before that, too. And there were the itinerants, the hoboes. Knew one named Tom Brown. He used to come to the farm and he'd work awhile.

"You never knew how long he'd stay. Sometimes it would be a few months, other times it would be only a short while. You'd wake up in the morning, and he'd be gone with never a word. When his star moved, he moved. Next thing you knew, he'd be back here again. Might be a year or two, but he'd come back and work a bit. Then, when his star moved, he'd be gone.

"He always had some project he'd work on. One time he plowed a piece of land up here and put in onions. We still call it the onion patch. And he mostly drained a swamp out here. Different projects. Sometimes he'd get them finished, sometimes not. There was a family over in Brownsville, Vermont, and he used to stop at their place, too. The last of his being here, he stopped at their place. Then he came up missing. Nobody thought anything about it, because that's the way he'd do. They found him a few mornings afterwards, and he'd died out in a pasture somewhere. Tom Brown wasn't his real name. That's what he went by. His brother had been a prospector up in Alaska. He come here to see Tom one time, and he gave mother a big gold nugget.

"Probably Tom's star moved again and he come back here, and then finally he, I guess he started to move when his star did, and he didn't make it."

COOKING AND HOUSEHOLD MATTERS

"Pies? We made pumpkin, squash, and custard. Then there was apple, mince, peach, rhubarb, strawberry, and raisin pies. She used to use sour cream and raisins—it made a delicious pie. And pineapple pie, too. Really, any kind of fruit pie. They would put hand-sliced apples on strings over the stove to dry. Store them in cloth bags, and then you'd have dried apples to use in winter. They soaked them in water to reconstitute them. We used any apples we had. I remember McIntosh, Duchess, Spies, and Wolf River. There were Transparents, too, the most beautiful apple you ever saw in your life. Alexanders—those were very big apples. We never used to have to spray apples. We didn't have the insects, and we had very good apples. You plant nasturtiums, and there were other plants as well, in an orchard, and they'd keep insects out.

"In the pantry they had a barrel of sugar and one of flour. Pail of lard, too. There'd be a bag of dried beans in there that they'd grown themselves, at least fifty pounds of beans. We'd raise them, let them dry in the field up on a pole, then thresh them and winnow out the chaff and dust on a windy day. Mother did her cooking out there in the pantry. By that, I mean she'd prepare the materials, mix them, and so on. Kept her cooking dishes and dough board out there. She didn't have to run for anything.

"Had salt in twenty-five pound bags. Coffee grinder on the wall. We'd buy the beans and grind our own coffee. We boiled our coffee. Boiled it in the pot, and sometimes we'd drop an eggshell in. Best coffee you can make. Another way was to make it in a pan on the stove. Put the water in and the coffee, and an eggshell to clear it. Then when it was done, put it through a strainer. Sometimes we put in a little salt too. The Italians made it with half hot milk. It was quite pale and sweet. Very good with hard Italian bread to break up in it for breakfast.

"And they drank a lot of tea back then. The stores got their tea in bulk in big boxes lined with metal foil. They had bins with tight lids on them. Four or five different kinds of tea, probably fifty pounds in a bin. We drank some green

114. Home-canned food in down-cellar storage, 1939.

tea, but most of it was black. Gram had her teapot on the stove all the day long. It was a gray enamel pot, and she'd leave those grounds in there and just add water and add more tea and keep on. Pure acid by the end of the day. It was pretty strong. Made a difference whether you were working for forty dollars a day or fifty cents a day.

"Were flies a bother? Yes. You took a newspaper and cut it in strips and tacked it to the top of the screen door. Shake the door before you came inside to dislodge the flies—stir 'em up. And we'd take a towel and start in one corner of the room and chase them outside. And we had fly coils. It had a red ribbon with

115. Three generations of farm women, McIndoe Falls, Vermont.

a thumbtack fixed to it. You pulled them out, and a long narrow strip of flypaper came with it. The end of it was the little round, cardboard container the whole thing came in. The paper strip was covered with thick tan glue. You hung it from the ceiling or somewhere you wouldn't run into it, and in twenty minutes, sometimes, the paper would be full of flies.

"There was another kind, too. A black sheet of paper treated with poison. Put it in a dish and put some water in it. And when the flies got a drink of that they said goodbye.

"We had screening for the windows, but it was cloth and it came in little squares. You tacked it to the window frame outside. After a meal was finished, we set the table up for the next one. It had an oilcloth cover. At Thanksgiving and Christmas, we used a white tablecloth. The plates went on upside-down, and the cups upside-down in the saucers. Glasses too. Silverware went under the plates. Salt, pepper, and sugar were always left right there, and the toothpicks in a little container. The spoons were kept in a glass container. Then the whole table was covered with white netting.

"The crockery was ironstone in a nice, brown, old-fashioned pattern. The forks were steel. They had three tines and wooden or bone handles. Knives the same make. The spoons I think were silver plate. There was a big pitcher of water on the table at every meal. The room was heated with a big box stove.

"When I was teaching in North Ryegate, I boarded with the Renfrew family once. Every day, before every meal, the elder Renfrew, an old man with a white beard, said grace. In the evening, after supper and chores, we went into the living room and sat down. The lamps were lit, and the old man opened his Bible and read a passage. Then we all read a verse, and he read another chapter, and he said a prayer. Every single evening.

"The houses did have wallpaper. Very old-fashioned, it would be today. Large patterns and a lot of color. Flowers for bedrooms; stripes and a lot of giltwork on some of it. A lot of the woodwork was grained. They'd lay on a ground color of paint. Then they'd go over it with colored varnish, and take a tool called a 'grainer' and go over the varnish while it was wet. The base color showed through, and the whole thing looked like wood grain varnished over instead of paint."

CARNIE MAN

"I knew an old blind man once. He'd traveled with the carnivals for many years, and he was in White River Junction [Vermont] for awhile. He had a white cane, and he was standing by the curb tapping it, trying to get someone to help him across the street. 'What's the matter? Won't anyone help you across the street?'

"'Damn them, no!' So I helped him across. At one time, he worked in the woolen mill in Hartford [Vermont]. Then he went blind and began to travel. He used to sell pencils on the street sometimes. He lived in a small, bare hotel room when I knew him. I remember sitting and talking with him a few times. All he owned in this world was a little radio and a small bag of clothes. Break your heart to see him, but there's a lot of old cusses like that.

"He was a very interesting old man—had a lot of stories. He said he was in Texas once, and they put him in jail for being a transient. They kept him a few days. Then one night, the sheriff came in, unlocked the cell door, and said, 'Come out of there.' Brought him out onto the road and gave him a bucket of paint and a brush. Said, 'Start painting that line down the middle of the road. When you get to the edge of town, keep going!' "

SLEEPING

"Used to heat soapstones and put them in the bed to warm it before you crawled in in winter. Heated them on the kitchen stove, good and hot. It was like walking into a warm room when you crawled in there. We had flannel nightgowns. The sheets were flannel in winter, too. One place we lived, we had two feather beds, one on top of the other. Crawled into bed, and the top one came right up around you. We had wool blankets. They were 100 percent wool, the finest blanket you could get. They came from the paper mill. They ran them on the rolls, and quite often one would tear or get damaged somehow, and they cut them up into blanket size and sold them to the help. The women would bind the edges. I'd rather have one than any three you can buy today. Sometimes the women would dye them; otherwise, they were a nice light tan color."

CHEESE

"We used to make cottage cheese for our own use. There's as much difference between that and what you buy in the store today as there is between salt and pepper. It was very dry, and a little gritty. It was very good. You can see that now they leave all the moisture in it because it sells by the pound."

PUDDING

"Puddings? There was Indian pudding made of cornmeal and molasses. Tapioca was popular, and rice pudding, though there wasn't as much rice around in those days. I think bread pudding was the most liked of all. They didn't throw bread away. When it got stale, they put it into a nice bread pudding. But that was in our village. You didn't have to go very far in those days 'fore one village lived entirely different than the other one."

SMOKING MEAT

"You may not believe this, but 99 percent of the farmers smoked their meat in a barrel. You put the meat in a pickle after you butchered. Then they'd take one of those tin pans they used to set milk in. Put sand in the bottom, and get a fire started in it, and put the corn cobs on that. Put a wooden barrel over it. Then they hung the hams and bacon on a broom stick, and hung them down in there, and threw a bransack over the top of the barrel. You dug a little trench out from the bottom so you could have a damper on the fire. Just lay a board over it to close off the air."

WEDGING AN AXE

First man: "You know, a fella told me the other day that whenever he wedges anything, he was told by his grandfather to always use hardwood to wedge softwood. And vicey versa."

Second man: "Yup. My father always told me when you get ready to put a wedge into an axe, drive a shingle into it and drive your wedge beside the shingle, and it'll never come out. If you drive an iron wedge into your hardwood, it'll get frosty, and using it in the woods, it'll jump out."

CLOTHING

"Children's clothing? Pants and blouses and middies, you know, like navy blouses. Knickers for the boys. Felt boots and overshoes, black with four buckles. They were cloth with a rubber bottom. Gaiters [like spats] to keep the snow out. Buttons all up one side. It took a button hook to get them on and off. Cowhide boots with copper toes—coldest thing you ever saw. Long underwear called union suits. On Wednesdays, the women patched clothes. They didn't just throw things away if they had a hole. And they darned things with a wooden egg. Mend back and forth, as smooth as could be, so it didn't hurt your feet."

BASKETS

"We had a lot of baskets. They were made of brown ash, and men and women both used to make them. Dad would fell a brown ash, cut a log, and drag it to the house. Take the bark off it and pound the log with the back of an axe to loosen the layers. You have to be careful not to bruise the log else you'll have a weak spot in your basket. Strip out the basket ribs and the filling from the thick and thin layers you took off. Cut them to width, strip off the fuzz with a jackknife, and weave your basket."

MEALS

"Everyone ate at once, hired men, relatives, anybody who happened to be there. A typical noonday dinner? Farmers had a lot of salt pork because they

116. Henry Waters, farmer, Lyman, New
Hampshire, in the 1930s.

killed their own pigs. They sliced salt pork thin and poured a little hot water
over it to get most of the salt out. Then they dipped it in flour and fried it up
crisp. Or they'd make milk gravy and add the fried salt pork to it and serve it
over boiled potatoes. And then, if it were in the summertime, they'd have their
vegetables. Always had pie for dessert. Milk, tea, and coffee to drink. There was
always a pitcher of water on the table. We didn't have refrigerators, so we canned
vegetables and meat in two-quart jars, smoked hams, cured bacon, and salted
pork. Made our own sausage.

"How did we make milk gravy? You heat the milk—not too hot. Take
some flour and mix it well in cold water and stir it slowly into the hot milk.
Keep stirring so it won't lump. If it's to have salt pork, put in two tablespoons of
hot pork fat, stir, and then add the fried salt pork.

"We used to put dried beef in milk gravy, too, and serve it over toast or potatoes. And we'd buy dried codfish and cook it in milk gravy. Just before it was done, you broke a few eggs into it and let them cook, sort of like a poached egg. That was very good.

"We had rye and graham flour for muffins. Yellow cornmeal for corn bread and cornmeal mush. Any mush that was left over you fried the next day. Barley for barley soup. And Thanksgiving was butchering time, so you'd have a nice pork roast for Thanksgiving. Take all the trimmings from the hog and grind 'em up with a hand grinder. Start frying that sausage as soon as the spices were added and it was made. Put it down in a twenty-gallon crock, and pour the grease from frying it in to cover the top. Have it year-round that way. Go down to the cellar anytime—June, July, August, September—take a knife and scrape the fat so you could get down and get at the meat. Take it up and fry it."

VEGETABLES

"Used to plant cabbages. We had a dirt cellar, and they'd go in the dirt when we brought them in. Carrots and beets were kept in bins built off the floor so the air could circulate. Filled 'em with sand. Sometimes the cabbages were hung by the roots from the floor joists, and they'd keep that way, too. Dad used to plant some kind of lettuce that kept all winter long. If you could get the snow off it, the lettuce was right there. Parsnips, too, you could dig in the winter. The potato bin had a slatted bottom to it. The men would dump in ten or eleven inches of potatoes and spread lime all over them, just sprinkle it on from a pail. Keep doing that till your potatoes are all in and your bin is filled. I think the lime kept the moisture from the potatoes."

ITALIAN PANCAKE

"My mother used to make pancake. It sounds horrible, but it tasted so good. She made it with eggs, a little flour and milk and onions cut very fine. She'd brown them in a frying pan and then pour this mixture over them till it browned, then turn it over and do the other side. It was delicious. She'd cut it like a pie."

HULLED CORN

"They used to make a lot of hulled corn. They made it with wood ashes; they poured water through wood ashes in a barrel and used the lye. Sometimes they used commercial lye or some composition, but it never tasted the same as with wood ashes. It was dried corn you know, very hard. The lye took the hulls off and softened it so you could eat it with milk. An old man used to sell it from house to house, that and homemade horseradish he carried in bottles in a box hung from a leather strap over his shoulder. Sunday nights we'd have something light like hulled corn, or bread and milk, for supper."

SOUP AND CRACKERS

"Mother would make potato soup: potatoes cut up fine and onion and salt and pepper and milk. She always served it with those big white St. Johnsbury crackers. Wonderful. They were like two pieces put together, and you split them and crumbled them up, and there was nothing like them. Sometimes we'd split them and toast them and put on plenty of butter. Mmmmmmm."

CUTTING WOOD

"We owned a big woodlot up on the mountain, three miles away. There's a footpath up over that mountain. I walked up there those two winters, and there wasn't anybody within miles of me. Some days my father came up and helped me; some days he wouldn't. Take my dog with me. I built a shelter up there out of old boards and a little old roofing and spruce boughs, where I could build a fire and eat my dinner. I went up there and chopped cordwood all day. I got up there by nine in the morning, and I left when the stars were starting to shine at night. And back up the next morning. Draw the wood home. Pile it up right out here, and saw it up with a gasoline engine and a sawing machine, and split it. Deliver it to the village in a dump cart for ten dollars a cord. You couldn't get one more cent if you tried, to save your soul."

HEATING

"We heated the house with woodstoves back then. The ceilings had a round hole to let heat up into the bedrooms, and of course the stovepipe heated things up a little. But it never was warm enough to sit down beside a window. There were no storm windows either. I remember the stove had a top that swung round, and I can remember Father putting in a big chunk to keep the fire, to keep the coals going till morning. But the kitchen stove never kept a fire all night. You shut the door and tried to keep one room warm. We had warming stones made out of soapstone to go in the bed and warm the sheets. Along in the 1940s we built a new chimney, and we had stoves for the parlor and living room. But we never used the parlor in winter."

PRESERVING MEAT

"Common help worked out for a dollar a day and dinner. Help that lived with you got twenty a month, board, room, and washing [early 1900s]. Dinner would be potatoes and vegetables, home-raised meat, homemade cheese and butter, and you lived well. We didn't can much in those times. We salted meat. Had a pork barrel down cellar. Put a layer of salt in the bottom of it, then a layer of pork laid on end instead of flat, and so on till you got the barrel filled. That was common salt pork laid up in brine. You put a stone weight on the pork to keep it down under the brine. Take out a piece whenever you wanted one, and slice it and fry it up. Salt pork comes from just under the skin along the hog's back. Then it grades down to the thinner pork, which has streaks of meat in it. The belly pork and that's made into bacon. We brined bacon meat and then smoked it with corncobs in the old smokehouse out there. Smoked it till it was brown outside, 'bout a day I guess.

"Pork legs and like that we pickled. There was a 'rule' [recipe] for a ham pickle. I remember it had molasses and salt in it. The salt pork we fried, and we'd have the fat for gravy. Had salt pork and potato and a vegetable. We ate cornmeal mush or oatmeal for breakfast. And they had Cream of Wheat way back. Father's favorite breakfast was egg toast, a doughnut, and cup of coffee. Kept squash upstairs in someone's bedroom where it wouldn't freeze—I've had squash in March."

THE START OF SUGARING

"Years ago we always got our line storm. 'Twould last for two or three days or more. Blow, sleet, maybe a little rain. Cold, nasty, dark! Why you'd think, by gorry, along about the eighteenth or twentieth of March, you'd think spring was never coming. By golly, when the storm cleared away and the big redheaded woodpecker over in the woods was slamming and banging around and the crows begun to squall, you could make up your mind that sugarin' was just around the corner. You'd better get your roads broke out, and your smokestack set up, and get things ready for business. 'Cause when it started to run [the sap], it was goin' to run, and run it did!"

HERBS AND BAKED HAMS

"There were natural herbs growing around—hops, sage, and peppermint. And caraway was a native herb. It was nice to get a bunch of caraway and just chew the seeds. Had it hanging up in sprays in the pantry. We had lots of different beans. Baked beans: you'd pick them over the night before. Make sure they were all good. Four-quart beanpot. Let them soak in hot water—soak all night. In the morning, change the water and boil them. Put in a little salt and boil them till they were soft. Drain the water off and put them in the beanpot. Then you'd add a little salt and some molasses. Some liked to put in maple syrup. The last run of maple syrup is apt to be dark and strong flavored, but it's just what the doctor ordered for baked beans. Put the pot in the oven and bake it. Add more water if need be. You'd start baking eight o'clock in the morning and have baked beans for supper. And there'd be beans for Sunday dinner after you'd got home from church. That and bread and butter and tea and a dish of sauce, and there you were. Applesauce was the standard dessert. That and pear sauce. Peel and quarter the pears, take out the seeds, add sugar, and that was pear sauce. And we canned pears, lots of them.

"Dinner was the big meal of the day, and it was at noon. That was the meal that got prepared, you know. Supper would be leftovers if there were any. Because after noon it was time to do something besides keep house. Pies, cakes, cookies, you'd make them mostly mornings while you were getting the big meal."

A NOTABLE SUPPER

"I think the supper I most remember was when I was twelve or thirteen. That year the wild strawberries were ripe and the peas were ready to eat at the same time. That didn't always happen. Mother and I went out, right after dinner, and went to picking wild strawberries. When we got a couple of buckets, we brought them in, and Father, who wasn't working out in the hayfield that day, he went to hulling strawberries. And then, when we got the peas picked, we all pitched in finishing the strawberries and shelling the peas. And five o'clock in the afternoon, time for supper, we had green peas and strawberry shortcake. And Mother had made two shortcakes that day, so Fred and Paul each had half of a shortcake and Father and I split the other one. I remember saying how good the supper was, and we'd eaten it in twenty minutes and three of us had worked all afternoon to get it ready. That was my idea of a supper—two big soup plates full of green peas and homemade bread with a glass of cold milk. And then the strawberry shortcake, which was biscuit dough cooked and separated like crackers and piled with wild strawberries and sugar and no cream on it. You didn't need the cream with that combination. The shortcake was well buttered. Sometimes supper was red flannel hash, or you might have a boiled dinner. So this one was very special."

117. Edward Clay, farmer, North Thetford, Vermont.

We old men are chronicles, and when our tongues go they are not clocks to tell only the time present, but large books un-clasped; and our speeches like leaves turned over and over, discover wonders that are long since past.

From a seventeenth-century tract

Postscript

Of the people in this book, all but one (born c. 1886) were born just this side of 1900. Theirs was the last generation to grow up immersed in a full-fledged Yankee culture. Their lives are proof that times do not necessarily undergo a sea change merely with the turning of a century—without exception, their cast of mind was nineteenth century, a period that only ended with the 1930s.

In the years I was doing fieldwork, I would rise early, put dinner, camera, and tape recorder in the car, and set off. Most of those days I left the twentieth century behind: when a mountain road led down into an unfamiliar village or to a remote farm neighborhood where things had changed hardly at all, or when I stood in a dusty corner of a barn listening to an old man explain the working of the worn and long-unused sidehill plow stored there. I recall spending several fascinating weeks one summer talking with Maurice Page and Ben Thresher as I measured and photographed their old mills in East Corinth and West Barnet, Vermont.

If I were to choose one informant to stand for all the rest, it might be Edward Clay of North Thetford, Vermont. His knowledge of rural life, like all the others, was encyclopedic. In his case, he came to it through a direct and lifelong experience of very old-fashioned farming. Like the others, he had an instinctive grasp of the importance of what older men and women could tell him. As a boy, he listened avidly to the stories the oldsters told. "Hand-me-down stories," he said. "And I filed all that away in my mind because it was interesting to me how they used to do things."

I remember Edward Clay as an innately courteous, indeed, almost a courtly person. He recognized that what he knew was vanishing rapidly, and he wanted nothing more than to have it saved. I visited him many times over the twelve years I knew him, and we became fast friends. He was a proud man, and for awhile it troubled me, as it has other folklorists, that I was getting so much without giving anything back. Once in awhile, Ed would accept a tin of Prince Albert for his pipe or a package of Earl Grey tea, which he greatly enjoyed sharing with me. But that was all, and every Christmas he'd have a bottle of Old

Crow whiskey for me. At last I realized he was pleased just to have me come and chat and record so much of what he knew. Each visit ended with his telling me, "Now when you come again, I'll tell you about cutting tanbark," or some other, now little-known aspect of farm life.

At first we walked around the farm while he told and demonstrated to me how things had been done. One winter, though, he fell on the ice, injuring his back so badly he was confined to a wheelchair. After that, our meetings took place around the table in his farm kitchen. I'd bring in a couple of armloads of firewood and feed the stove, while he put the tea kettle on to boil.

After swapping the news, Ed would begin to tell me about some bygone aspect of farm life, and I'd turn the recorder on. He seemed to know, without being asked, how important detailed information was. If he was talking about the shingling of an old barn when he was a kid, he'd tell me just how long the shingles were, describe how they were hand split from old-growth pine, and explain exactly how they were laid. Or he might mention that his grandfather got along with the Gypsies by planting two or three rows of corn and potatoes for them along the edge of the field and letting them camp on his land. As a consequence, the old man, unlike some other farmers nearby, was never bothered by stealing.

One day I visited Ed, only to find the house empty. He was in the hospital, as I learned from his brother Ernest, and there he stayed until he died that summer.

On a warm August afternoon, I went to his funeral in the small North Thetford graveyard where he had been sexton for more than thirty years. There was a large crowd in attendance: city people Ed had met over the years; people from nearby villages; farm men and women, the men a little awkward in their Sunday best, the women in clean, colorful housedresses; relatives and assorted children; and what struck me most, a small crowd of men in work clothes who had come straight from their work and would be going back to it—loggers, mostly, with a few men from the feed store and garage. Ed, like the others in this book, had touched a good many lives.

My last real visit with Ed had occurred on an afternoon of bone-chilling cold in late November. He seemed reluctant to have me leave. I agreed to a last cup of tea, and when finally I rose to go, it was almost evening and a fine, hard snow had begun falling. As we shook hands, he looked out at the snow and gathering dark and repeated a poem he had learned as a schoolboy.

> Heap high your golden harvest,
>   Heap high the golden corn.
> No richer gift hath Autumn bestowed,
>   From out her lavish horn.
>
> Heap high the golden harvest,
>   For the chill winds soon will blow.
> And o'er the empty harvest fields,
>   Will drift the flying snow.

Then he grinned a rueful grin and said, "There's no more like us."

Appendix

Archaic Words and Terms

A gold mine of archaic words and expressions can be found amongst the older generation in the Yankee Highlands, people in their seventies and eighties. The following list includes some of the terms I picked up during work in the field.

and the like a' that

angle dog or *mudworm* (earthworm)

a whoop and a holler and fourteen axe handles (to describe the distance to a neighbor just down the road)

Barm Gilliyud (Balm of Gilead)

belly bunt (sliding belly down on a sled)

belly-wash (a soda such as ginger ale)

bent or *bay* (the section of a barn between framing posts, usually sixteen feet, which accords with the old English rod)

bonnyclabber (sour milk)

bruk ("The hoss bruk his leg.")

ca boss (calling the cows down from the pasture)

ca jock (to call horses in from the pasture)

change works (exchanging work stints with a neighbor)

choice (term for a favorite thing as, "I'm pretty choice of that.")

clim and *clum* (for climb and climbed)

coal hod (coal scuttle)

cocked as a cannon (drunk)

confisticated (for confiscated)

copperas (copper)

corn mill (grist mill)

daow (used as a strong negative—"You going to the meeting?" "Daow!")

deef (deaf, as in "Deef's an adder," an ancient saying)

Devil's darning needle (dragonfly)

dooryard (in former times, the space between the back door of the house and the barn) *drawing* (as in drawing a load of wood)

dutch cheese (cottage cheese)

fell (for fallen, as, "It was all fell apart.")

fetched up (brought up)

frailed out (flailing, that is, "We frailed out the beans.")

gord stick (goad stick used in driving oxen)

grandther (grandfather)

greens (cooked dandelions or spinach, etc.)

greensward (sod)

grist (a quantity of corn to the mill to be ground)

groom's man (best man)

haggley (rough)

hay corks (hay cocks)

head axe (poll axe)

headlands (a clear space at either end of a plowed field that resulted when using the old, one-way plow)

hed (had)

high beams (the highest cross beams in the barn; upon them were laid loose boards to hold hay)

his'n, her'n, their'n, our'n

hoe cake (griddle cakes of cornmeal and flour baked on a griddle or in a spider)

I be all right

intervale, sometimes *interval* (broad, flat river meadows along the Connecticut River)

in the mustah (militia)

kickabout (a man who moved about a good deal)

ki daik (to call sheep)

kitchen tunk, or *junket* (farm neighborhood party)

lolly or *lolling* (a kind of panting an ox does in hot weather because of its inability to sweat)

mistrusted what he was doin' (suspected)

'mongst ye

mortification set in (Infection in a wound)

mudsill or *tole log* (a great log laid in a dug trench across the bottom of a stream upstream of a wooden dam; to it are fastened the frames and planking of the dam)

nawn (none)

nigh horse or *nigh ox* (near horse, near ox)

nooning (lunch)

only fit to bottom a chair and look out the window (said by an invalid)

ox sled or *ox dray* (stone boat)

periodicals (men taking strong drink on a regular basis)

plowsword, also *plowsward* (a plow coulter)

pummice (pomace, ground apples for making cider)

right smart

riz bread (raised bread)

riz doughnuts (raised doughnuts)

rock maple (the sugar maple)

ro-ud or *rud* (road)

rowen or *rowing* (second hay crop)

sassholes (root cellars dating from Indian times)

scaffle (scaffold of loose boards for extra hay storage)

scoot (farm-made wooden sledge)

set (as in, "Hemlock bark 'sets' if you don't spud it right off.")

sick at the stomach

so bossie (to sooth cows while milking)

spider (iron frying pan)

stooking horse (wooden horse used to make the conical piles of hand-cut corn called stooks or shocks)

strawboard (old-fashioned, red-colored building paper)

sugar orchard (sugar bush)

teeter board (seesaw)

than the most of the folks (She was smarter than the most of the folks)

the sun riz (rose)

this'n

thundershower mill (small saw or grist mill requiring heavy rains to swell the small streams that power them)

trace (several ears of Indian seed corn whose husks have been turned back and braided together; hung from the rafters to dry and to keep it from the rats)

traverse (bobsled)

tumble (four thicknesses of hay folded together and pitched up onto the hay wagon)

'twa'n't good for ye

'twa'n't much better than sugar for beans (in reference to poor-grade maple sugar)

up onto

wa'n't but four or five years old

whinner (nicker, the noise a horse makes while eating)

yeast bread (raised bread)

Illustration Credits

Illus. 2. Courtesy of Maurice Page, East Corinth, Vermont.

Illus. 46, 47, 48, and 51. Courtesy of William Gove, Randolph, Vermont.

Illus. 49 and 50. Courtesy of John St. Clair, Hartford, Vermont.

Illus. 55, 96, 103, 105, and 106. USDA Farm Security Administration; photos by Arthur Rothstein, 1937.

Illus. 63, 73, 74, and 75. USDA Farm Security Administration; photos by Marion Post Wolcott, 1940.

Illus. 72. USDA Farm Security Administration; photo by Jack Delano, 1941.

Illus.76 and 108. USDA Agricultural Adjustment Administration; photos by L. C. Harmon, 1940 and 1941.

Illus. 77, 78, 79, 80, and 81. Models by James Nott.

Illus. 104, 107, 112, and 114. USDA Farm Security Administration; photos by Russell Lee, 1939.

Illus. 109. USDA Agricultural Adjustment Administration; photo by Boyer, 1941. Courtesy of Jean Conklin, Woodstock, Vermont.

Illus. 110 and 113. USDA Farm Security Administration; photos by Louise Rosskam, 1940.

Illus. 111 and 117. Courtesy of Edward Clay.

Illus. 115 and 116. Courtesy of S. E. Hastings, Sr.

Figs. 2, 3, 4, 5, 6, 7, and 8. From sheets of architectural and site drawings produced by the Historic American Engineering Record under the general direction of Douglas L. Griffin.

Fig. 11. Courtesy of Billings Farm & 1890 Museum, Woodstock, Vermont.

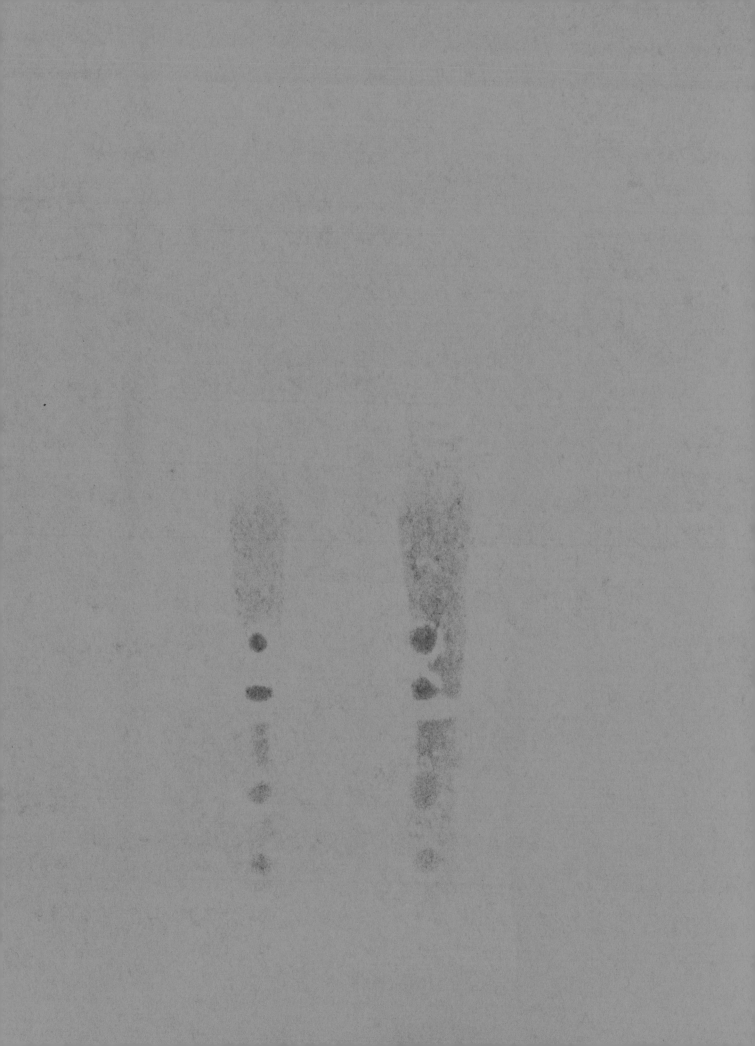